J'adore New York

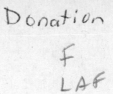

ISABELLE LAFLÈCHE

J'adore New York

A NOVEL OF HAUTE COUTURE AND THE CORNER OFFICE

HARPER
WEEKEND

Harper Weekend

J'adore New York
Copyright © 2010 by Isabelle Laflèche.
All rights reserved.

Published by Harper Weekend, an imprint of HarperCollins Publishers Ltd

Originally published by HarperCollins Publishers Ltd in an original trade paperback edition: 2010
This Harper Weekend trade paperback edition: 2011

HarperCollins books may be purchased for educational, business,
or sales promotional use through our Special Markets Department.

HarperCollins Publishers Ltd
2 Bloor Street East, 20th Floor
Toronto, Ontario, Canada
M4W 1A8

www.harpercollins.ca

Library and Archives Canada Cataloguing in Publication

Laflèche, Isabelle, 1970–
J'adore New York / Isabelle Laflèche.

ISBN 978-1-55468-124-2

I. Title.
PS8623.A3585J3 2011   C813'.6   C2010-907026-7

Printed and bound in the United States
RRD 9 8 7 6 5 4 3 2 1

To my parents
and to Patrice

A woman's perfume tells more about her than her handwriting.

—Christian Dior

Edwards & White is one of the leading global law firms, with forty-five offices across Asia, Australia, Europe, and the Americas.

Our New York City office is our most dynamic, with more than five hundred lawyers, and is the cornerstone of our international network.

We are seeking talented and ambitious associates from our international offices to transfer to our ever expanding team in New York. These positions offer the opportunity to work on high-end transactions with the world's leading corporations, financial institutions, and governments. The New York office enjoys a collegiate and partner-directed, not partner-dominated, work environment, which offers excellent career development opportunities. You will receive a highly competitive remuneration, including a generous relocation allowance.

Chapter 1

"MASSACHUSETTS! Where's the goddamn paperwork for Massachusetts?" A tall man holding his suspenders with both hands is taking long strides down the hallway, punctuating each step with the name of a state. "New Hampshire!" He stops in front of a boardroom where associates are furiously stuffing envelopes with piles of paper. "Maine! Are we friggin' ready in Maine?" He continues his pacing, mops his brow with a handkerchief, and pokes his head into another conference room where it looks like other associates are about to drop dead from the stress.

I peer into the boardroom, spying on the chaos while I wait for the office administrator. Six young lawyers are sitting around a large mahogany table littered with polystyrene cups. The men have their shirt sleeves rolled up and their ties loosened and the women have removed their suit jackets. They look as if they haven't slept in weeks.

The man in suspenders looms in the doorway. "FOR CHRISSAKE, WHERE THE FUCK ARE THE PACKAGES FOR NORTH CAROLINA?"

The associates nervously scramble to fill the envelopes under his watchful gaze.

"What's going on?" I ask a light-haired man sitting next to the door after Mr. Suspenders has moved on to his next group of victims.

"Major investigation. We're filing applications with the regulators in all fifty states. One of our biggest clients is facing jail time."

"Who's the guy in suspenders?"

"Harry Traum, head of litigation. He specializes in white-collar crime defence."

"Oh."

"A former army general and a tough man to please," he adds under his breath. "I'm Alfred, by the way. Who are you?"

"Catherine. Just transferred from the Paris office."

"Great, welcome aboard," he says to my chest.

"Thanks." Relieved that I accepted a transfer to the firm's corporate group, I walk back to the reception area where a middle-aged woman with a perfectly coiffed head of fire red hair and matching nails is waiting for me holding a box of business cards.

"You must be Catherine. Welcome to New York. I'm Mimi, the office administrator. You'll be sitting in that office over there in the corner." She says, pointing, her arm glittering with gold bangles.

"A corner office?"

"It's only temporary, hon." She pats me on the shoulder. "Until the new partner moves in and your office is finished. No one gets a corner office until their tenth year at the firm. But don't you worry, in time you'll get yours," she adds in a conspiratorial tone.

I kick myself for being so wide-eyed. In big law firms, a corner office represents the ultimate symbol of success, the carrot dangled before the most ambitious associates who believe that years of sweating it out are worth it to obtain a corner view, which in reality is nothing more than another space in which to bill more hours. Is this ridiculous? *Yes.* Do I want it? *Absolutely.*

We walk side by side and other than Harry Traum's voice reverberating in the background, a tomblike silence pervades the hallway. The minimalist decor, marble floors, and contemporary art give the office a cold, impersonal feel.

"Anything you need, you get," Mimi advises while giving me the grand tour. "We ranked first in law.com's annual survey of best places to work," she boasts with a radio announcer voice. "There's a full breakfast every morning, the car service is paid for around the clock, all lawyers fly first class."

She glances over at me to make sure I'm impressed.

I nod with a smile, having enjoyed similar perks in Paris.

"I almost forgot to mention that we've recently added a few items to the list, including concierge services and pet insurance."

Pet insurance? What lawyer at this firm has time to take care of a pet? Isn't that like offering child-care services to a group of monks?

"And we recently initiated a new Friendship Program where partners and senior associates are encouraged to say hello, thank you, and good night to junior associates. Isn't that sweet?" she exclaims, her eyes flashing with excitement, as if such gestures were extraordinary.

It's obvious that I'll need to adjust to a new set of social rules here.

"Well, here's your office. Let me know if you need anything. I love your French accent, by the way—it's adorable." She shakes my hand warmly.

As soon as I put down my handbag, I hear a knock on the door.

"Catherine, dah-ling, welcome to New York!" As I look up, a striking Indian man dressed in a slim-fitting black suit is standing in the doorway. He has a radiant gold-coloured complexion, a tall, slender physique, and speaks with a sultry English accent. I instantly recognize Rikash; we had spoken several times while I was working on a mandate for the New York office. Given his penchant for French haute couture, we had instantly bonded over the phone, and I was ecstatic when I found out he would be my assistant in New York.

"Rikash! I can't believe we'll be working together! I've never had a male assistant before, especially one who has better skin than I do."

"I know, isn't it fantastic? I can't wait to take you out on the town. You're in my shopping territory now."

"I can't wait either. You have such great taste."

"I won't disagree with you on that front."

"Remember that limited-edition Goyard suitcase you had me pick for you a few years ago when it first came out? I'm still jealous you got one."

"That old thing? You can have it, sweetie. It's so passé. From now on, what is mine is yours, except for the men, of course."

"Thanks, I'll keep that in mind. How's your documentary coming along?"

"Which one? I'm working on a few at the moment." He lights up, obviously thrilled I remembered. I'm thrilled too—I'm going to need him on my side to survive here.

"The one about child labour in India."

"I'm hoping it gets selected by an independent film festival in Mumbai."

"With your talent, I'm sure it will."

"I'm keeping my fingers crossed. Anyway, if you need anything at all, I do mean anything, just let me know. I'm always happy to help. Talk to you later." He twirls on his feet and sashays back to the reception area.

The excitement of being here tingles through every inch of my body. I had been waiting for the perfect moment to request a transfer to New York and it had finally arrived. Out of thirty applicants from international offices, only three candidates had been chosen, and I was the only one assigned to the corporate group. I'm determined not to disappoint.

An attractive woman in her late forties oozing power marches in. She has a luxuriant mane of chestnut hair cascading down to her shoulders and is wearing a gorgeous fuchsia wool bouclé suit. The impeccable cut of her jacket follows her svelte silhouette, while the hemline of her skirt is about ten inches higher than mine. On her feet are a pair of black patent-leather Christian Louboutin's with a three-inch gold heel that I had drooled over while window shopping in Paris before I left.

"Hello, Catherine," she says, looking me up and down. She strides toward my desk and shakes my hand with vigour, nearly breaking my pinky. "Welcome aboard. My name is Bonnie Clark. I'm the partner in charge of mergers and acquisitions. I do most of the *real* legal work around here. So you worked in our Paris office?"

"Yes, I did," I answer, my hand still throbbing.

"What were you doing there?"

"A variety of different things: securities law, corporate—"

"I hope you have some experience dealing with M&A matters," she cuts me off. "I need you on a deal right away."

"Yes, of course."

"Good, I'll get you started on it."

She marches out of my office without saying goodbye. The strong scent of her Joy de Patou lingers in the air.

"How fast can you get to the airport?"

"To go where?"

"Don't ask any questions, Catherine, I'm the one doing the asking," Bonnie hollers through the intercom not two minutes later. "I need you to conduct a due diligence review on a deal."

"No problem. I'll just pop home to pack and head straight for the airport."

"There's no time for that," she cuts through my voice impatiently. "The Town Car is waiting downstairs."

I glance down at my grey tweed Tara Jarmon suit and black patent Roger Vivier pumps and realize this is what I'll be wearing for the next forty-eight hours. Oh well, I've done it before, I'll do it again.

She hangs up without providing any more details.

"AND BY THE WAY, THIS IS MY BIGGEST CLIENT, SO DON'T SCREW THIS UP, OKAY?" Her voice comes back through the intercom to hit me one more time.

Rikash rushes into my office with a travel itinerary, a BlackBerry, and a look of desperation.

"You're going to Booneville, my dear. Nutron is the largest steel producer in the country and is one of the firm's biggest clients. They're looking to acquire a company called Red River Steel Mills. Here are the details." He drops a thick black binder on my desk.

My fingers flip swiftly through the tabs and I feel fuelled by the challenge. I always get a major adrenalin rush from working on high-profile acquisitions and this sounds like a deal I can sink my teeth into. It wasn't exactly how I planned to spend my first day in New York, but it's the perfect chance to prove myself.

"Honey, you need to a-cce-le-rate, you're going to miss your flight. It's in less than two hours and this is rush hour. Go NOW!" He orders, pushing me out of my office as he hands me a black canvas toiletry bag.

"It's the firm's last-minute travel kit."

I take a peek: it's filled with travel-sized Kiehl's deodorant and cream; Tom's of Maine natural toothpaste and mouthwash, Bulgari shower gel and shampoo, and Jo Malone Grapefruit Cologne.

"I don't have any clean underwear to take with me."

I cringe at the thought of buying underwear in a place called Booneville; I never buy lingerie in a store where I can also find toilet bowl freshener, dog food, or canned tuna.

"I say go without. You'll be the most popular woman in town," Rikash shouts as the elevator doors close.

I rush down to 42nd and don't see any available Town Cars so I opt for a cab. As I climb into the first available one, a woman gets in on the other side.

We both sit staring at each other.

"What the fuck do you think you're doing? Get the hell out of my cab!" she screams, her face menacingly less than two inches from mine.

What lack of class! Outraged, I wipe off some of her spit from my cheek and rush out onto the sidewalk.

A black Lincoln sedan stops in front of me. The driver nods and stands to greet me but doesn't say a word as he quickly opens the door and I climb in. Classical music is playing on the radio and there isn't a single trace of the previous occupant. I breathe a momentary sigh of relief and then dive into the binder on my lap.

I can just see the sign announcing the entrance to the Holland Tunnel when the car comes to a screeching halt.

"Excuse me, lady. I think I have a flat tire."

"What? Are you serious?" A wave of panic washes over me. I nervously look at my watch and I'm already flirting with missing my flight. My heart racing wildly, I take several deep breaths to calm down. *Don't fucking screw this up,* I replay Bonnie's words in my head. There's no way I can face her dramatic reaction when I tell her I missed the one flight to Booneville. Despite reciting to myself *Be calm, be calm,* I can feel the sweat seeping through the only blouse I'll have to wear in the foreseeable future.

"Yes, lady, I'm very serious."

He opens the door and tiptoes along the curb to check out the tire situation.

"It's totally flat. Sorry, miss. Maybe you can get the next flight?"

"There isn't a next flight to where I'm going."

I grab my overflowing briefcase and laptop bag and rush into the oncoming traffic in three-inch heels.

"Are you crazy? You'll get killed!"

I'd rather die from being run over than from humiliation.

I lift my arm and flag down a taxi in the fourth lane over. The cabbie waves and barely avoids colliding with seven cars to get to where I'm standing, creating a cacophony of honking that forces my driver to cover his ears with both hands.

"Newark airport. Please hurry, I'm *very* late."

"No problem, dear, hang on."

The cabbie slams on the accelerator and I grab the passenger handle next to the window. He aggressively dodges traffic and cuts in front of every car via the right lane, causing even more honking. I close my eyes and try to control my angst. Is a flight to Booneville worth dying for? At this second, it feels like I just might. Overcome by a mixture of panic and nausea, I open the window to get some air while I cover my mouth to help keep the motion sickness in check.

My heart pounding, I arrive at the check-in counter with thirty minutes to spare. The airline attendant advises me that the flight is closed.

"Aren't you aware of travel regulations? You're supposed to be here at least two hours in advance."

"I'm very aware, but my taxi got a flat tire on the highway and I *need* to get on this flight, please."

"I'm sorry, you're being bumped to the next flight, which is tomorrow."

I spend five minutes begging, pleading, and (barely) faking a nervous breakdown. I've never actually committed an act of air rage, but in those three hundred long seconds, I clearly envision myself hitting the attendant with my two-ton litigator's briefcase while yelling, "Let's see who's bumping who now!"

After what feels like an eternity of major theatrics, she hands me a boarding card.

I sprint to the security checkpoint and the first guard I meet confiscates my new bottle of J'adore by Dior, a gift my mother gave me before I left Paris. Although I have a tendency to be heavy-handed in the eau de toilette department, I've never heard of anyone actually being spritzed to death. Fuming, I hand it over.

The second security guard gives me a suspicious evil eye after glancing at my French passport. Ignoring him, I put my laptop on the security belt while struggling to hold my briefcase in one hand and my can-be-reached-at-all-times gadgets in the other. I must look like a complete disaster.

I'm still juggling my briefcase when my BlackBerry rings.

"Catherine, where are you?"

"Hi, Bonnie, I'm about to go through security. Can I call you back?"

"No, you cannot. I have the client on the other line and I need to make sure everything is on schedule."

The security guard gives me a dirty look. "You need to give me your phone, miss."

"Bonnie, I really have to go."

"Tell the stupid-ass security guard that this is way more important."

I inhale deeply to prevent a career-limiting response.

"Everything is going *very* smoothly so far and yes, we *are* on schedule."

"Let's keep it that way."

I hand over my phone to the guard's loud sigh of exasperation and rolling of the eyes as he throws it into the plastic bin.

After the plane takes off, I quickly return to poring over the documents in the binder. Performing due diligence is a process where lawyers provide other lawyers with such massive amounts of information and paper that neither they nor their clients have any clue about the mess they're getting themselves into. Practically speaking, it involves spending several days reviewing legal documents in a dusty data room located in the middle of an industrial park in hell's half-acre, with no windows, no air, and, apparently, no clean underwear. Over the last six years, I've developed an uncanny ability to review gargantuan amounts of documents in record time and sum them up in a few lines. This assignment is no different from the other due diligence mandates I've worked on in Paris and will hopefully show Bonnie what I can do.

I speed-read through a few pages before I'm interrupted by a woman who brushes by me wearing—*Quelle horreur!*—a bright coral tracksuit made out of towel-like fabric and big white running shoes. To make matters worse, the track pants are at least two sizes too small, revealing bobbles of cellulite on her thighs. Why do some American women do that to themselves? I desperately want to hand her a bottle of Elancyl slimming gel to help her manage her skin-circulation issues. Unfortunately, the only thing I have on hand is the firm's travel kit and there's no cellulite-busting cream in the bag. I must advise Rikash to stock up on *important* toiletries when I return.

I look away from the velour horror show and continue my reading. I only have three hours left to review the entire contents of a five-inch binder. I slip in my iPod earphones to help block out noise and focus intently on the table of contents: Red River's annual report, its most recent public filings, as well as a due diligence questionnaire. This last document is fifteen pages long and lists each document that I need to retrieve from the data room. I quickly annotate the margins and categorize them by order of importance.

I peer out the tiny window to look at the receding Manhattan skyline and imagine the inhabitants of these luxury high-rises: successful entrepreneurs and professionals who most likely once worked long hours to pay their dues. The idea of being holed up in a small, musty room with boxes of documents fastening Post-it Notes to folders for thirteen hours a day is far from glamorous, but I keep my chin up. Perhaps one day, once I've made partner, I'll live in one of those high-rises. The thought makes me giddy with excitement.

A Cadillac Escalade awaits me at the airport. I've never actually been inside a vehicle this size; I swear it could be used as a second home. Standing next to it is a petite woman in grey flannel trousers and a bubblegum pink twin set holding up a card with my name written in bold print. She is very blonde, her hair is piled very high, and her nails are very mauve.

"Catherine, is that you?" she shouts joyfully with a Southern drawl.

I nod. She pounces.

"Sooo nice to meet you, honey! My name is Jacqueline.

I'm the secretary to the general counsel."

"Very nice to meet you too, happy to be here."

I try to climb into the vehicle in my narrow pencil skirt and heels. Jacqueline gently nudges me on the rear so that I can actually make it onto the back seat. The driver is manoeuvring the stick shift with one hand and a vat-sized coffee mug in the other. As we merge onto the highway, he steers with his elbow while taking sips from his gigantic cup and speeding like a maniac. I try to catch a glimpse of the Southern countryside, but the erratic driving keeps me swaying from side to side. The vehicle reeks of tobacco, and our two-hour ride in the extreme heat makes me want to vomit, a feeling that is intensified by Jacqueline's cheap perfume and incessant yakking.

At Red River headquarters, Jacqueline takes me through security to get an access badge, a painful process that involves having my picture taken. In no mood for a photo shoot, I try my best to smile for the camera. The result is only a half-step up from a mug shot.

We take the elevators down to the basement where a long dark hallway leads to a dreary grey room. Dozens of boxes are piled to the ceiling. I'm ready to roll.

"Hi, I'm Rob." A deep voice reverberates through the

basement. "The general counsel of Red River Steel Mills." A stocky, dark-haired man stands at the entrance of the dungeonlike room. He is wearing a moss green suit, a purple shirt, and a matching wide tie along with an expression of doom and gloom.

"Hi, Rob. I'm Catherine."

"Yes, you are." He checks me out like Hannibal Lecter did when meeting Clarice for the first time. "So you're here to spy on us, are you?"

Something tells me that this charming jurist is about to make my next few days a living hell.

"I wouldn't exactly call it spying. It's fair game when you're looking to be acquired."

"I'm very leery of anyone coming into our company and reviewing our highly confidential information. These are important trade secrets."

"It's all part of the fun." I try to lighten the mood. "And I should be out of your hair shortly. Once you show me where things are stored, Jacqueline can help out with the photocopies and it should all go pretty quickly."

His face goes from not-so-happy to pissed in a fraction of a second.

"First of all, *I* have no time to help you go through these documents. And secondly, no copies are allowed. Jacqueline will stay here with you because I want her to make sure you don't take anything. *Nothing* is to leave the premises." His voice abruptly switches into a demonically cheerful tone. "But she can bring you coffee if you want. Here at Red River, the coffee is free for everybody."

I stare at them, feeling both dumbfounded and outraged. Even though I can summarize the material terms of a contract in fifteen minutes flat, this is a bit much. How can I pull this off quickly without taking any photocopies? I take a deep breath and remind myself that this project is my ticket to earning Bonnie's respect.

"I better get started then."

My phone rings. Bonnie.

"Catherine, how far along are you?"

"I haven't started yet."

"What are you waiting for?"

"I just got here. Did you know I can't take copies of any of the documents?"

"Tsss. Of course, it's standard practice. Haven't you done this before?"

"Yes, I have, but in France the standard practice is to make copies. I think you better send some people down here to help me out. It'll take me forever to go through all of this."

"That's completely out of the question, Catherine. Why do you think we pay you the big bucks? You're not in Kansas anymore, Dorothy."

You're right, I'm not. I'm in Munchkinland, but there's no yellow brick road in sight. "Okay then, I'll do my very best to get this done quickly."

She hangs up the phone.

After I've spent six long hours painfully transcribing notes from various agreements onto a yellow notepad, Jacqueline approaches my table.

"Would you like some coffee? Here at Red River, the coffee is free for everybody."

A quick peek into her porcelain cup reveals a gross-looking, watered-down brownish liquid.

"No thanks."

"Are you planning to stay much later, Catherine?" Jacqueline's makeup is starting to melt and sprigs of her updo have come undone.

"Probably for another five or six hours. You can go home if you want."

"Oh no, I'm under strict orders to stay with you at all times."

Not knowing whether to feel worse for myself or Jacqueline, I go back to taking notes. After she has purchased every possible item of clothing online and played a few dozen games of solitaire on her computer, Jacqueline surprisingly blurts out, "Okay, I think I'm going to call it a night."

"Are you sure? I thought you needed to stay here to check on me."

"No, it's fine, I think you're a good girl. Besides, we have cameras everywhere," she says after giving me the signature Red River diabolical grin. "Don't forget to help yourself to some more coffee. I've just brewed you a fresh pot."

After she leaves, I scuttle over to the vending machine, looking for something that will keep me awake for the next few hours and that doesn't taste like café à l'eau. I select a can of Coca-Cola from the dispenser to avoid falling into a deep coma. Fuelled by caffeine, I'm ready for another few hours in the dungeon.

I attack a box in a corner on the far side of the room that I didn't see earlier. After rummaging through old correspondence, I come across a nondescript dark green folder. In it are yellowed letters between senior management and the company's trade union dating back twenty years. I sift through them quickly until a starkly white piece of paper catches my eye. What is this? *Très curieux.*

I pull out the page from the folder and am shocked by my discovery: a letter dated about one month ago on Securities and Exchange Commission letterhead alleging that Red River's executives had committed fraud relating to the backdating of stock options. *Oh!* This is huge. I scan the rest of the letter; there's another allegation of fraud against both the CEO and CFO for attempting to cover up the stock options scheme.

I make notes, then put the letter back in the folder. It's almost five in the morning in New York, but I'm guessing Bonnie's already up. What should I do? After staring at my phone for several minutes, I call her number and she jumps on the line.

"This better be important." I can hear a treadmill whirring in the background.

"I found a letter from the SEC dated a month ago alleging that the CEO and CFO committed fraud."

"OH. MY. GOD." The line goes dead.

I go back into the data room and grow more nervous by the second, anxiously awaiting further instructions from Bonnie, which don't come. My blouse is now completely soaked and I feel like a piece of rotten Camembert.

I make my way to the ladies room with my travel kit and take a large swig of mouthwash and pop a few Aspirins to calm my pounding headache. I'm perched on the counter, dabbing some Kiehl's deodorant on my silk blouse to cover the stains when a teary and frazzled Jacqueline rushes in. She grabs my arm and drags me to the first-floor lobby where a security guard escorts me out of the building as if *I* were the criminal.

A taxi is waiting for me. I guess the Escalade is out of the question.

I thank Jacqueline for her warm hospitality before I zoom off somewhere over the rainbow.

On the plane I order a glass of celebratory champagne. I'm exhausted but sit beaming with pride; I just saved the firm's biggest client millions of dollars on my first day. And even better, I can bill every single one of the last twenty-four hours. When I get back to the office, I assume Bonnie will thank me for a job well done. Maybe she'll even mention partnership track.

It doesn't happen.

Welcome to New York.

Chapter 2

"Why aren't you at the weekly M&A meeting?" Bonnie's voice bursts out of my speakerphone. Day two on the job, day one in the office.

"I'm sorry, the what?"

"You're late. Get down here immediately!" she screeches before the line goes dead.

I spend five minutes trying to find Rikash so he can tell me where the meeting is, fifteen minutes desperately searching for the conference room in a giant maze of cubicles and offices, and finally arrive, out of breath.

As I'm squeezing quietly through the door, I look down and notice a long, perfectly straight run that mars the entire length of the pantyhose on my left leg. *Merde*. In the boardroom, a group of aggressive-looking attorneys are attentively listening to Bonnie, who is drawing a series of charts on a whiteboard. She gives me an evil stare as I shuffle sideways to avoid showing the run in my stockings to the entire group.

"ABC Acquisition Corp., an affiliate of Pear Partners, has announced its intention to acquire shares of Bella, Inc., and China Enterprises, Inc. We're counsel to ABC."

She draws a blue square for each legal entity and red lines between them to show their affiliations. "Bella also holds forty-five percent of Bingo Industries, and China is a holding company that owns fifty-five percent of Bella." She points to the board while flipping her hair back in the same way that women in shampoo commercials do. I imagine her seductively whispering, "Don't hate me because I'm beautiful" like in those old television ads. She then bends slightly forward to read her notes and strategically reveals an impressive décolletage emphasized by her one-size-too-small black lace brassiere. I'm taken aback, but the corporate raider types are delighted.

Ten blue squares and twenty-five red lines later, I realize that in my rush to make it to the meeting, I have nothing to take notes with. I pull out an old credit card statement from my handbag and start drawing squares and triangles similar to the ones on the board with my lip liner. *Ah, merde!* Out of space! I rummage in my bag as quietly as possible, finally coming up with a crumpled Duane Reade receipt. I continue drawing as I attempt to hide my shoddy notetaking with my left arm. At the end of the meeting, I wait for everyone to exit the room before running to the ladies room to remove my ruined pantyhose.

I'm suddenly filled with anxiety. Being involved in high-profile acquisitions was one of the reasons I had requested a transfer to New York. But working on these acquisitions with Bonnie might bring some challenges. I'm going to have to do a lot better than lip-liner notetaking.

Back at my desk, a tense-looking man with dark brown eyes and dark curls rushes into my office at breakneck speed. He's wearing a lavender shirt with matching cuff links and is weighed down by a pile of binders and documents.

"You must be Catherine. Here are some files I want you to start working on immediately."

As he gets closer, his eyes meet mine. I'm struck by the

intensity of his gaze and how it contrasts with his soft boy-ish features.

Ooh la la. . . . I could bill a lot of time just staring into his eyes. I purse my glossed lips and give him a doe-eyed look à la Amélie Poulain. Then I snap out of it. Focus, Catherine, focus!

He must be Antoine. During my interview with Scott, the head of the corporate group, he mentioned that I would be taking on the files of a lawyer transferring to the Paris office in the upcoming months. For just a split second, I wish I had stayed in France.

"This is for you." He points to the large binder he places on my desk. "It's a collection of precedents I've prepared. It contains every possible type of document that clients could request, and I've separated them by client name, type, and by date."

A quick glance at his binder reveals that it is indeed a grand legal work of art. Perfectly outlined summaries of each document and precedents are meticulously placed between coloured tabs. I clearly have big shoes to fill.

"Also, here's a copy of the Securities Act. You should read it as soon as possible. It will be your working tool on a daily basis."

Read the *entire* Securities Act? The mere thought of having to read more than a thousand pages of legal minutiae makes me feel queasy. I've already fallen behind in my load.

As soon as he's placed the massive volume in my hands, a woman's voice comes through the intercom.

"*Ann-twone*, there's a call from the SEC on line one. The director of registrations needs to speak with you urgently."

"Put him on hold. I'll be right there." He runs out of my office without saying another word.

I guess he didn't get the Friendship Program memo about saying hello and goodbye.

I'm surveying the aftermath of Antoine's visit when Mimi calls.

"Do you have any questions about billables?"

Having worked for the firm for six years, I'm already extremely well versed in the firm's formidable billable hours requirements. Big Law Firm economics go something like this: as an associate, you are paid about a third of what you generate as billable hours as a salary, another third goes toward paying the firm's expenses, and the last third goes into the partners' pockets. The Big Firm partners make lots of money on the backs of associates, which explains why they hire so many and why so few make it to the top. It's like a giant pyramid scheme, except that pyramid schemes are illegal and this is about as legal as it gets.

The New York office has the highest quota of billables and to get where I want to be, I'm going to need to bill at least twenty-two hundred hours this year. Which means I need to start *now*.

My desk is already covered with documents and binders. Maria, Antoine's assistant, calls me. "*Ann-twone* wants to know whether you prefer Chinese or Italian. He wants to review some files with you over dinner in the boardroom tonight at nine."

Just then, cold hard New York reality strikes me between the eyes.

I'm ready for the challenge.

Chapter 3

"I say we skip the crappuccino."

Rikash stands beaming in my office doorway wearing an immaculately tailored linen coat with a Prada messenger bag strapped across his chest.

"Would you like an espresso? I'm going down for a coffee and a drag. I can't stand the caca they serve from the breakfast cart."

"That would be great. I'd kill for some good coffee."

I dig into my wallet for some change as he takes a seat.

"How are you settling? Have you found an apartment yet?"

"Not yet. I'm living in the firm's temporary apartment. I'll be taking care of that over the weekend."

"Good. What about summer plans? It's coming rather quickly."

"The summer? It's only May."

He rolls his eyes.

"Sweetie, let me explain something to you. The heat in this city is completely unbearable in August. You have to have somewhere to escape to. If you don't find a summer rental ASAP, there'll be nothing left and you'll fry to death, *alone.* Let me make a few phone calls, maybe I can get you into a share in Quogue or something." The disdain in his voice implies that he might as well get me a place in hell.

"Thanks, Rikash, I really appreciate it."

After he leaves for his coffee run, I attack the correspondence in my in-tray. I sift through a few copies of the *New York Law Journal* and invitations to attend various legal seminars: there are so many to choose from in the city, it's dizzying. And I'm already getting the distinct impression that they constitute a rare opportunity for lawyers to catch some sleep on firm time.

Under the heavy pile of seminar invitations and legal bulletins, I find a catalogue with *J. Crew* written in bold print.

Oh. Mon. Dieu.

I'm hit with a rush of excitement so strong that it borders on the orgasmic. I flip through the pages and desperately want to be in these pictures. Carefree and smiling women wearing candy-coloured shorts and T-shirts are riding bicycles and cavorting with surfers on the beach. Even the dogs look happy. Now *this* is American style at its best. And these fabulous outfits can be mine with the click of a mouse! The French are somewhat reluctant to purchase anything online; as a people we'd rather wait in line for hours to obtain mediocre service and engage in hour-long discussions with the sales staff. Personally, though, I prefer anonymous clicking. (It even sounds naughty.)

A knock on the door makes me jump from my seat. I hide the catalogue under a copy of the *Law Review*.

"Good morning, I'm Nathan. I didn't mean to startle you."

Fair-haired and appearing to be in his mid-thirties, he's wearing the standard law firm uniform; a navy suit, a white shirt accessorized with a red-and-blue-striped tie, and a pair of tortoiseshell glasses.

"No, no. I was just, um, reading the news. It's important to keep up with what our clients are up to."

"Right."

He approaches my desk and gives me another crippling New York handshake but quickly pulls away as though he might pull out a bottle of Purell from his trouser pocket.

"You're new, huh?"

"New to this office. I'm a transfer."

"From Paris?"

I nod.

"So you've decided to cut the vacation short?"

"Excuse me?"

"Come on, it's not like you guys actually get any work done over there. We all know what really goes on in the satellite offices."

I could start explaining that despite the long lunches, I did work my derrière off in Paris. I was constantly at the mercy of the demands of American clients and needed to be available for conference calls late into the night because of the different time zones. Thinking better of my little tirade, I decide not to provide an answer to avoid it being used against me at some later date, but clearly I'll need to overcome this perception that I spent most of my time on lunch.

"Did you go to a French law school?"

"I did, but I also participated in an exchange program here in the States."

"Which one?"

"Pepperdine."

He rolls his eyes.

"*Another* vacation."

I want to deck him.

"Mmm." I bite my lip.

"So, the corner office. What's that about?"

"It's only temporary. Until some new partner moves in."

"Oh right." He looks suddenly relieved. As he relaxes, I can see him scanning my desk and computer screen for anything interesting.

"What's your main area of practice, Nathan?"

"I like to be involved in the firm's most important files. I billed more than twenty-five hundred hours last year. I'm up for partnership this year so I'm working like crazy."

Ah, this is my first encounter with *zee* competition. In front of me stands an overachieving, potentially backstabbing, sadistic machine: the New York associate on partnership track. I take a deep breath, smile, and try to switch to a friendlier tone.

"Nice suit."

"Thanks. Coming from a Parisian, I'll take that as a compliment. Are you into fashion?"

"Guilty as charged. I love to window shop."

"I can see that." He nods toward the poorly hidden J. Crew catalogue.

"Hmm. Not mine."

"Maybe you should take advantage of it. I'm not sure when you'll have time to go window shopping here." He gives me a condescending smirk.

I respond with a half-smile and a nod: message received loud and clear. I throw an annoyed glance toward the door to suggest he should resume his billing activities. He's now got major competition to deal with.

Turning away from Bonnie's ABC file for a second, I take a sip of the coffee Rikash picked up for me and look out onto the street. From my desk, I can see Grand Central Station and hundreds of people walking hurriedly to work.

My reverie is interrupted by Antoine's voice coming through the intercom.

"I hope you don't have any plans for lunch. We're taking some clients to Brasserie."

Ah, meeting important clients. That's right up my alley. My heart trills in anticipation.

"Perfect. Who are we meeting there?"

"Two hedge fund managers from PCL Investments. They're a big account."

"Sounds good."

"Bonnie's coming too," he adds in a distinctly unenthusiastic tone that leads me to suspect that the two of them are not on the greatest of terms.

"What time?"

"Our reservation is in half an hour, but I'm leaving now. I need fresh air. Bonnie will meet us there."

As we walk along the streets of midtown, I let myself spend a minute thinking how I might impress these reputable PLC fund managers. Maybe I could mention the transaction I expertly negotiated for Swiss Bank last year? Or should I first bring up the Picasso exhibit I saw at the Grand Palais to break the ice? Antoine, on the other hand, manages to talk non-stop on his cell phone while also BlackBerrying the entire way. I wonder if he can bill for the time he spends on both gadgets.

At the restaurant, I take in the decor as the maître d' leads us to our table: stunning modern design commingles with a not-so-modern business crowd. Bonnie is sitting in a rear corner with two men. One has a paunch and what appears to be a toupée and the other is a tall man with a large gold chain nestled snugly in his thatch of exposed hair and a matching ring. Both are wearing ill-fitting suits. The paunchy one stands to greet us. "Nice to meet ya, counselaaar. Mel Johnson is the name, and this is my colleague Jack Stone."

"Nice to meet you gentlemen," I smile as I shake their hands, trying to conceal my disappointment at their lack of polish.

Mel takes a lecherous look at Bonnie and me and, with a glint in his eye, asks, "So are the two of you 'partners'?" emphasizing his pun with finger quotes. He then mischievously winks at Antoine and turns to his colleague with a big, satisfied smile.

I mentally roll my eyes after his cheesy *jeu de mots* and imagine jabbing my pointy stiletto heel into his *parties intimes*, but I smile politely instead.

Our lunch lingers on for far too long as Mel and Jack make failed attempts at practising their French-language skills and recount every single trip they've ever taken to Paris, including the several bachelor parties where they ended up ogling half-naked *danseuses* at Crazy Horse. Mel isn't exactly the ticket to partnership I was hoping he'd be.

Antoine interrupts Mel's storytelling to advertise my previous work experience. "Catherine's been involved in a lot of international regulatory work in Europe. She'll be perfect for handling your international expansion plans."

"Fan-tastic," Mel replies while playing with his tooth-pick.

I glance over at Bonnie, who sighs loudly. Not good at sharing the spotlight, she glares my way before she stands to leave. She pulls out a gold lamé business card holder and casually flings a few cards on the table.

"Gentlemen, it's been a real pleasure. I'd be happy to help you out, but I charge a *lot* more by the hour than Catherine and Antoine. But then again, you get what you pay for."

Stunned, my spine stiffens into the back of my chair. Why did she just put us down in front of a major client?

Mel intently surveys her backside as she walks toward the exit.

"What a party-pooper that broad is. It's too bad. She's got a hot bod. With an attitude like that we wouldn't want to have her around the office, would we, Jack? But we'd gladly take Catherine anytime."

Take Catherine? I suck it up, my physical revulsion matched by my determination to impress.

Antoine shoots a dirty look at Bonnie's retreating figure and attempts to justify her abrupt departure. "I'm really sorry about Bonnie leaving so quickly. She has her hands full these days."

"Listen, *Ann-twone,* don't waste your breath defending Ms. Tight-Ass-Snobby-Pants 'cause we'd much rather work with Catherine anyway."

After what feels like an eighteen-hour lunch, Mel finally brings up something work-related as we make our way toward the exit. He enthusiastically mentions that he's working on his firm's proposed expansion in Europe and that he'll need my help in the upcoming weeks to obtain certain clearances with the European Securities Authority.

"We'll be talking very soon, counselaaar." He ends with a wink and a too-close-for-comfort handshake.

"Wonderful. Looking forward to it," I reply, trying hard to disguise my true feelings.

Chapter 4

There's no accounting for taste and most of my colleagues' offices prove it. They are typically decorated with golf tournament trophies, Lucite IPO tombstones, empty closing dinner champagne bottles, and various unattractive knick-knacks from "exotic" four-day vacations. But Antoine's office has a different vibe; it's like walking into an upscale interior design shop. On a windowsill sit some tulips in a delicate red Murano glass vase and works of modern art are hung over his mahogany desk. Silver cups holding sharpened pencils and a leather agenda are neatly placed next to organized stacks of black binders and brown accordion folders.

He stands to hand me several new files and I catch a glimpse of the silk lining of his Paul Smith jacket and a whiff of Vetiver by Guerlain. Here is a man with refined taste, a refreshing change in a sea of Brooks Brothers suits, messy offices, and strong cologne.

"These files have looming deadlines. I need you to review them ASAP."

I know this is a test to see what I am capable of, and I am determined not to disappoint. I flip open the top one to take a look at the cover page. "This is the Allen Partners deal they were talking about in the *Journal* this morning, right?"

Surprised by my response, he smiles and offers me a Tootsie Roll from a large glass jar.

"Here, take a few. They'll help you get through these documents."

I accept his settlement offer and reach for a treat.

"Thanks."

"I'm happy to hear you have some experience. I was worried they had transferred a complete neophyte," he says in a friendly, conspiratorial tone.

"I've had my share of late nights with these types of transactions."

He grabs a Tootsie Roll before changing the subject. "Catherine, did you handle any intellectual property matters in Paris?"

"Yes. I did some contract work for a few French software companies."

"So you're familiar with international copyright laws?"

"Absolutely."

"Good. I'd like to bring you in on an important mandate for a French client that has major business activities here."

Expecting him to hand me some work for France Telecom or a large French bank, I nod in agreement.

"No problem. I'm happy to handle it."

"It's for Christian Dior."

I nearly fall off my chair. I've always dreamed of doing legal work for my favourite *maison de couture* but was repeatedly told that the company was off limits as a client since a major French law firm handled most of their legal matters. I never imagined that moving to New York would give me an opportunity to do so.

"But I thought Pineau La Rochelle handled all their legal work?"

"In Europe they do, but they've retained us for a specific project here in New York."

"Oh?"

"They want us to help crack down on the sale of counterfeit luxury goods in Manhattan."

My eyes must be as big as saucers. I imagine successfully shutting down an international ring of organized criminals who sell knock-off Dior bags on New York street corners. My reward? Being presented with La Légion d'honneur as I wear a made-to-measure John Galliano dress as Carla Bruni-Sarkozy proudly looks on.

"I'm definitely interested in helping out!"

"Great, I was going to hand it over to someone in the IP department, but since you speak French, you can liaise more easily with Pierre Le Furet, Dior's IP director, who is spearheading this initiative."

"When can I start?"

"You should get going on the research right away. Your starting point should be the PRO-IP Act that was recently enacted. Apparently the act increases civil and criminal penalties for copyright infringement and requires courts to enforce stiffer forfeiture penalties against convicted infringers. I would also read the report prepared by the

Anti-Counterfeiting Coalition and then call the Trademark Infringement Unit of the NYPD. I'll give you the name of the inspector overseeing it, he should be helpful."

I scramble to take notes and picture myself working alongside the NYPD while they raid a warehouse filled with fake merchandise in Chinatown. I knew moving to New York would be exciting but never dreamed it would be like an episode of *Law & Order.*

"Okay, will do."

"It might be a lot to handle with all the work Bonnie's been giving you," he says, crossing his arms and looking peeved. "So let me know if you become overloaded. This file is really important to the firm."

"Of course."

He stares at me hesitatingly before standing up and closing his door.

"Catherine, you need to understand how this office works if you're going to survive here."

"Okay," I answer eagerly, excited about getting a competitive edge.

"I know you've been with the firm for several years, but New York is totally different. You need to think of it as a feudal system."

"Right." I nod but have no idea what he's talking about.

"You see, the senior partners are the warlords. They lead their battalions—their departments—into battle to gain control of more territory: clients, files, and billable hours. The victory is a major payout at the end of the year."

Warlords? Battles for more territory? Paris was competitive, but this is nuts! I stare at Antoine, wondering if he strips off that Paul Smith jacket at the end of the day to play World of Warcraft. I giggle, assuming that he must be joking, but his expression remains severe.

"You need to form an alliance with a warlord who will continuously supply you with work and protect you when times get tough. No warlord, no future at Edwards and White."

He's dead serious. What does this mean for me?

"There's a lot going on right now at the firm. You need protection."

Protection? This is starting to sound more like a mafia ring than a feudal system.

"Who's your warlord?" I ask.

"Scott."

"Who should mine be?"

"I think it should be Bonnie."

Bonnie? But he seems to hate her. Is he trying to trick me?

"I don't think she'd be my warlord. She seems way too busy." And, I don't mention, bitchy.

"Catherine, you need to get real," he says, looking exasperated. "Everyone around here is very busy. You need Bonnie to provide you with a steady stream of work. A steady stream of work means a clear route to partnership."

"Okay, I get it." I think.

"Good. One last thing. Did Scott talk to you about doing pro bono work?"

"No, he didn't."

"We're all encouraged to do some, Catherine. But it's *not* a substitute for meeting the billable hours requirements."

"Have you done any?" I ask, trying to find out whether this is actually something successful associates do—or just something they pay lip service to.

"Yes, for a school in Harlem for kids with learning disabilities. They're moving into a new building to accommodate their expanding art program and I'm helping them negotiate the lease." His voice softens. "It's extremely rewarding."

I'm surprised that an apparent workaholic like Antoine

takes time out of his busy schedule to help Harlem school kids.

"That's amazing! I'd love to be involved in something that important. But, honestly, when do you find the time?"

"I just make the time—mostly on weekends."

My weekends in Paris that I didn't spend at the office were mostly filled by browsing at Le Bon Marché, checking out art galleries, or occasionally lying in bed recovering from a bit too much red wine after a night out with my girlfriends. I feel embarrassed by my lack of altruism.

This unanticipated piece of information makes me want to know more about Antoine and I have an urge to dig deeper into his private life.

"Can I be nosy? Why are you leaving for Paris?"

"For personal reasons." He looks away before responding.

Feeling awkward about his closed response to such an intimate question, I cover my tracks with flattery. "The Paris office can definitely use the bench strength. They don't have anyone of your calibre."

He responds with a grateful smile.

Leaving his office, I can't stop wondering about the reason for Antoine's upcoming move. Whatever it is, he's a bit of a mystery.

I take the long way back through the reception area and catch a glimpse of Bonnie's office. Unlike the other darkly ornate offices, hers is sleek and modern. A long white leather couch sits in front of the window and two matching Barcelona chairs face her glass and stainless-steel desk. The look is cool and icy and from what I've seen so far matches her personality.

Back in my office, I find my agenda placed in the middle of my desk with *Rikash's Birthday* in big red letters covering today's date. *Ah, merde.* I need to do something about this *tout de suite.* Any lawyer knows that a good rapport with her assistant is crucial. It's like the relationship between an actress and her makeup artist.

I scurry over to Mimi's desk, since she seems to be a master of office culture.

"Mimi, can I bother you for a minute? I need help with something."

"Of course, sweetie, how can I help?"

"It's Rikash's birthday today and I want to take him out to lunch. Do you know his favourite places to eat?"

"Sorry, I don't. But it's 'restaurant week.'" She rummages in a drawer. "Here's a *Zagat.* Go for the names in bold print."

"Thanks. I owe you one."

I hustle back to my desk and start dialling numbers. Four Seasons, *Fully booked*. Le Cirque, *fully committed*. Aureole, *nothing before 3:30 pm*. I try a few more places before I stumble upon the listing for the 21 Club. "*Yes, we do have one table for two available at 1:00.*"

"Wonderful. I'll take it."

"This place is such a boys' club. I wish we were people watching at the Café de Flore."

Obviously my choice isn't the hit I hoped it'd be.

"Okay, it isn't exactly the trendiest scene, but I read that it used to be a former Prohibition-era speakeasy. It's kind of exciting, don't you think?"

"Pfff, the days of Prohibition are long over and thank god for that. I'd die without my gin and tonic after work." He removes his sunglasses from the top of his head.

"Gin and tonic? I thought you'd be more of a flavoured martini type."

"Don't be fooled my sweet exterior. I enjoy my liquor strong, straight up, and with no artificial flavours."

I go through the menu and decide on one of their classic

lunch offerings. "I'll have the 21 burger with fries and a glass of red wine. What are you having?"

"How do you eat all that fattening food and stay so thin?"

"I'm French, remember?"

"Oh right, and I'm not, so I'll have the house salad. Bathing suit season is just around the corner."

"Do you want some wine?"

"No thanks. I have a strict rule about waiting until after five."

"I probably should too, but having a glass of wine is a ritual that I just can't go without."

"I'm sure you were introduced to it early in life. In India, I drank contaminated water as a child. Luckily, I can go without."

"So you've opted for gin and tonic instead?"

"Yes, it stimulates the palate and the mind."

"Wine also stimulates the mind. Baudelaire once said that there would be a major void in human intelligence if wine didn't exist."

"That void already exists at our firm, in case you haven't noticed. And if my memory serves me right, Baudelaire studied law, developed a fondness for booze and hashish, contracted syphilis, and died, so I'm not sure I would follow his lead."

I laugh, amused by his wry sense of humour, but stop when he doesn't join in.

"Why the long face, Rikash? It's your birthday. Come on, lighten up."

"Sorry, sweetie, I'm just a bit pissed off. Bonnie the ice queen made me miss something really important yesterday."

"What?"

He hesitates before answering. "The Dolce and Gabbana biannual sample sale," he says with equal parts pout and reverence.

"Why didn't you ask someone else to cover for you?"

"Like I didn't think of that! I did everything I could to get out of the office, including kicking and screaming in reception, but Bonnie wouldn't budge. I had to finish one of her documents since Maria and Roxanne were both out shopping at Daffy's." The disdain is nearly dripping off his face.

"Rikash, it's just a sale."

As soon as the words come out of my mouth, I know they're a dumb thing to say. He gives me a look that suggests I've violated a sacred oath.

"Just a sale? Are you serious? That sale is the cornerstone

of my wardrobe. God, I even sleep in Dolce."

"Okay, sorry. I guess I'd be upset if I missed a Dior sale."

After I commiserate, his face softens. I'm dying to tell him about my new Dior mandate but decide to wait until we get back to the office to avoid leaking sensitive information to fellow diners.

"Anyway, I got my revenge. Bonnie asked me to order a Town Car yesterday afternoon for an important meeting downtown and I 'forgot.'"

"*Non?*"

"Since she couldn't get another car during rush hour, she had to take the subway. I would have loved to be a fly on the wall as she wobbled down the stairs to catch the F train in her Jimmy Choos."

I'm surprised by his confession but full of admiration for his spunk. I also make a mental note never to prevent him from going to a sample sale.

"Did she say anything about it?"

"Are you kidding? She doesn't address assistants directly. She had Roxanne yell at me on her behalf."

"You've got guts."

"It's all about survival. You've got to stick up for yourself."

He tucks his serviette in over his designer tie. "Anyway,

enough about *me*. You need to find an apartment. You don't want to stay in that dreary corporate suite for much longer. Where are you going to look?"

"You won't approve, but I'm thinking of the Upper East Side."

He shakes his head.

"Soon you'll be wearing penny loafers and quilted jackets."

"It may be a bit staid for your taste, but I like the fact that I can walk to the office and at least I'll get some sleep at night."

"Who moves to New York City to sleep?" He takes a bite from his salad. "Speaking of getting no sleep, have you started dating yet?" he asks with a mischievous glance.

I take a sip of Beaujolais before answering. "Rikash, it's not a priority for me right now."

"Ah yes, the old not-a-priority syndrome."

Unaware that I was afflicted with a syndrome, I pry for more information.

"What do you mean?"

"I've met so many women your age, totally consumed by their careers and ambition, going out bar hoping, luxuriating in the blush of money, not one bit concerned about finding a mate, and then one day, poof!" He snaps his fingers. "They reach forty and freak out."

Startled by his abrupt gesture, I nearly jump from my seat.

"You know, they join those dating sites, buy a book about how to find a man, and become aggressive huntresses. Don't let that happen to you, dah-ling. Get in the market while the going is good and you don't have cheek implants."

I reach for my glass and swirl my wine pensively before finishing it in one large gulp. Although I know he's right, I'm not ready to face the reality he's describing; it seems so distant. After all, I'm in my early thirties and I don't have time for a committed relationship.

"You're probably right, but for the moment, work is my priority, not finding true love."

He nearly chokes on his salad.

"True love? Who's talking about true love? I just think you need to get out there and get some. It'll help your practice. Look at Bonnie." He covers his mouth and I know he's just revealed some juicy information.

"What about Bonnie?"

"I really shouldn't say."

"Oh come on, you can't do this to me, Rikash! Spill it."

He looks around the room before answering.

"Okay, I won't say much, but I'll say this. She's sleeping with someone at the firm and she's very territorial about it."

"Who?"

"Can't say."

"How can I stay out of her way if I don't know who it is?"

"Just watch, you'll figure it out. Like I said, be careful or she'll make your life a living hell. And you definitely don't need that right now. There are enough turf wars going on at the office as it is."

"How do you know all this?"

"Information circulates at lightning speed, especially *that* kind of information. Rumour has it Bonnie was engaged a few years ago to a senior partner in London, but he broke it off a week before the wedding. She never got over it and has been fishing in the office pool ever since."

Stunned, I lean back into my chair. I then try to analyze my reaction: If Bonnie were a man, would I be so shocked? Of course not. But doesn't she know that a woman's reputation at work can be destroyed faster than you can say *déshabillé*?

"Okay, now tell me about the turf wars."

"I wish I could, dah-ling, but I don't know much. I overheard someone in the elevator say something about a senior partner leaving, but I have no idea who it is. All I know is that there have been lots of closed-door meetings lately and that everyone seems to be on edge."

"I'm not surprised. There's always some kind of drama going on. What about Antoine? What's his story?" While Rikash is dishing, I might as well ask.

"He's a fantastic lawyer, but I've had a hard time trying to figure him out. He keeps mostly to himself. I think he's sexy and I was hoping he'd be otherwise inclined, but I've come to the conclusion that the only sheets I'll ever see him in are his damn time sheets."

"I know. I've had trouble sizing him up too. He's so intense. One minute he's yelling, the next he's offering advice. But you're right, he is pretty sexy."

"He just needs to take that highlighter out of his buttocks."

I giggle. "What about you? You always have an interesting project in the works."

Rikash rambles on about his recent amorous conquests—"Men are like fish, the longer your rod, the better their bod"; his upcoming documentary about an Indian transsexual, "The title is *Mahotmama*"; India fashion week, "Have you ever heard about the nipplegate scandal?"; Bollywood movies, "You definitely get your money's worth with a thousand pelvic thrusts a minute"—until our talk turns back to office gossip.

"Please stay away from Harry Traum," he warns. "He's in the middle of a messy divorce so he's a real nightmare. And you better watch out for some of the secretaries, they're real bitches: Roxanne is psychotic and Maria's on the verge of a nervous breakdown; you'll see, sooner or later she'll crack. Antoine and Bonnie have been working her around the clock."

When Rikash mentions Antoine and Bonnie, I nervously look at my watch. Our lunch has gone on for an hour and a half and now I'm seriously behind in my work. I'll be stuck in the office late again tonight.

"Sorry to cut our lunch short, but we aren't in Paris. I need to get back to the office and bill some hours."

"Thanks for cheering me up, dah-ling. This lunch gave me a nice little morale boost. Now I'll make it through the afternoon without having to pop any pills."

❧

"I need you to create a new client profile for me." I stand beaming in front of Rikash's cubicle. "Christian Dior."

"Are you serious? You can't kid around about things like that. I don't think my heart can take it."

"I'm not. They're a new client. Exciting, isn't it?"

He jumps up from his chair with hands stretched high above his head. "Yay! Finally an interesting file that isn't named after some barbaric war or military program!"

I can't help but smile at Rikash's reaction. It's true that many acquisition files are opened under secret code names such as Operation Gulf War, Kandahar II, or Minuteman Missile Project. I guess they're appropriately named given the internal wars being waged at Edwards & White these days.

Antoine passes by en route to the reception area.

"Going out to grab lunch. Catherine, don't forget to finalize those files for tomorrow morning."

I nod and close my office door to get some work done.

At six thirty, after printing out the PRO-IP Act and reading the white paper prepared by the Anti-Counterfeiting Coalition, I emerge from my office. Rikash has left, but Maria and Roxanne are whispering away. They immediately stop and try to look innocent. I've obviously walked in on some heavy gossip.

"Working late?"

"Yep. We have four files to finish for Antoine tonight," Maria replies, looking annoyed that I've interrupted their dishing session. In her late thirties, Maria has a penchant for long-sleeved T-shirts that have slogans like *Here comes trouble* or *No more problems please, I'm trying to quit* written in sparkly glitter across her large bosom. Today's shirt reads, *Keep calm and carry on.*

I follow her shirt's advice and go back to reading the anti-counterfeiting white paper. Its contents are fascinating; it describes the broad range of products counterfeited in America, which range from helicopter parts to Viagra. It further explains that counterfeiting has been linked to terrorism, human trafficking, and child labour. Buying fake merchandise clearly isn't as harmless as I thought it was, and I make a mental note to tell friends who occasionally pick up a knock-off bag on the street. At nine thirty, I open my door again and Maria is still typing away while intermittently nibbling on her General Tao chicken and crispy Grand Marnier prawns.

"Want a prawn?" Maria asks. "They're really tasty."

"No thanks."

I remain completely engrossed in Dior until ten thirty,

when my empty stomach wakes me from my trance and forces me to rove the various boardrooms looking for old meeting food. Despite the lavish meals the firm offers, I am never able to order any before the cut-off time and end up munching on leftover ham sandwiches with wilting lettuce.

At eleven thirty, after putting together a closing binder for Allen Partners, I decide to turn off my computer. Not for the first time, I catch myself wondering why it is that other professionals can leave their offices at a decent hour, while attorneys are expected to meet and greet the cleaning staff.

"Want a lift home?" Maria asks as she puts on her coat. "I have a car waiting downstairs. We'll drop you off."

"No thanks, I need some air. I'll walk you to the elevators, though."

On our way out, we walk by Bonnie's office. She is shoeless and has both feet on her desk, which is nearly buried beneath a huge pile of documents and dotted with empty cans of Diet Coke with smears of red lipstick. Her hair is piled high on her head and secured with a Montblanc pen, and she has a Hermès scarf tied around her neck.

Based on the information Rikash shared earlier, I can't help but wonder which lawyer is getting tied up with her scarf tonight à la *Basic Instinct*. Could it be Alfred? Maybe Alfred is good in bed.

Antoine catches up with Maria and me as he shrugs on his suit jacket. He makes a point of looking the other way when passing Bonnie's office and there is no exchange of "good nights." I'm beginning to suspect that the Friendship Program memo got lost in the mail.

"Going home?"

"No, I'm meeting someone for a quick bite. I'll be back later."

Back later? It's almost midnight. Who's he meeting at this hour?

After he's left the building, Maria looks at me and rolls her eyes. "He does this all the time. Never sleeps."

I decide to stroll up to Madison Avenue on my way home to the corporate apartment at 74th and Fifth. I need a little time for window shopping. Back in Paris, it was how I'd wind down from work. I'd spend Sunday afternoons on the rue du Faubourg Saint-Honoré nursing a latte and stopping in for a quick peek at Colette before making my way to Place Vendôme. The vibrant colours and the sheer beauty of high fashion are the perfect counterpoint to the high pressure and piles of manila folders I spend most of my day with.

I stop in front of Dior's majestic store on 57th and take in every detail. They have multi-tiered beaded heels on display and ruffled leather handbags that make my jaw drop. I still can't believe I'll be doing legal work for Dior. I take a deep breath and feel totally intoxicated by the idea. I then move on to Madison and peek into Barneys' windows. I love looking at the cuts, the fabrics, and the way the designers play with proportions. All the stores I've only read about in American *Vogue* and seen on my favourite French fashion blog, Garance Doré, are here in front of me. I let the world of prospectuses, memos, and legal briefs slip away for today. Now I'm ready for dreams of taffeta, organza, and mousseline.

Chapter 5

"What the hell is this?" Antoine marches into my office looking thoroughly pissed off, brandishing the binder I worked on yesterday.

"Um, it's the binder I put together for the Allen Partners closing next week." My mind is spinning through last night. Why does he look so angry? What could I possibly have done wrong?

"Is that right?" His furious flipping of the binder's pages is punctuated by the tapping of his cuff links on my desk.

Given the serious look on his face, I remain silent.

"This is absolute garbage, Catherine. Did you actually look at this before putting it in the binder?" He points to a page marred with yellow marker and bullet points.

Merde. In a panic, I nervously check my email to see which file I sent to Maria before leaving the office yesterday.

"You're right, those are the drafts. They aren't the documents I asked Maria to print for me."

"Maria?" he asks, his voice getting increasingly louder and more aggressive. "Are you telling me that you rely on *my* secretary to review *your* work?" His face turns a deep mauve that matches his tie.

"No . . . um. I just thought that I could trust her to print the final document correctly."

My stomach is in knots so tight they could hold together the sails on a tall ship navigating through the Bermuda Triangle.

"I can't fucking believe this! Catherine, you're the lawyer, not Maria. Thank god I caught this. Can you imagine how bad it would make me look if this had been sent out to Allen Partners?"

I sit in my chair, mortified. I'm sure I sent her the right document but should have checked the final product anyway. Ashamed of my oversight, I stand to apologize, my hands shaking.

"I'm really sorry about this, Antoine. I'll double check next time."

He takes a deep breath and stares coldly into my eyes. "There better not be a next time, Catherine." He storms out of my office.

Merde. Merde. Merde. What do I do? Part of me desperately wants to run after him into the hallway and get down on my knees begging for forgiveness while kissing his Boss shoes, but my rational self realizes that literally prostrating myself would cross the line from screwing up to sucking up.

How could I have been so careless? This could cost me something vital: *his respect.* I try to dive into Bonnie's ABC file, but it takes me an hour before I can focus. I've spent six long and painful years trying to climb the ladder to become a partner, an accomplishment reached only by a minority of women in big law firms. And now my chance at making it to the top might be up in smoke because of a careless oversight.

I try to do some work on the Dior file to get my mind off things, but I get only temporarily distracted before Mel Johnson manages to track me down.

"Counselaaar! Are you ready for our conference call?"

"Hi, Mel, yes, yes. Can we start now? I have another call at noon with a Brazilian client."

"You're such an international woman of mystery, I love it. Hang on."

I sit on a call for more than an hour with Mel and his colleagues discussing their company's international expansion plans while staring out the window. Not wanting to sound unprofessional, I try to clearly answer questions about European securities registration requirements even though I'm secretly hyperventilating because of the episode with Antoine.

"Can we talk further over drinks after work?" Mel asks once the conference call ends.

"Sorry, Mel, I'm going to be tied up with a big project tonight."

"You're going to be tied up tonight? Wow, I just love it when a woman talks dirty."

In no mood for his double entendre, I cut the conversation short.

"I had so much work to do yesterday, all I ate was half a yogurt," a tall blonde announces to her enthralled audience.

I stop by the staff breakroom around noon to pick up a bottle of water and accidentally drop in on a conversation among three young female lawyers from the litigation group.

A short brunette responds eagerly. "God, I was in court most of the day and all *I* ate was a carrot stick during recess."

"Wow," the blonde responds, clearly impressed.

The third participant puts her hands on her hips before blurting out, "Jeez, ladies, if you think that's bad, I was stuck in the library doing research for Harry Traum until two in the morning and didn't eat a thing all day!"

To my dismay, a look of admiration comes across the other two women's faces. Could they be proud of starving themselves for the sake of work? Or is it that as a group, lawyers are so fiercely competitive that we feel the need to compete in every single thing we do, including not eating? I'm convinced that competitiveness is the answer, as it's fair to say that most lawyers have a type-A personality. Here in New York, most lawyers fit into the AAA category; sort of like the batteries but with levels of energy, competitiveness, and ambition that never run out. There is no need for chargers here, as the fuel is in endless supply: money, power, sex, peer recognition, and ego stroking.

It's no surprise then that conversations by the proverbial

water cooler at the firm typically revolve around upcoming triathlons *(when do they train, in their sleep?)*, exotic or physically challenging trips *(climb Mount Kilimanjaro for fun anyone?)*, and time-consuming cultural or artistic endeavours such as learning a fourth language or to play a musical instrument *(during extensive bathroom breaks?)*.

I read an article in *Psychology Today* recently that outlined the major character traits of type-A personalities: 1) insecurity about status, which translates into excessive competition; 2) time urgency and impatience, which causes irritation and exasperation; and 3) free-floating hostility, which can be triggered by the most minor incidents.

I seem to fit somewhere in between types A and B. I'm definitely competitive, there's no question about it. I finished at the top of my class in law school, competed on a ski team, and have engaged in my fair share of office politics, but I consider myself pretty easygoing, level-headed, and, while I get frustrated, I have never raised my voice or been hostile toward anyone at the firm. At least, *not until now.*

"Maria, run down and have my jacket dry cleaned. I spilled Diet Coke all over the front and I have a client meeting this afternoon," Bonnie demands, standing in the middle of the hallway holding her suit jacket in one hand. The silk of her ruffle blouse is so thin and the cleavage so revealing that she's practically standing in her brassiere. I guess she's unaware that a transparent silk square barely covering her unmentionables does not a blouse make.

I can't help but smirk a little. Why go to the trouble of getting her jacket dry cleaned when Bonnie will pull her usual *femme fatale* routine of making some remark about the room temperature, then slowly but strategically unbutton her suit jacket so every straight man in the room will lose track of the conversation. She could be reciting her favourite pumpkin pie recipe and nobody would even blink an eye. From what I've seen, Bonnie knows how to close a deal and it rarely involves wearing a suit jacket.

"Catherine, I've been thinking," she calls after me as I fail to sneak into my office unnoticed. "I need to know where the best dry cleaners near the office are. Why don't you research that for me? Today."

Dry cleaners? Excuse me? Did I go to law school and bust my derrière for the last six years to research *dry cleaners*?

"Is that billable to any particular file?" I mutter under my breath.

"No, it's not. Also note that I like any research done for me to be presented in memo format," she shouts into the hallway before slinking back to her office. (Refer to character trait #3 of type-A personality.)

I slam my door so hard that they must have heard it in Brooklyn. Rikash buzzes me on the intercom, but I don't respond.

"*Salope!*" My hatred is so intense that "bitch" doesn't even begin to describe her.

I'm tempted to call Scott and let him know how I'll be spending the next few hours of my billable time, but I swallow my pride to start doing the research. If that's what the ice queen wants, that's what she'll get.

Edwards & White Office Memorandum

To: Bonnie Clark
From: Catherine Lambert
Re: Dry Cleaners on the Upper East Side

I *Purpose*

The purpose of this memorandum and the attached exhibit is to identify the highest quality dry cleaners near our office. While there are about ten dry cleaners at every intersection in

Manhattan, their levels of quality and service diverge greatly. Hereinafter is a list of those top-quality cleaners that I would most recommend.

II *Madame Paulette Dry Cleaners*

Madame Paulette Dry Cleaners would appear to be the top choice for your dry cleaning needs. They boast a long list of distinguished couture designers such as Dior, Chanel, Givenchy, Gucci, Prada, and Hugo Boss[1] as faithful clients. Conveniently located on Second Avenue between 65th and 66th streets, their website offers rave reviews and glowing testimonials from well-known, satisfied customers. "It's very exciting, in the dry-cleaning end of things. They turned a delicate silk blouse from sad yellow back to white."[2] In addition, Madame Paulette has been described as the dry cleaner of choice for the perfectionist and the merely finicky.[3] It is famously snooty but well worth the effort because it has rescued many a garment from the edge of ruin.[4]

---

1 *New York Magazine*, May 2009.

2 Nora Ephron, *New York Times*, October 31, 2009.

3 *New York Times*, January 7, 2010.

4 *Lucky Magazine*, January 2009.

Finally, it is worth noting that they specialize in the maintenance and preservation of wedding gowns, both old and new. "The only establishment I trust to maintain, renew, and preserve my bridal collection is Madame Paulette."[5] So that you can examine their high standard of care, I have attached for your convenience as Exhibit 1 a jacket dry cleaned this afternoon by Madame Paulette Dry Cleaners.

III *Alpian's Garment Care of New York*

They are located a stone's throw away from our office, at 325 E. 48th Street.

"Alpian's knows garment care" is their motto. Their website offers a reassuringly precise description of services available. Their attention to detail is impressive: employees are trained to look for loose buttons, open seams, lint, and unresolved stains. Furthermore, they use a wide array of devices to make your garment look its best in your closet, in your suitcase, and, most importantly, on you.

In order to ensure the absence of material misrepresentations in the above-referenced website, a few of Alpian's clients

---

5   Vera Wang, *InStyle Magazine*, November 2009.

were interviewed by a junior associate this afternoon. Most clients questioned for the purposes of this memorandum declared themselves completely satisfied with Alpian's services.

IV *Anel French Cleaners*

They are located on Columbus Avenue between 69th and 70th.

Although further written evidence about the services they offer is scarce, I was immediately drawn to their name. How could a business that was wise enough to select a name that rhymes with Chanel and have an Eiffel Tower as its logo fail to be equally astute in its execution of dry cleaning services? In addition, a sign in the window promises that "satisfaction is guaranteed."

It should be noted, however, that in a recent court decision, *Roy Pearson vs. Custom Cleaners*, this type of guarantee was interpreted and it was concluded that a customer cannot demand any type of service he or she desires based on such a sign. As a result, a D.C. judge's $65 million lawsuit against the cleaners, which allegedly lost a pair of his pants, was dismissed.

Anel's most noteworthy feature is its fast and reliable delivery services, which will allow you to focus on work or extra-curricular activities.

V *Conclusion*

In conclusion, it can be successfully argued that within a close distance from our offices, your garments can be cleaned rapidly, safely, and satisfactorily. I hope the above information will be helpful in assisting you with your dry cleaning needs in the future. Please do not hesitate to contact me should you have any questions (or excess lint).

After I press send, I stare at the blank wall wondering why I followed her silly memo instructions. Why stoop as low as to draft a memo on dry cleaning? Why didn't I just tell her to go to hell? After all, I've been with the firm for six years and developed a good rapport with some senior partners in Paris. I square my shoulders and tell myself the truth: this is a childish game to see what I'm made of. If I dare object, complain, whine, shed a few tears, or threaten to jump ship, she wins and I lose. And I've worked way too hard to lose now. Am I willing to give up my place in the race for partnership?

Non, I'm ready for the next round.

Isabelle Laflèche

Chapter 6

"I'm glad you like it. But don't assume that it's yours just yet." Brian, my eager real estate agent, tells me as we leave a bright, well-maintained prewar one-bedroom apartment on the corner of 68th and First. Brian and I have just spent six hours looking at more than two dozen apartments, most of which require a major overhaul and cleaning job. Exhausted, I'm in no mood to look at any more places unless I can figure out a way to bill this time back to a client. I'll do whatever it takes to get this place.

Barely large enough to contain the antique dresser and

bed inherited from my grandmother and shipped over from Paris, my new home, located on a relatively quiet street within walking distance of the office, has windows overlooking a small courtyard that reminds me of my old apartment in Saint Germain. This tiny jewel is exactly what I want.

"You need to get approved by *Elad*," he says with a menacing look and one eyebrow dramatically arched, like a character out of a vintage horror flick. "And he's *very* difficult."

"Who's Elad?"

"He manages the building. He has final say on *everything*. You need to come with me to his office to meet him in person and fill out an application."

Brian escorts me to a dark, ghoulish waiting area in a dreary office building and shakes my hand. "Someone will be with you shortly. Good luck."

I imagine him laughing like Vincent Price in the "Thriller" video as he walks out of the building.

"Come in," a woman's voice blurts out from a mysterious intercom system as I walk through a dingy waiting room to the other side of the office. Completely buried beneath a towering mountain of paper, Elad sits in a low swivel chair. It's impossible to see anything about him other than the top of his balding head. Which isn't pretty.

"Who the hell are you?"

"Um . . . I'm Catherine, I'm applying for the apartment on 68th Street."

"Which one? I have hundreds of places on 68th. Who's the broad in my office?" he shouts into his phone.

"The French lawyer," the mystery voice responds.

He mumbles something undecipherable under his breath.

"Okay, sit."

As I approach, his dark eyes look right through me.

"First, let's talk money: I want three months' rent in advance and a security deposit. Any damage to the place, you'll never see that money again, got it?" he says with a rapid-fire New York accent.

"Elad, the woman from Washington is here to sign the lease for her daughter," the mystery lady interjects through the intercom.

"Tell her that she's too late. Once I'm through with the lawyer, I'm going home . . . Tell her to come back next week."

"But, Elad, she flew in all the way from—"

"Not my fucking problem," he shouts back into the phone.

"With her daughter—"

"LIKE. I. SAID: NOT MY FU-CKING PROBLEM."

Today's horoscope predicted great luck in real estate matters; it was silent about the hellish landlord.

"Now where were we? Ah yes, the broker fee. You pay a broker fee, which is fifteen percent of your first year's rent, and we also charge a three-hundred-dollar paper processing fee."

I nervously sit up in my chair and try to calculate how much all this is going to cost me. I've been spoiled by France's pro-tenant laws and hadn't expected to pay more than two months' rent in advance. I guess the laws are different in New York. For a split second, I consider raising the subject but think better of it. Looking into his eyes, I see homelessness.

"Okay."

"Do you have any credit history in this country?"

"No, not yet."

"You'll need to find yourself a guarantor with a New York City address who makes a few hundred grand and who will guarantee the lease."

Merde. Now I'm really screwed. Who do I know in New York who will guarantee my lease? A few of my father's relatives lived in New York, but I hadn't spoken to them in about fifteen years. I couldn't just call up and ask them to guarantee my exorbitant rent, could I? There was my friend Lisa, whom I had met at law school and who was now living in New York, but I couldn't bring myself to ask her either. Maybe the firm would sign? After all, I'm not the first foreigner to transfer to the city.

"No problem," I reply, keeping my sangfroid.

"Now let me tell you something," he says, pointing his index finger while lowering his voice for emphasis: "There are two types of tenants I don't care to have in my buildings: models and lawyers. Models don't pay their rent and usually skip town on me, and lawyers are real shit disturbers. They're always quoting me some fucking section of this act or that code to avoid paying their rent. I don't want any problems, you hear me? I have no qualms about evicting anybody." He snaps his fingers dramatically.

I nod back, gritting my teeth, amused to hear that for once in my life I fall into the same category as a model. I'm also happy I kept my big mouth shut rather than blabbering on about irrelevant French laws. If I had even broached the topic of French *locataire* rights, this guy would've had me out on the street faster than a dead cockroach.

"And there's another thing."

Okay, now I'm really scared. What *else* is this guy going to come up with?

"The superintendent in your building is walking a very tight rope with me at the moment." He joins his thumb and index finger together in mid-air, mimicking a tight rope. "So I expect you to report back to me anything he does that ain't kosher, got it?" he tells me, his index finger still pointing. "So when are you moving in?"

"Next weekend?"

He dials a number on his phone. "There's a French chick in my office. She's signing a lease for apartment 7A. She'll be coming over to pick up the keys and she's moving in next weekend. No fucking screw-ups this time!"

It takes me a second, but I figure out that he's having a one-way conversation with the superintendent in my building, for whom I suddenly feel a tremendous amount of sympathy.

After signing about fifty forms and handing over a ridiculous amount of money, I stand up to leave his office, *très fatiguée* by the whole experience.

"Miss, send me the signed guarantee by the end of the week or I'm giving the apartment to someone else, *capice?*"

He smiles proudly as if he had just pronounced a word in French.

"I want the postcoital flush."

"That's my girl." Rikash pats me on the back.

"I can't believe I just said that to a Sephora salesclerk."

After an exhausting first week in New York and a traumatic rendezvous with my new landlord, I treat myself to a relaxing Sunday afternoon in Soho in the company of my confidant/personal shopper/beauty consultant.

"I love the NARS Super Orgasm collection," Rikash coos while dabbing a bit of colour on his cheeks. "This blush will make you look like you've been getting some action."

"At least it'll give me some colour. I look half dead."

"You look better than most lawyers in the office. They look like they passed decades ago."

I apply the blush to my cheeks and the pink tone with specks of gold gives my dreary complexion an immediate boost.

"I think you should get the matching eye shadow and lipstick," Rikash comments after the salesclerk hands me a box of pleasure-simulating face powder. "The ad in your magazine does say, why only have one when you can have four orgasms?"

I had picked up a copy of French *Vogue* on our way to brunch in the West Village this morning, and we had gushed over the new trends and giggled at the provocative ads.

"Good idea. I've never actually faked one, but now I'm going all the way. You're a bad influence, Rikash."

"I know, and I love it!" He wrinkles his nose.

Afterward, he takes me to see a friend's art exhibit at a gallery on West Broadway, where we discuss contemporary art before we stop in at the Moss store to pick up a stunning pair of Plexiglas lamps for my new apartment. We then head to Balthazar to grab some coffee and French pastries.

"I still can't believe you're moving to the Upper East Side. It's way more fun downtown. You could shop here every day."

"I'm staying clear of all possible distractions and temptations. I'm here to work."

He rolls his eyes.

"Don't forget to smell the camellias, my friend. That firm will suck your soul dry if you let it. I've seen so many enthusiastic young associates come in all eager and whatnot, and leave a few years later running on empty."

I look away for a moment, trying to dismiss the doom and gloom of his statement.

"And don't think it actually gets better once you've made partner. It's like a giant–apple pie eating contest where all you win is more crust."

"I could handle a *pain au chocolat* eating contest." I point to our bag of goodies jokingly.

"Ah yes!" he sighs, his mouth covered with confectionary sugar from his almond croissant. "Me too."

"Don't worry about me, Rikash, I'm pretty tough. I'm not going to let myself get beaten down by the workload, not now."

"It's not the workload I'm referring to but the slave-driving cads running the show. They can drive you mad."

"I've managed to maintain my sanity so far."

"That's what you think!"

"Ha! Very droll!"

"Let the galley slaves row together!" he shouts into the streets while mimicking a rowing gesture. "Row! Row! For fourteen, sixteen hours a day until you keel over and they throw your overexerted body to the sharks!"

"Shhh. Not so loud!"

"Are you embarrassed by my behaviour? You better

get used to it, sweetie, 'cause you ain't seen nothing yet."

"*Mon dieu*, I'm not sure I can handle it."

"Oh puh-leaze, don't be such a bore."

"I should probably get home soon. I need my beauty sleep. There's only so much Mr. Nars can do to boost my skin tone."

"Let's get you a cab then, dah-ling. You definitely need to get some rest before you start your second week in la-la land."

Chapter 7

"I need this *yesterday*," Antoine announces while marching toward my desk.

It always makes me a little crazy when someone says they need something "yesterday" or "two weeks ago." Why not go completely retro and say you need it back in 1895? (Refer back to character trait #2 of a type-A personality.)

"What is it?" I feel my shoulders stiffening. Whatever it is, I need to make up for last week's major faux pas.

"Have you heard of the plain-English disclosure rules?"

"Of course. They're the rules the SEC adopted several

years ago to make financial disclosure more understandable to investors."

His face softens. Contrary to Bindergate last week, I'm not a total idiot.

"I need you to convert some of the language from an old prospectus into plain English so that it complies."

"Will do."

"Do you have a second to talk?"

"Of course."

He shuts the door before walking closer to my desk, and I feel momentarily intoxicated by his cologne. It catches me off guard. Could I be attracted to a man who treated me like a piece of papier mâché just a few days ago? No, it's probably just that my hormones and pheromones are a bit out of whack from the stress—I'm reacting to any testosterone that comes within a five-foot radius of my body.

He looks out my window before taking a seat in one of the chairs.

"You really lucked out. The view is amazing."

"Not for long. Everyone around here is making a point of reminding me that it's only temporary."

"They're just jealous." He runs a finger along one of the petals of the pink lilies I picked up to soften the masculine surroundings. "Catherine, I'm sorry I was abrupt with you the other day. I'm under a lot of pressure." His eyes remain focused on the flowers.

Surprised by his apology, my body relaxes.

"It's okay, I understand. Besides, you were right. I should have reviewed those documents more carefully."

"I agree, but I shouldn't have snapped at you like that."

"Apology accepted."

He pauses, then shoots me a shy grin.

"I heard Bonnie made you draft a memo on dry cleaners."

"How did you find out?"

"Rikash sent it to the entire support staff, and my secretary sent me a copy. Bonnie can be a bit demanding."

A bit demanding? How about a lot of a dictator? I keep that one to myself.

"What do you think she's trying to prove with that nonsense?"

"That she's the boss. She's worked really hard to get where she is, and I suppose she wants to share the pain."

"She's doing a fine job of it."

"She was like that with me at first. But she eventually warms up," he says unconvincingly.

"I bet she warms up to me like a polar bear does to a sea lion."

He chuckles as he loosens his tie. It's the first time I've seen him smile.

"Catherine, I'd like to continue working with you on the Dior matter even after I've moved to Paris."

"Of course," I respond, trying to keep a straight face.

"It will be a good way for me to stay up to date with what's going on in the New York office. I feel like I'm going to get disconnected from base camp."

Sensing that he's about to open up, I wait for him to continue.

"I'm worried that moving to Paris will mean taking a step back in my career."

"Not necessarily, there's lot of great work in that office, and the partners are exceptionally smart."

"How was it for you? Did you have a good rapport with them?"

"I'd say yes. I had occasional run-ins with some of my colleagues, but they're a talented bunch, and I completely respect them."

He continues to stare at the floor as a moment of not-uncomfortable silence passes between us. The look on his face makes me wonder if his move was his decision.

"And I'm sure you could come back to New York if you wanted to."

"Not once I'm out of the loop. I just hope this won't ruin my chances of making partner. I'm up for it this year."

"I'm sure it won't. It seems like you're one of the best they've got."

He smiles tenderly before standing.

"Thanks, Catherine, I really appreciate it."

"No problem. My pleasure."

"I really mean it, thank you." He turns around to look my way before crossing to the doorway. "Oh, and I meant to tell you that I really like what you're wearing today. That dress looks brilliant on you."

Surprised by his compliment, it takes a moment before it actually registers. I want to reply that he doesn't look too shabby in his impeccably tailored pinstripe suit either.

"Thanks."

He walks out into the hallway, both hands in his trouser pockets, looking sad, and my heart drops at the thought of no longer seeing him on a daily basis.

❀

Now that Antoine and I have connected on a personal level, it's time to knock his socks off legally. I turn to my new plain-English project, which is actually much more interesting than it sounds. I'm all for getting rid of as much legal gobbledygook as possible, and I love the challenge of rewording legalese into plain English. I begin with a disclaimer located on the inside of the cover page:

NO PERSON HAS BEEN AUTHORIZED TO GIVE ANY INFORMATION OR MAKE ANY REPRESENTATION OTHER THAN THOSE CONTAINED OR INCORPORATED BY REFERENCE IN THIS PROSPECTUS, AND, IF GIVEN OR MADE, SUCH INFORMATION MUST NOT BE RELIED UPON AS HAVING BEEN AUTHORIZED.

Hmm, this is what I'd like to write:

Don't read anything other than this document. If you do, you obviously have way too much time on your hands.

But my professional self jots this down instead:

PLEASE RELY EXCLUSIVELY ON THE CONTENTS OF THIS PRO-
SPECTUS. NO OTHER DOCUMENT HAS BEEN AUTHORIZED BY
THE COMPANY.

I then turn to the "Use of Proceeds" section, which
highlights what the company will do with the money it
raises in the proposed offering.

WE INTEND TO USE THE NET PROCEEDS FROM THIS OFFERING
FOR GENERAL CORPORATE PURPOSES, INCLUDING DEVELOP-
ING OUR INFRASTRUCTURE, PRODUCTS, AND SERVICES, ALL OF
WHICH WE HAVE YET TO IDENTIFY.

My own plain-English version:

*We do not yet offer any products or services of any value
nor have we decided what to do with your hard-earned
money. Basically, if you invest in our company, you're
the living proof that there's a sucker born every minute.*

Legally correct plain-English version:

WE ARE IN THE PROCESS OF IDENTIFYING AND DETERMINING WITH CERTAINTY THE INTENDED USE OF THE MONEY RAISED THROUGH THIS OFFERING.

I move on to the "Risk Factors," a list advising prospective buyers about the potential risks associated with purchasing this company's stock. This one catches my attention:

WE MAY NOT EFFECTIVELY MANAGE OUR LONG-TERM OBJECTIVES; OUR MANAGEMENT TEAM HAS BEEN HERETOFORE INEXPERIENCED IN THE MANAGEMENT OF A LARGE PUBLICLY TRADED COMPANY.

My plain-English version:

We have absolutely no freaking clue what we're doing. Do you?

Correct plain-English translation:

MANAGEMENT MAY REQUIRE ASSISTANCE IN MANAGING THE CORPORATION.

I make my way cautiously but quickly through the entire fifty page prospectus. Satisfied with my work, I hit send and then move on to my favourite file: the battle against counterfeit goods.

As requested by Antoine, I go through the memo prepared by Dior's intellectual property director, M. Le Furet, which outlines the adverse impact counterfeiting has had on its U.S. business and then start drafting a detailed summary of the PRO-IP Act. Finally, I go to *Harper's Bazaar* fakesareneverinfashion.com website and am reading helpful tips for how to spot a fake bag when Rikash buzzes through on the intercom.

"Sorry to interrupt the shopping, but I have Mel on the line."

"I'm not shopping. I'm actually doing research. Put him through."

"Good morning. How's my sweetie doing?"

"Great, thanks." I mentally prepare for his advances.

"I have an urgent question about our Paris office."

"Yes?"

"We're in the process of hiring a managing director over there and need some assistance with his registration application with the European securities regulator."

"No problem. I've completed hundreds of those forms."

"Perfect, I knew my favourite little lawyer would take care of this."

I bite my tongue after he uses the adjective *little*. Could he be more condescending?

"I'm emailing you a questionnaire right now. Can you ask the director to complete it and send it to me for review?"

He pauses, something I realize I've never heard him do. "What kind of questions do they ask?"

"The usual questions about integrity; whether they've committed fraud or have been convicted of any financial crime."

There's a long second silence.

"Well . . . our candidate has been reprimanded for something pretty minor: money laundering. We were hoping you could ask the securities regulator to overlook it, *madame*. You smell what I'm cookin'?"

Seriously? Is this guy for real? I stare out the window for a brief moment and regain my composure. If I asked this question to any of the regulatory staff at the securities commission, they would laugh me off the phone. How can someone like Mel be managing hundreds of millions of dollars of people's money?

"No, Mel. There's absolutely nothing I can do."

"Oh come on, counselaaar, we're not going to let something minor like that get in the way of hiring a good candidate, are we?"

"Mel, we're talking about a serious financial crime here. The regulator will never go for it. The answer is no." I repeat firmly, hoping to resolve the matter definitively.

After I stick to my guns, Mel agrees to find a new candidate and I go back to defending Dior's interests.

Chapter 8

"I know what you're doing, dah-ling, and it's not *bill-able*."
Busted. I know that it seems contrary to the straight-line lawyer side of me, but I love to occasionally check my horoscope. Despite the naysayers, some astrological forecasts are startlingly accurate. A close friend in Paris gave me one for my birthday and it had predicted every disappointing relationship and misstep in my career, including the time I fell flat on my face during a client presentation as I attempted to explain complex banking regulations in four-inch heels. Friends sigh with disbelief when I tell them

that their lost luggage or misplaced car keys are caused by Mercury retrograde or that their Chinese sign incompatibility is the *real* reason why they never hear back from a date, but deep down I know astrology holds most of the answers.

"I'm just taking a few seconds to read my horoscope. What's the big deal?"

"God, you sound like my mother. She had my astrological chart prepared when I was born but probably fainted when she read that her eldest son was going to be gay."

"Did you keep a copy?"

"No, I smoked it."

"Come on, Rikash, stop making fun. I actually believe in this."

"Okay, what's my sign?"

"You're a Taurus monkey."

"That makes sense. It's monkey business all the way."

"And monkeys are spunky and charming."

"Well, thank you, I'll take that as a compliment. Surprisingly, I haven't received any yet today so that will do just fine. What about you, what's your sign?"

"A Virgo dog. You know, the dedicated perfectionist type."

"Yes, but remember that dogs are insecure and usually have their noses up someone else's rear end."

"Thanks for the reminder. I wonder what Bonnie's sign is. Probably a dragon or a snake."

"No, I'd say she's a rabbit." He gives me a dirty wink.

After a final sip of my espresso, I gather the courage to ask Scott to be my lease guarantor.

As I make my way toward his office, I overhear him speaking with Antoine.

"How's Catherine doing?"

"Not bad, so far," Antoine replies. "Not sure her billing is up to par, though."

Not bad so far? Her billing not up to par? *Merde!* Is this what I get for spending every waking minute of last week in my office tied to my desk eating day-old sandwiches, writing dry cleaning memos for Bonnie the Vampire Slayer, putting up with ridiculous come-ons from gross-me-out clients, and still billing no less than fifty hours in my first week in New York?

I try to calm down, but anger bubbles in my brain. How can Antoine stab me in the back after being so friendly?

I guess it's every lawyer for herself in this crazy jungle. I tiptoe closer to Scott's office and am about to aggressively chime in to defend my honour when I hear Antoine's voice softening.

"Anyway, Mel seems to really like her and she did a fantastic job on some plain-English disclosure I gave her. And the fact that she speaks French will help us with the Dior file. I'll hand her a few more files today to see how she handles the pressure."

As Antoine stands to leave, he sees me standing in the doorway and looks startled.

"Good morning."

"Oh, is it?" I ask before entering Scott's office.

He gives me a bewildered look before walking away.

"Hey, Catherine, have a seat. How's everything so far? I hear Mel enjoyed meeting you last week."

"He seems . . . interesting."

Scott laughs. "That's a good way to put it. I may have an even more interesting project coming up for you. We're involved in a beauty contest and vying for the financing of a large technology company. If we get it, it'll be a great deal to sink your teeth into."

"Sounds amazing," I hear a voice that sounds like mine

blurt out. God, can I handle another matter on my to-do list? How will I manage to stay on top of the Dior counterfeiting project? I might need to quit sleeping.

"Antoine was just telling me how lucky we are to have you. He thinks you were a great transfer."

"Really? I thought—"

He cuts me off.

"Antoine is as hard on others as he is on himself. He's a perfectionist at heart."

"I've noticed. Nothing wrong with that." Relieved that I didn't barge in on their conversation, I finally relax into his leather wing chair.

"So how's the apartment hunt? Any luck?"

"Well, I was actually, um, going to ask you about the process. I hear that landlords sometimes ask for a guarantee."

"Just call Mimi, we'll have someone in accounting take care of it. We do it all the time."

My horoscope must have been right when it said today was a good day to ask my boss for a favour. Now I can send the guarantee back to Elad and start making his life miserable.

"If you don't have any plans after work, I have two tickets for a party the American Bar Association is hosting at the Gramercy Hotel. You should go. It will be a great way to meet new people in the city."

This is a little unexpected, given the conversation he was having just minutes ago about my billable hours not being up to par. But if the boss is asking, *pourquoi pas?*

"Rikash, how about joining me for an ABA party at the Rose Bar?"

"You mean socialize with lawyers after my shift here is over? No thanks, I'd rather cut my right arm off."

"Come on, Rikash, please."

"Nope, sorry, dah-ling, I already have plans. I'm going to see some hot men dance on tables. It's way more fun. Don't you have any other friends in the city?"

I decide it's time to call Lisa. She was my closest friend the year I spent at Pepperdine, and she and I had kept in touch through sporadic birthday and Christmas emails, but I haven't seen her in years. Like me, she ended up working for a large white-shoe law firm, one of those London-based international firms that form part of the Magic Circle.

"Hello, *ma chérie,* guess who? Long time no speak, *non?*"

"Oh my god, oh my god, oh my god, Cathereeen! How are you?"

"Great! You'll never guess where I moved to?"

"Let me guess. Some exotic French island like Martinique?"

"*Bien sûr que non,* I'm not even close to semi-retirement. No, I'm here in New York!"

"*Aaahhh!* That is so fabulous! When did you move? And why didn't you tell me sooner?"

"It happened so quickly. The firm posted an announcement a few months ago saying they needed a few associates in New York and next thing I knew I was looking for an apartment on the Upper East Side."

"You moved to the Upper East Side?"

"Yes."

"Oh my god, we're neighbours. Let's go out to celebrate!"

The more things change . . .

Back in university, Lisa was the ultimate party girl. Not only was she a social butterfly who knew everybody on campus, but she was also the treasurer of the student body, a position that not only helped her prepare for a career in international bank financing but, more importantly, provided her with an invite to every party.

"My thoughts exactly. How about meeting up at the Rose Bar after work? There's an ABA party tonight."

"I'll be there at seven. Can't wait!"

Chapter 9

I'm excited about my first big night out in the city that never sleeps. Sitting in the back seat of a cab flying down Park Avenue, I feel like a native New Yorker going out on the town. I catch a glimpse of the Chrysler Building's jewel-like crown and a shiver goes down my spine. Who knows what awaits me tonight? The suspense makes the cab ride feel even more exhilarating.

I arrive at the Rose Bar, an art-filled space in the Gramercy Park Hotel, and quickly pick out Lisa in the crowd. Always dressed in her trademark ultra-feminine attire, she is wearing a black sheath dress with a hot pink cardigan, a triple-strand pearl necklace, lace stockings, and the highest heels. Her hair is tied back in an elegant ponytail. She is chatting up the young bartender, who looks totally mesmerized by her big green eyes and outgoing personality. I'm so excited about our reunion that I cut through the crowd using my (ahem, new) J. Crew red satin clutch.

"*Bonjour, ma chérie.*"

She jumps into my arms and gives me a triple air kiss.

"Catherine, I'm so happy you're here!"

"So am I, I'm really excited!"

"You look great as usual." She studies my outfit. "I see the French flair hasn't disappeared with your move to the States. Wait. Is that a J. Crew bag? Don't tell me you've gone American on me!"

"As a matter of fact, I have!"

"Welcome to America! The land of online shopping!" She hands me a glass of champagne. "Here, I ordered your old favourite: pink Taittinger. Let's toast to your move to Manhattan!"

She turns to the bartender.

"Jamie, why don't you pour yourself a glass to toast my friend Catherine—she just moved here from Paris!"

The bartender willingly obliges and the three of us lift our glasses in perfect bubbly unison.

"Here's to being single, drinking double, and sleeping triple!" she toasts.

"I see that you haven't changed at all. And I mean that in a good way."

She giggles.

"This is a great party, despite all the lawyers!"

I scan the room: champagne is flowing by the case-load; a young woman wearing a tiny silver bikini who looks straight out of a Skyy Vodka ad is standing on top of the bar and pouring iced vodka into the martini glasses of drooling attorneys. Another woman wearing a tight strapless gown is standing behind a table serving oysters, smoked salmon, and caviar.

"I can't believe you finally moved here, Cat!"

"I can't believe it either. Even though I've already billed close to a hundred hours, signed a lease with Robespierre, and visited half the dry cleaners in Manhattan, it hasn't really sunk in yet."

She wrinkles her nose. "Why all the dry cleaners? Did you lose something?"

"Trust me, you don't want to know." I try to change the

Isabelle Laflèche

subject to something more uplifting. "You'll never guess who my new client is: Christian Dior! I'm so excited, Lisa, this has definitely confirmed my decision to move here."

"Oh my god, that's amazing, Catherine. I always thought you should work in fashion. What will you do for them?"

"I can't say, but I'll let you in on it as soon as I can."

She gives me a knowing smile; she understands that we are ethically bound not to divulge any client secrets.

"Enough about my work. How are things in the Magic Circle?"

"You mean the Magic Kingdom?"

I laugh. "I'm glad to hear the firm hasn't billed you out of your sense of humour."

"You can say that again. But don't worry, I'll show you a good time in this city."

"I'm sure you will. Remember all our crazy girls nights when we would go out in stretch limos and drink wine coolers until we fell over on the dance floor? We didn't look like future legal gatekeepers."

"We were very classy back then, weren't we? Believe it or not, I still do it! I have a group of fun girlfriends that I go out with. It's good to let off steam once in a while."

"I haven't done that in a long time. I've been so busy

planning my move here. I could use a girls night out."

"You absolutely need to join us on Thursday night then, no excuses allowed." She points a manicured finger at me.

"Yes, *madame*."

After we joke around a bit, she becomes serious. "I have an important meeting tomorrow with my boss."

"What about?"

"My future at the firm."

"Oh?"

"I think I might be up for partnership."

My stomach drops. Thanks to her heavy partying agenda, I had better grades than Lisa in law school and had scored much higher in the moot court competition. Today, she's made a giant leap forward in the great race for the legal Holy Grail. Still, I'm thrilled for her.

"When do you think it's going to happen?"

"I'll find out tomorrow. It's the big talk."

"Wow. I feel like it'll probably be another ten years before I get the big talk."

"Stop it, Cat. Be a little patient. You're the sharpest lawyer I know."

"You need to repeat that to my warlord."

"To who?"

"Never mind. Let's not talk shop anymore."

After we order another glass of champagne, Lisa zeroes in on her favourite topic: men.

"So I guess you're still single if you moved to New York, hunh?"

"Oui, ma chérie."

"That won't last long. French women do very well here. You're viewed as exotic, so that accent will do wonders for you."

"Oh? Like birds?"

"Exactly. Like exotic birds with fast metabolisms!"

"I didn't move here to find a man, Lisa. I moved here for my career."

"How bo-ring."

"What about you? Are you seeing anyone?" I ask the question, even though I know that Lisa can't stay single longer than a bee at the height of mating season.

"Mmm-hmm. His name is Charles. He's a senior associate at the firm."

"Things are going well?"

She looks away for a moment before responding.

"I feel like I'm always the one making the effort. I'm getting a bit tired of it."

I stare back into her green eyes for a few seconds and realize how grateful I am that we've slipped right back into our old friendship.

"Why do *you* keep making the effort? Aren't relationships supposed to be give and take?"

"I know, but he cares about me. I guess he just has his own funny way of showing it."

This sounds so familiar. I hold back from rehashing the same advice I used to give her years ago. She always had a big appetite for toxic relationships and had dated every bad boy, narcissist, and egotistical scumbag on campus. She had blamed her father, an eccentric, philandering oil magnate, for her complicated relationships with men. I blamed peach schnapps.

"When did you last see him?"

"Two weeks ago."

"Two weeks ago? That seems like a long time when you work in the same office."

"He's been so busy with work. He was out entertaining clients all last week. And my work schedule has been insane . . . you know how it is."

"And what did you guys do on your last date?"

She develops a sudden fascination with the stem of

her martini glass, avoiding my gaze.

I've heard this sad story before: Lisa stays by the phone waiting for her man to call after he's finished drinking his tenth beer with the boys at some bar. And when he does make the call, she jumps in a cab, and, like a Chinese food delivery, arrives at his place within minutes. A pattern that inevitably causes men to lose interest faster than you can say, do you want an extra egg roll?

"Well?"

"Well, we didn't really *do* anything. I just went over to see him."

It always amazes me that highly intelligent and educated women like Lisa (and me, I must admit) get involved in complicated, roller-coaster romances with dubious, uncaring, afraid-of-commitment types. Maybe the overuse of our left-hemisphere brain cells kills most of the cells on the right side? Or maybe we're just desperate for some fun at the end of a long day.

"He called me after having dinner with clients downtown and I met him for a drink at his place."

"Lisa, that's *not* a date."

"Stop being so hard on me. We're supposed to be catching up, not arguing."

"I don't like to see you getting used by some jerk."

She gives me an offended look. "Wow. Don't hold back, Catherine. Charles is not a jerk."

Seeing tears well up in her eyes, I apologize and swiftly change the subject to something lighter: shopping.

"Can you get me into any of those great sample sales my assistant has been telling me about?"

She instantly brightens.

"Absolutely. My friends and I get invited to all the great sales. I can get you in anywhere you want—I'm assuming Dior is still top of the list?"

"*Bien sûr!*"

"*Vous êtes Française?*" A young man wearing a suit picks up on my accent and elbows into our space. Lisa raises her eyebrows at me and turns to chat with Jamie.

"My name is Patrick, I'm from Lyon." His strong tobacco breath nearly knocks me out.

"*Enchantée.* What do you do here in Manhattan?" I ask.

"I'm in finance. I work for Swiss Bank."

"What are you doing at an ABA party?"

"Great place to pick up lawyer chicks. What about you?"

"I work for Edwards and White," I reply hesitatingly, trying to avoid a cheesy pickup line.

"Hey, I know a guy named Antoine who works in your office."

"Really?" I ask, surprised. "How do you know him?"

"He's dating a friend of mine. She hardly sees him though, he's always working."

Very interesting. Between the crazy hours he keeps at the office and his pro bono work on the weekends, when does Antoine find the time to date?

I go for a final run at the bar after I air-kiss Patrick good-bye.

"Let's split," Lisa suddenly announces, holding her jacket. "I know a great Moroccan restaurant not too far from here that has live music on Mondays. You'll love it, it's *very* French."

We arrive at L'Orange Bleue on Broome Street and not a moment too soon: I'm completely drunk. The room is a whirlwind of colour and a belly dancer is doing her thing to the thumping drums of musicians from North Africa.

"Lisa, is the restaurant named after the Paul Éluard poem?"

"Huh?"

"Was L'Orange Bleue named after the poem by Paul Éluard?" I scream at the top of my lungs.

"Who's Paul? Did I date him in law school?"

"Never mind."

"Here, drink this." She hands me a martini glass containing an unknown toxic substance. I take a few sips and attempt to circumvent the belly dancer when a dark-haired man grabs my arm and drags me onto the small dance floor. Lisa claps her hands with excitement.

"Go, Cat! Go!"

After a few rounds of hip gyrations, I find myself perched atop a chair doing my own version of *la danse du ventre*. After the crowd urges me on for a solid ten minutes, I suddenly trip over and wind up on the restaurant's very hard floor.

"Oh my god, what happened?"

"Lisa, I need some food. *Fast.*" She sees from the look on my face that I'm dead serious and rushes to the dining room to order something to eat.

In the meantime, I run to the ladies room and collapse demurely in one of the stalls.

A knock on the door and Lisa's voice wakes me from my dizzy spell.

"Catherine, are you okay?"

"I'm fine. I'll be out in a minute."

I open the door and catch a glimpse of my reflection in

the bathroom mirror. I look like a cross between Courtney Love and Amy Winehouse. I don't recall throwing up, but the large wet stain on the front of my jacket confirms that I regurgitated the mystery drink on my suit only seconds ago. Embarrassed, I grab a tissue to clean up the mess. Suddenly remembering that I have meetings and conference calls in the morning, I realize I need to get home now.

I wake up to a pounding headache caused by a mélange of African drums, champagne, and martinis. I witness last night's ugly reality: my agnès b. pantsuit is strewn across my living-room carpet, my grandmother's pearl necklace is dangling from my bedside reading lamp, and one of my stilettos is balancing precariously on top of my bookshelf. The other one is nowhere to be found.

I show up at the office around ten thirty completely hungover. As soon as I set foot in the reception area, Mimi whispers, "Hi, doll. Listen, Antoine has been looking for you. I think he's a bit upset."

Noticing that I've just arrived, Rikash rushes into my office and shuts the door.

"Dah-ling, you're in major trouble. Antoine has been

looking for you for the last hour." He comes near me, then takes a quick step back after smelling the alcohol on my breath.

"Oooh. You were a bad girl last night!"

"How d'you guess?"

"The smudged mascara is always a dead giveaway."

"I'm not feeling too good. I don't know how I'll get through the day."

"Don't worry. I do this all the time. I actually come to work straight from the clubs and nobody can tell because of my little trick: a Gatorade and a dosa. I'll run downstairs and fetch it for you; it works miracles. In the meantime, take deep breaths and stay put."

"Thanks, Rikash. You're a lifesaver."

As he opens the door, I see Antoine waiting outside, pacing with his hands on his hips. He looks like a thunder-cloud.

Bordel.

"Catherine, I was counting on you to be on the conference call this morning for the PLC file. Now that I sat through it myself, I'm totally behind and I have six deadlines today."

I feel horrible, and not just physically. I can feel my cheeks redden as a sense of shame comes over me.

"So how was the ABA party? Any good?" Scott asks as he stops by.

"Um, it was fantastic, thanks." *Zut*, Antoine's going to be mad.

As I expected, Antoine's face turns purple. I suspect that while I was downing bubbly at record speed and belly dancing to North African beats, he was at the office working till the wee hours. I'm done for.

When all else fails, resort to sex.

"Antoine, I met someone who knows your girlfriend last night."

"Really?" He responds, looking embarrassed to admit having a personal life in front of Scott.

"Yes. A banker named Patrick."

"Patrick? I don't know any Patrick."

"Well, he knows you."

"Oh, Patrick. Yes, yes, I do remember him," he adds after Scott has moved out of earshot. "Listen, I don't *have* a girlfriend, okay? She's just a friend." The purple in his face has now turned to a bit of a blush. "Can you call Mel back on the PLC file? I'd really appreciate it. Thanks."

After I'm done with Mel, I call Lisa to get the details on what happened last night.

"Quite a night, wasn't it? You were smashed."

"I know. How did I get home?"

"I put you in a cab and paid the driver a little extra to make sure you got there safely."

"I don't even remember. How did your meeting with your boss go?"

"Great! He confirmed that I'm up for partnership in the next year."

A sudden wave of envy washes over me. I should be completely thrilled for Lisa, not jealous, but I can't help it. I do my best to sound sincere.

"Congratulations! We need to celebrate! But not tonight, I'm totally dead."

"Don't worry. I'm meeting Charles after work tonight. He's treating me to dinner at the Gramercy Tavern."

I regret having thought badly of Charles—that's really thoughtful of him. For a split second, I feel sorry for myself but try to regain my composure.

"How sweet of him."

"I told you he cared about me," she says pointedly. "Anyway, we need to work on your drinking endurance. It's way too low."

Our conversation is interrupted by screaming in the hallway. I hang up and rush toward the photocopier. In front of Antoine's office is the kerfuffle that Rikash had predicted only last week.

"It's a simple fucking document!" Antoine screams from his office.

"I've just about had it with you and your goddamn simple documents. You can shove them you know where," Maria screams from behind her desk. "Ask someone else to change the font twenty-five times 'cause I've really fuckin' had it. I'm going home and might not be back. Ever."

She puts on her coat and makes her way down the hallway with her breasts bouncing beneath her *I don't give a rat's ass* shirt.

Rikash stares at the scene with his manicured hand pressed to his mouth, Mimi shakes her head in disbelief, and Roxanne runs to meet Maria near the elevator. A heavy silence looms as all the other lawyers in our department remain behind their desks, speechless.

Antoine walks out into the hall a few minutes later looking visibly distraught. "I don't understand her behaviour, it's completely unacceptable." He walks into Scott's office and slams the door behind him. After about an hour, Antoine exits Scott's office, puts on his coat, and leaves for the day, shocking everyone with his early departure.

This is my chance to go home and get some sleep.

Chapter 10

It is better to be silent and be thought a fool than to speak and remove all doubt, my father always used to say. I try to keep that in mind when Nathan saunters in for a visit.

"When's the new partner moving into this office? I thought this was only temporary?"

"Not sure. I heard there might be a delay with his start date."

He answers with a frown, then reaches over to shut my door. "Did you see the article about the firm in today's *Wall Street Journal*?"

"No. I didn't get the chance to read the paper yet."

"Well, you're missing out on some important info." He leans against one of my visitor chairs with his arms crossed on his chest.

"Oh?"

"I'm assuming you're aware that large New York firms have raised lawyer salaries in recent years?"

"Of course."

"Apparently the partners are a bit resentful and there's talk that they'll be raising the minimum billable hours quotas. Have you heard anything about *that*?" he asks while surreptitiously scanning every item on my desk, looking for evidence that I might know something he doesn't.

"Not a thing."

Raising the billable hours quotas? Is that humanly possible? I'll have to set up a tent and shower in between my desk and door. On second thought, a set-up like that might not be so bad if it could help keep people like Nathan out. I find his insecurity to be disconcerting (refer back to character trait #1 of type-A personality); he couldn't possibly bill more hours unless the firm added a Johnny-on-the-spot in his office and delivered his meals intravenously.

"Have you heard that some senior partners are leaving to start their own firm?"

Rikash had mentioned it at lunch, but I'm not going to let on that I know anything.

"Really? Haven't heard about that either."

He squints in disbelief. For some reason, he thinks that I would know more about firm politics than he does. It's oddly flattering.

"If you do, can you please let me know?" he says with obvious exasperation at my lack of inside information. "If the most senior partners leave, it'll be all about the survival of the fittest around here." He gives me a look of superiority as if to say that a) I am definitely not part of the fittest, b) my chances of survival in the event of a reorganization are close to nil, and c) he will rule the new world order. I shoot him one back that suggests d) he might want to be a little more careful until he knows where he stands.

After Nathan leaves, Maria knocks on my door. She's wearing an uncharacteristically conservative navy suit and frilly beige librarian blouse.

"I would like to formally apologize for my behaviour yesterday. It was completely unacceptable and I promise to never do it again."

I try not to let my shock register on my face. "No apology necessary. Listen, you've been working long hours these last few weeks and it's okay to feel tired. It could've happened to anyone."

Surprised by a sympathetic ear, her face brightens.

"I'm completely exhausted. Antoine and Bonnie have been working me around the clock. I haven't had a day off in nine months and I've been here most nights 'til midnight."

"I know."

"It takes me an hour and a half to get home; and then when I do get home, I have to do laundry and, if I'm not too late, cook dinner and help the kids with their homework. I don't know if I can keep this up for much longer."

Her daily routine boggles my mind. I can't even begin to fathom what it must be like; I usually collapse on my couch after a ten-minute walk from the office.

"I understand. Listen, if you ever want to chat, my door is always open, okay?"

"Thanks, I appreciate it. Not many lawyers around here care about the support staff."

"It can be a bit of a cold place."

"A bit cold? How about freakin' freezing." She looks down and hesitates before going on, but my willingness to listen prompts her to continue. "It's getting pretty nasty around here . . . I'm not sure what's going on." She pauses again, hoping I might say something, but I remain silent. "Everyone's been playing dumb, but I'm not stupid . . . I see what's going on . . . and just so you know, I don't play games. I tell it like it is."

It occurs to me that our entire department seems preoccupied with the poisoned firm climate. Maybe *I* should start worrying too.

"You're right. Honesty's always the best policy."

She stands and walks toward the door with a pained expression. "Not always."

It must be difficult to put up with childish power plays and the tiresome behaviour of spoiled lawyers. I'd be exasperated if I were carrying her load. I vow to myself never to treat Rikash with disrespect.

My phone rings seconds after Maria leaves.

"Counselaaar, where's the memo you promised? We're anxiously waiting for it."

"Hi, Mel, I'll have it to you by ten o'clock."

At 10:04, the phone rings again.

"Counselaaar, no sign of your memo in my inbox yet."

"It's on its way, Mel. Just give me another twenty minutes or so. I need to proofread it before I send it to you."

"Maybe your little secretary should stop filing his nails and type a bit faster. He doesn't work at a spa."

"Listen, he's not to blame here. I need a bit more time to make some final revisions, okay?"

At **10:10**, Mimi calls to remind me of an upcoming meeting about the firm's new employee benefit program.

At **10:13**, Antoine wants to know if I've had any dealings with Hart-Scott-Rodino. In the split second before I admit that I haven't had much direct involvement with this legislation, I can't help but think that he's referring to a) a B-movie actor represented by our entertainment group, b) a new form of prenatal childbirth classes, or c) the leader of some local Italian mafia ring.

At **10:15**, the NYPD inspector in charge of the Trademark Infringement Unit returns my call.

At **10:19**, the SEC wants to discuss a recent filing for one of Antoine's clients.

At **10:22**, the delivery guy from the corner deli calls from the lobby to deliver my breakfast. (I missed the firm's breakfast cart *again*. I'm now becoming seriously addicted to American-style egg sandwiches: I need to pick up that book about French women not getting fat otherwise I'll soon become an exception to the rule.)

At 10:23, my new Citibank representative wants to know if I want to invest in mutual funds.

At 10:25, Bonnie is looking for a precedent she asked me to find for one of her acquisitions. (And doesn't understand why the hell it is taking me so long to find it.) "You better make damn sure I have those poison pill documents for my meeting tomorrow. If you can't get the fucking job done, I'll get someone else to work on it."

Poison pill? It sounds like something I'd like to drop into her morning coffee.

At 10:27, Nathan wants to know how many hours I've billed so far this week. (I lie and tell him that I've billed twice what I've actually docketed.)

At 10:28, Bonnie calls again, telling me that I need to check with her before accepting any new mandates from Scott or Antoine since she has complete dominion over my time and workload.

At 10:29, Lisa wants to know whether I have time to join her for a manicure and pedicure at Rescue Beauty Lounge before our dinner tomorrow night. (Completely out of the question.)

At **10:35**, the phone rings again.

"Catherine, it's Mel again, and he's getting quite rude with me on the phone," Rikash complains.

I pick up the call. "Listen, Mel, I'm doing my best here. It'll be there shortly," I plead, gritting my teeth.

At **10:55**, Rikash types the final revisions to the memo and I send it off. I'm completely famished but have no time to eat breakfast since I'm due in Scott's office for a conference call in less than five minutes.

At **10:57**, Scott's ecstatic voice comes through my speakerphone. "Hey, Catherine, great news! Remember that beauty contest? We got the deal. Browser hired us and we'll be lead counsel on their first round of financing. I'd like you to be my point person for this transaction. Can you be at a meeting at the Swiss Bank offices tomorrow afternoon? Unfortunately, I can't make it. I have another meeting."

"Sure."

At **10:58**, I stare out my office window for a brief moment, when Rikash buzzes me on the intercom.

"If it's Mel, put him into my voicemail."

"No, it's your mother. She says she has some good news for you."

"*Bonjour, ma chérie,* you won't believe this. Your cousin Françoise just found an amazing job in Paris. She'll be a senior buyer for Chanel. She'll be travelling all over Europe and will have an unlimited expense account and clothing allowance."

"Wow, that's really amazing." I picture my gorgeous cousin jetting off to the fashion shows wearing a tailored bouclé jacket, a pair of oversized CC sunglasses, rows of delicate pearls around her neck, and a large leather quilted bag, while my business trips involve sweating my way past aggressive security guards in smelly three-day-old suits.

At 11:03, Roxanne calls me on the intercom. "Catherine, Scott is waiting for you in his office for the conference call. You're late."

I drop my head on my desk and want to weep.

Chapter 11

"It's a vintage Louis Féraud from Les Puces."

At seven on Thursday night, Lisa picks me up in front of my office building in a taxi. She compliments me on my dress as soon as I set foot in the cab.

"Ah yes, Les Puces! I remember being so jealous of the stuff you found there back in school."

"You have to try it—I find the most incredible things there."

"I wish I had the patience to pick through pre-worn stuff. I like my clothes to be fresh off the rack."

Lisa has always been into labels and current trends. For me, it's not the price tag that counts, it's how you put it together. I decide to change the subject.

"What's Charles up to tonight?"

"He's in Hong Kong for business. He left yesterday."

"How was your celebratory dinner?"

"Wonderful," she responds with the dreamy look of someone in love.

"I'm sorry I was so judgmental about him."

"No worries. You just don't want to see me hurt."

"It's true. And I'm so happy about your promotion. First drinks are on me."

"Thanks, Cat. I hope it wasn't a problem to leave the office early?"

"Not really. Convincing Rikash to cover for me only cost a triple Marble Mocha Macchiato and a chocolate eclair."

We arrive at the Blue Owl, a trendy lounge in the East Village that's completely packed with men in suits and model types holding a rainbow of martinis.

"Cat, meet my friends Amanda, Leanne, and Beverley." Lisa waves to three women in their early thirties clad in head-to-toe Prada, Gucci, and Chanel respectively.

I reach over to shake three of the most perfectly mani-cured and heavily jewelled hands I've ever encountered.

"Hello, nice to meet you."

"Catherine, Lisa told us that you've just moved here from Paris. We love Paris, don't we, ladies?" Beverley (Cha-nel) says, holding up her martini glass in a mini-toast.

"Oh, yes, greatest shopping ever!" Leanne (Gucci) jumps in eagerly.

"Great? How about fantastic! I nearly emptied the YSL store during my last trip," Amanda (Prada) throws out.

"Lisa told us you were a lawyer. What type of law do you practise?" Leanne asks.

"Where did you go to law school? Have you taken the New York bar exam?" Beverley asks before I can answer Leanne's question.

"I went to law school in France and met Lisa during an exchange program at Pepperdine and no, I haven't passed the local bar yet."

"My brother passed the exam last summer. He said it was a walk in the park," Beverley comments.

I've heard many stories about the bar exam, but most of them make it sound more like a journey to hell and back than a walk in the park.

"Are you working at Skadden or Sullivan? You must keep crazy hours these days," Amanda jumps into the question period.

I'm obviously under serious cross-examination by the bling brigade.

"No, I don't work at Skadden, Arps or Sullivan and Cromwell. I'm with Edwards and White, and yes, you could say that I'm working crazy hours these days. How about you, what do you do?" I ask my interrogators before they can get another question in.

"Amanda's at a hedge fund, Leanne's a trader, and I'm a doctor," Beverley answers in a rehearsed manner.

"You must know what it's like to work long hours."

"Yes. It's been a wild ride," Amanda replies. "I practically live on an airplane these days. But at least *we* get paid. You lawyers don't make much by the hour given the amount of work you do."

Ouch. You're picking up my bar tab for that one, missy. Speaking of which, I need a drink. After reviewing the colourful cocktail menu, I opt for the Comtesse; channelling my inner French royalty will make me feel a little less inferior among these princesses. I order two drinks, one for Lisa and one for *moi*. I ask the bartender to make them strong.

"I hope you don't mind, we made reservations at Daniel for dinner. It's our absolute favourite. The cheese plate is scrumptious and they have an incredible wine list."

"Oh, not at all," I say, pretending to be quite at ease with the idea of spending on dinner an amount that could pay for a day at the spa or cover half the cost of a new armchair for my apartment.

"Why don't you girls go ahead? Cat and I will catch another cab and meet you," Lisa suggests while they simultaneously drape themselves in their expensive-looking trench coats.

"Okay, see you there," Beverley shouts, waving her Burberry scarf.

"How did you meet these women?" I ask Lisa as soon as they're out of earshot. "They're kind of, well, obnoxious, don't you think?"

"I met them at a garden party last summer in the Hamptons. They're actually pretty harmless."

"Harmless? They seem more like piranhas in designer suits to me. Did you hear what Amanda said about lawyers being underpaid? That was rude."

"Listen, you better get used to it. That's how people are in New York. We're trained to be fiercely competitive."

The tone of her voice tells me it's time to back off.

"Sorry, I guess I'm used to people being a bit more discreet. In France, talking about your salary is considered gauche." I pick up my bag and pass her her scarf from the bench beside me.

"It's different here. Your salary is worn like a badge of honour. You have to go out there every day and fight for it."

"I guess I just prefer to keep the details of my financial situation private," I say as we slip out the door past the hostess and I raise my hand to flag a cab.

"Come on, Cat, lighten up! That's what makes living in New York so exciting!" Lisa exclaims as we climb into the stuffy car. "Making the money and spending it. These girls are so much fun, you'll see."

Although Lisa and I get along, when it comes to friends and acquaintances, we can be oceans apart: I can't stand mindless chatter and prefer to stay at home watching a movie or reading a good book, while Lisa's a social animal who needs to go out even when the entourage sounds like a high-maintenance version of Alvin and the Chipmunks.

"Okay, if you say so."

For the sake of our friendship, I keep quiet for the rest of the ride. I mentally prepare for our upcoming competitive dinner conversation as we make our way uptown to the Upper East Side.

My jaw drops at the sight of Daniel's decor: soaring ceilings, sparkling crystal glasses, Bernardaud china, and clusters of roses meticulously placed throughout the room. We take our seats, and, as anticipated, the tone of the evening's conversation is set.

"I can't wait for Memorial Day," Amanda starts. "My boyfriend rented a house for us in East Hampton. We love taking our new Porsche for a ride out there."

And they're off!

"Unfortunately, I won't be there this year. I really need a break from the city. I'm heading to a private island." Leanne moves into first place.

"So, Catherine, what are *you* doing for the Memorial Day weekend?" Beverley asks perkily.

I give Lisa a panicked look. Long-weekend planning isn't billable so it's been the last thing on my mind. Suddenly, I wish I had mobilized Rikash on my summer plans.

"Um, don't know yet. Frankly, it's hard for me to make plans these days with work being so hectic."

All three of them stare at me in silence with a look of disappointment. Clearly we're not going to be best friends. Despite the fact that I have no interest in being one of these girls, I suddenly feel completely uninteresting and bland.

"Give Catherine a break, she just moved here!" Lisa tries to rescue me from my pathetic social life.

"I can't wait. I'm getting my hair done at John Frieda next week." Lisa changes the subject to outrageously priced beauty treatments. I hope she hasn't lost her down-to-earth side to become as precious as her friends.

"Oooh," they all coo at the same time.

"I'm going for a peel next week at Elizabeth Arden. My skin is so dull looking, I look like I'm in my late thirties—so scary."

The waiter finally arrives to take our order and saves me from spa hell.

"*Mademoiselle,*" he addresses me first. His piercing blue eyes look right through me and this gives me a frisson.

"*Bonsoir, monsieur, je vais prendre le ravioli en entrée ainsi que votre filet de sole, merci.*"

The three of them gape at me. Score one for Catherine; go ahead, ladies, and try to match that. I watch gleefully as all three awkwardly place their orders, steering clear of pronouncing anything in French on their menu. I spend the next fifteen minutes thoroughly investigating Daniel's red wine list. Once our meals arrive, Lisa and I dig into our ravioli while the rest of them fiddle with their dressing-free arugula salads.

My savouring the pasta is interrupted by the buzzing of my BlackBerry. I've received an email from Antoine.

> I need to discuss an urgent matter. Do you have a couple of minutes?

I excuse myself from the table and rush to the ladies room. I need to respond to his message without letting on that I'm out on the town and have had a few Comtesse cocktails and glasses of wine. Just keep your cool, Catherine, and remain vague.

I reply with:

> Of course. Can you tell me what it's regarding? I'm working remotely this evening.

I figure the expression *working remotely* is ambiguous enough that I could be at the courthouse library buried under a pile of statutes and case law. I hold my breath in the marble stall and nervously click on his reply:

> I'm going over the American Bank prospectus and need your help with the capital requirements section. You're the pro on this, not me.

> No problem, just send me the draft. I'll be happy to look at it once I polish off what's on my plate.

Proud of my smooth comeback, I relax and plant my feet against the stall door. Keep it up, Catherine. So far so good!

> It sounds like you're swamped, wherever you are.

> Yes, totally inundated.

> Do you need to be rescued?

God, do I ever. Please save me from the conspicuously shallow trio. I try to end our email exchange before Lisa sends the waiter after me and busts my cover.

I'll manage, but thanks for the offer. I'll pop by your office tomorrow morning to go over the requirements.

If it wasn't so late, I'd suggest reviewing it over a glass of wine.

I'm surprised by the flirty tone of his response. If I wasn't stuck making polite conversation with a bunch of navel-gazing divas, I would gladly accept the invitation. But these are Lisa's friends, and I need to play nice.

That would be a welcome treat, but this is no time for temptations. I've got other fish to fry at the moment. *Bonsoir*, Antoine. X.

I can't believe I just ended my email with a kiss! What if he thinks I'm a complete idiot? Or maybe he'll just think of it as being a French custom. I scramble to find the recall feature on my BlackBerry when it vibrates a few seconds later. I hold my breath and nervously click on his reply:

Bonsoir, Catherine. X to you too!

Hmm. Not bad. I guess he's not so square after all. Proud of having got him to play a little and of deflecting a potential outburst over my night out with the girls, I get back to our table for a final round of the over-the-top one-upwomanship contest.

My dining companions give me a strange look as I take my seat.

"So sorry, work."

"Cat, look what our waiter brought over just for you!" Lisa exclaims.

A plate of delicate chocolate truffles is placed in front of my seat.

I now recognize the look on their faces: *envy.*

"I think he has a crush on you!" Lisa gushes. "How sweet."

If that's the case, that's just fabulous news for my ego. I give the waiter a grateful smile. Despite Lisa's questionable choice of friends, it hasn't been a bad evening after all: I managed to leave the office at a decent hour, enjoy a cocktail fit for a queen as well as a fantastic dinner in one of the city's most fabulous restaurants, and flirt like a bandit with not one but two men. Not bad, *n'est-ce pas?*

"I'll have to excuse myself. I'm on my way to San Fran first thing in the morning for a business meeting over the weekend," Amanda says as she gathers her all-Prada cell phone, keychain, and handbag.

"Bye, girls, see you next week at spinning class."

Amanda leaves the table without offering to pay her share of the bill.

"Oh, she probably forgot; we'll just cover for her. She's so busy these days with work," Beverley says, staring at the bill.

Busy with work? Nice excuse. I wasn't exactly in the mood to pay for some obnoxious stranger's expensive dinner. Especially not for someone who insulted me less than two hours ago. At almost $300 each, this hasn't exactly been a Thursday-night snack with the girls.

After I air-kiss our waiter on my way out and thank him for his generous gesture, he whispers in my ear, "Don't worry, *mademoiselle*. I'm heading to Staten Island for Memorial Day."

Chapter 12

As mornings-after go, there are few combinations more deadly than a BlackBerry, too much alcohol, and flirting with a colleague—no matter how subtle. I wish I could channel my inner Edith Piaf and hum, *"Non, je ne regrette rien,"* but it just isn't so. I wish I'd been able to call back that last email to Antoine—I knew it as soon as I hit send last night; I knew it when I woke up blushing with embarrassment this morning; and I really knew it when I ran into him in the photocopy room and he didn't even acknowledge my presence.

I stare at my computer screen and wonder what this will mean for our relationship going forward and, more importantly, my career. Why would he give me the cold shoulder? Does he think I have a crush on him? After all, he's the one who brought up going out for a drink! Catherine, you can't let stress and too much wine make bad decisions for you.

Rikash dashes into my office holding a stack of receipts.

"What's wrong? You seem preoccupied."

"I need your help, dah-ling. I'm under tremendous pressure."

"How so?"

"Bonnie just snapped at me for not having finished the expenses for her most recent trip to Europe. I've been working on them for three days, but I can't seem to reconcile the receipts."

"Why not?"

"There's one I'm not sure how to handle . . . It's for a garter belt and a bra from a lingerie shop in London."

"What? You're joking?"

"Does a thirty-four C cup from Agent Provocateur sound like a meal to you?"

"I can't believe she would expense that. Why would Bonnie expense her underwear? She makes enough money to buy the entire lingerie company. Then again, her under-garments are as key to closing a deal as her sharp legal mind. On second thought, forget what I just said. They're her main negotiation tool."

"What should I do?"

"There's got to be something you can do. Wait, lots of restaurants use numbers in their names, right? Eleven Madison Park, Candle 79, and Five Napkin Burger. So why not Thirty-Four C Regent Street?"

"Brilliant. Absolutely brilliant, thanks, love. By the way, are *you* okay? You look a bit down and out."

"I'll be fine. Just busy with work."

Despite a steady increase in women's enrollment in law school and legislation to promote equality between the sexes, it looks like women are still heavily outnumbered in the world of high finance. I show up at the meeting Scott arranged at the Swiss Bank offices and there are only two women in the room: the woman putting together the coffee cart and me. The large boardroom is filled with young men speaking rapid-fire financial jargon while taking notes on a thick draft prospectus; I feel a bit lost in an ocean of

J'adore New York 147

Dockers and blue shirts. For a split second, I wish I was in Dior's boardroom discussing counterfeit Lady Dior bags. But I quickly dismiss it; this testosterone-charged high-profile deal is exactly what I need to forget Antoine's silent treatment. I'm seriously regretting that silly email exchange. How could I let my guard down so easily, especially in a time of war? It's a tactical mistake and a tough lesson to learn. Catherine, never go to battle without your suit of armour. My thoughts are interrupted by a man's deep voice.

"Good afternoon, everyone, and thanks for making it to our meeting on such short notice. My name is Jeffrey Richardson. I'm the CFO of Browser." A stunning man with dark hair and broad shoulders is standing at the front of the boardroom wearing a light pink shirt and a tailored pinstripe suit. He looks like Nacho Figueras, the Argentinian polo player and Ralph Lauren model. Any lingering thoughts about Antoine quickly disappear.

"Just so everyone is aware, we've selected the firm of Edwards and White as our lead counsel. Is anyone from Edwards present this morning?"

My pulse begins to race.

"Yes, hello, my name is Catherine Lambert."

"Very nice to meet you, Catherine. Glad you can be with

us here today," Jeffrey welcomes me with a bright smile. My palms turn sweaty and I fear I will soon turn into a babbling idiot. Be professional, Catherine! Remember the lesson you learned just this morning!

"The main contact at Edwards on this deal, I presume?"

"Scott Johnson, our department's managing partner, will be the senior lawyer on the file, but I'll be the main contact."

The others around the table introduce themselves but I have trouble paying attention: I am totally mesmerized by Jeffrey's good looks and warm smile.

"How quickly can we expect your firm to complete the due diligence process?"

My neighbour's hand taps me on the shoulder. "Excuse me, miss, I think that question was directed at you."

"Oh, sorry, can you repeat the question?" I awaken from my trance.

"Yes, hello, Catherine. My name is Howard Greenblatt. We represent the underwriters. What's your firm's expected time frame to get the documents ready for the due diligence process? We're trying to get a handle on the upcoming deadlines and establish a legal timetable."

"Of course, yes, yes. To answer your question, I don't

foresee any delays and I can assure you that this file will be a top priority for me, I mean, for *us* at Edwards and White." Not the most eloquent answer, but it does seem to satisfy Howard. Come on, Lambert, you're not going to let a hot guy distract you like this, are you?

"Perfect. Thank you."

A question period starts after the introductions are over.

"What's the burn rate of the company?" one banker asks.

"What is the company's EBITDA? How many rounds of financing have you gone through so far?" asks another.

I try to keep up with the fast-paced questions by frantically transcribing every question and answer on my laptop. After an intense two and a half hours, Jeffrey thanks the crowd and tells everyone that we will continue at the next meeting.

I'm packing up when Jeffrey walks over.

"Very pleased to hear this file will be a priority for you. I guess that means that you and I will be talking on a regular basis from now on, doesn't it?"

"Yes, I guess it does." I pass him my card.

"Great. I'll ask my secretary to add your name to the working group list."

"Perfect."

I catch him glancing at my outfit. "Beautiful suit."

"Thanks." I look up and his eyes meet mine; despite willing myself not to with every fibre of my being, I begin to blush.

"Like the woman wearing it."

My heart stops; I fumble for words. Pull it together!

"I should be getting back to the office now. Um, I'll talk to you soon." I stammer, colour still rising in my cheeks.

He winks in response. I want to die.

I walk through the glass doors toward the exit while he stands in the lobby watching me; he waves goodbye.

Mon dieu, it will be difficult to refrain from flirting with *him*. I stroll along Park to get back to the office and can't help but think about Jeffrey. I replay our brief conversation in my head; it's obvious that there was mutual attraction, but I'm not prepared to navigate the murky waters of dating an important client. No thank you.

"Rikash, can you please open a file for Browser, Inc.?"

"Browser? I read about them in the *Herald Tribune* over the weekend."

"You read the *Herald Tribune*?"

Rikash never ceases to surprise me. I knew he was cultivated and well read but never thought he'd be reading international newspapers.

"Of course. I like to be well informed. I hope you have direct access to their senior management."

"Why's that?"

"Their CFO is one seriously attractive male."

He totally catches me off guard and I'm sure he can read the look of surprise on my face.

"How do you know?"

"There was a picture of him next to the article. I could definitely show him a whole new meaning to the expression *playing with the numbers*."

Hmm, so could I, if only he wasn't a firm client . . . But dishing about his good looks with Rikash is not off limits.

"God, tell me about it. I almost fainted when he shook my hand. He's not attractive, Rikash, he's drop-dead gorgeous. His name is Jeffrey, by the way."

"Do you know which way he goes?"

"Not your way, I'm afraid."

"In that case, you need to jump his bones because if I can't have him, someone I know needs to."

Here we go. Put on your seatbelt, Catherine. I'm sure that Rikash will try to lead you astray.

"He's a client and I want to keep it that way."

"Just remember, dah-ling: good girls go to heaven, bad girls go everywhere."

Before I can go on with our conversation, Scott walks into my office.

"How did the meeting go?"

"Extremely well."

"Great, happy to hear. I've been invited to attend a Browser function at Carnegie Hall next week, but I can't make it. Now that you're involved, I'd like you to attend on my behalf."

"Carnegie Hall?" I hesitate before answering. Scott had also asked me to attend a benefit Mel's wife was hosting for the St. Matthew's Society next week and I need to get my billables up. If only I could bill the hours I'm going to spend at these functions, at least then they'd be worth my while.

He senses my apprehension. "I know I'm asking you to attend a lot of client functions these days, but I'm afraid it comes with the job. Clients need to be wined and dined."

"Of course, I understand. I'd be delighted to go."

"Great, I'll ask Jeffrey's assistant to contact you with the details."

A few minutes later, Nathan walks into my office looking perplexed.

"I heard you'll be working on the Browser IPO."

"You heard correctly."

"Won't that interfere with your other mandates? You already have most of Antoine's files on your desk."

"I can handle it."

"If I were you, I would delegate some of my work. You don't want to be accused of malpractice. It can totally happen under a heavy burden, you know."

This is a *very* weak attempt at appearing concerned about me. It is true that my load is getting a bit heavy and I've fallen a little behind in my Dior research, but there's no way I'll let him get his grubby fingers on Browser's IPO; it could be my ticket to partnership. It's been said that to get ahead you must bite off more that you can chew and then *just chew it.*

"I appreciate your concern for my professional well-being, but I'll be fine, really."

A frustrated Nathan walks out of my office empty-handed.

"It's Mel. Do you want to take it?" Rikash calls me on the intercom.

"Sure, put him through." I put my finger in my mouth in mock gagging.

"Hello, counselaaar, looking forward to seeing you at the St. Matthew's charity ball on Monday."

"So am I. I'm especially looking forward to meeting your wife." I wonder whether my nose is getting longer.

"She, um, can't wait to meet you also. . . . Do you have some time now to go over the memo you prepared?"

"Sure, let me get my file."

Fifteen minutes of questions later, my other line rings and *Browser* pops up on the screen. I glance at Rikash to make sure he gets it. He answers and waves at me with big hand gestures.

"Mel, I'm sorry, but can I put you on hold for just one minute?"

"Catherine, it's Jeffrey on your other line."

"Great, put him through."

"God, he even sounds gorgeous."

"Rikash, put him through."

"I can take a message for you if you're busy."

"Rikash, transfer the call."

"You know I like to have my beefcake and eat it too."

"PUT HIM THROUGH NOW!"

"Okay, okay, there's no need to be such a party-pooper!"

"Hello, Catherine, it's Jeffrey. Scott told me that you'll be joining us next Thursday evening."

"Yes, that's right. Although I'm afraid Scott can't make it."

"That's too bad. Can we meet for dinner beforehand to discuss details? I want to make sure this IPO goes as smoothly as possible."

"Um. Sure."

He senses my hesitation. "Strictly business, I need some legal advice—it'll even be billable."

Music to my ears. "Yes, of course."

"Perfect. I'll make reservations and email the details over."

I reluctantly jump back to the other line.

"Mel, I'm sorry, where were we?"

"That was way more than a minute, counselaaar. I hope you stopped running your meter while you were on the other line. No double billiiiing!"

"Don't worry, Mel, I won't charge you for it."

"A legal freebie? Wow, that's a first. Can we go over the memo now?"

"Sure, but the meter is going back on."

After a half-hour legal discussion, Mel ends the conversation.

"I've got to run, so I'll see you at the Waldorf. Don't forget it's a black tie and the cocktails start at seven."

"I'll be there; wouldn't miss it for the world." I giggle as I hang up, surprised at my ability to make the statement sound sincere.

Chapter 13

Françoise Sagan once said that a woman shouldn't wear a dress to impress or dazzle other women. Rather, she should do so to be undressed by the man she loves. The sad thing is, I'm now slipping into a red floor-length sequined gown to meet Mel and his wife.

Roxanne and Maria walk in as I spritz some J'adore on my wrists.

"Aren't we looking glamorous?" Maria remarks as she stares at me from head to toe. "Oh my god, love the shoes."

Roxanne stands before me in stone silence and gives me her usual dirty look.

"Hot date?"

"No, Scott asked me to attend a benefit with Mel Johnson and his wife. Apparently Mrs. Johnson is on the board of trustees for the St. Matthew's Society."

"Really?"

Maria and Roxanne stare at each other.

"Have a great time."

God, those two are odd.

"Counselaaar, you look marvellous." I nearly run into Mel at the entrance.

"Thank you, you don't look too bad yourself." I return the compliment despite the fact that he's wearing a tuxedo a few sizes too small, making him look like the Michelin Man squeezed into Azzedine Alaïa.

We climb two broad flights of stairs and walk down a large hall that leads directly into a procession of elegant lobby spaces before we arrive in the Grand Ballroom. I crane my neck to look all the way up to the gorgeously painted ceilings.

"Would you like a glass of champagne?"

"Love one. So where's Mrs. Johnson?"

"She's tied up at some meeting. She'll be joining us a bit later. Why don't we walk around? I'll introduce you to some friends and colleagues."

We approach a tall man standing close to the bar and holding a cigar.

"Frank, let me introduce you to our lovely French lawyer, Catherine. She's taking care of our paperwork with the securities regulators."

"Nice to meet you, Catherine. I'm very fond of the French language. It's the language of *looove*," he says, making a tiny circle with his lips.

"Ah yes, the language de l'*amoowr*," Mel adds, trying to show off his foreign-language skills.

After a painful half-hour of similarly stimulating conversation with Frank and Mel, I'm thrilled when we are asked to take our seats for dinner. Strangely though, there is still no sign of Mrs. Johnson.

"What about your wife, Mel? Should we wait for her before taking our seats?"

"I'm not entirely sure that she'll make it tonight. She seemed a bit under the weather this morning when I left home."

Is she sick or in a meeting? Something's up because

Frank is winking at Mel and giving him the thumbs-up. *Oh mon dieu, quelle horreur!*

"So how long has your wife been on the board of the St. Matthew's Society?"

"For as long as I remember. She runs the whole thing," he answers in an uninterested manner.

"Ladies and gentlemen." A man takes the microphone to thank the organizers after our main course is served. As expected, there is no reference to a Mrs. Johnson. Shortly after the dessert, the band starts to play and several couples are dancing on the dance floor.

"Counselaaar, would you do me the honour?"

"Sure," I answer reluctantly.

He grabs my hand and leads me into a poorly executed fox trot.

"I hope you're having a wonderful evening. My colleagues are so pleased to meet you."

"Yes, Mel, I'm having a good time. Thank you for inviting me. I'll probably be on my way shortly, though. I have an early morning meeting tomorrow."

"Nonsense, the night is still young. We're just getting started," he replies as he awkwardly twirls me on the dance floor, almost making me trip on my dress.

"Counselaaar, I love your dress. It's electric. It brings out the fire in me."

Oh god, someone please call the fire department.

"You are zee one for mee!" he whispers in my ear. I move my face to look away, but he leans into the other ear. Get me out of here.

"And you are so veery deeesirable!"

As he leans his face closer to mine to kiss me, I turn my cheek the other way to avoid the strong stench of Scotch and cigar on his breath.

"Listen, Mel, I hope there's no misunderstanding, but I want to keep our relationship professional."

"Oh, counselaaar, I love it when a women gets feisty with me." He twirls me again, this time making me bump into the charity chairman.

"What about Mrs. Johnson? You're married, remember?"

"Well, as you lawyers would put it, I misrepresented the facts slightly."

"How so?" I stand immobile before him, having stopped the fancy footwork.

"Well, there is no Mrs. Johnson, only several ex–Mrs. Johnsons."

Okay, Catherine, act shocked—this is your exit card.

"What? You lied to me?"

"Have you never told a little white lie to seduce the apple of your eye? You're having a great time, remember? Don't be a party-pooper."

"A party-pooper? I only accepted your invitation because you're a client."

"Voolay voo kooshay avek mwoi ce swoire?" he whispers with a ridiculous accent and a forced come-hither look that could be a cross between Pepé Le Pew and Rodney Danger-field. He then parks his hand on my butt.

Okay, that's it, this party is definitely over.

"Listen, Mel, in case you didn't understand what I just said, I'm not interested."

I break away and run to the ladies room, dialling Lisa's cell as I go.

"Lisa? It's me."

"Where are you?"

"I'm in a stall in the ladies room at the Waldorf. Can you hear me?"

"Yes, what's wrong?"

"I need your advice," I say, perching awkwardly on the top of a toilet seat in three-inch stilettos to get better reception. "I'm at some charity ball with this client and he just tried to kiss me and grabbed my derrière. He's totally grossing me out. What should I do?" I ask, nearly falling flat on my face just as a woman walks in to use the facilities.

"Say you got called to the office and don't say anything else. He'll leave you alone after that. Don't let him push you around, but stay professional."

"You're right. Thanks, Lisa, you're the best," I whisper loudly as I hold my dress up to get down from the wobbly toilet seat.

Mel is waiting for me in the reception area.

"Just got a call from the office. I need to go."

"I would be very careful if I were you, counselaaar. I would seriously think twice about my next move." I can't believe he's threatening me. I channel Lisa: stay professional.

"Good night, Mel. "

I grab my evening bag and head for the exit, my red sequined hemline flapping from side to side as I try to walk as quickly as possible with painfully blistered feet.

I hail a cab outside the hotel and see Frank near the entrance smoking a cigar with a group of men. "*Bon swoire*, Catherine," he shouts.

My head spinning, I sink into the back seat of the cab.

It wasn't bad enough that Mel regularly made me squirm with his lascivious jokes and belittled me by calling me his "favourite little lawyer." No, this time he had to go for gold.

"We're making a quick stop on 42nd street. I need to pick up something from my office."

The combination of a tight evening gown and shooting pain in my toes turns getting out of the cab and walking through the lobby into a major achievement. As the elevator doors open on the twenty-eighth floor, it could very well be four in the afternoon given the loud clicking of keyboards and the whirr of photocopiers. I recognize some of the night staff, on the job at 12:30 a.m. to ensure that marked-up drafts left behind are typed up and on lawyers' desks first thing in the morning.

In no mood for light chit-chat, I slink past the support staff work stations and toward my office. To the delight of my cramped feet, I slide into my worn pumps, then throw a blazer over my bare shoulders. I sit in my swivel chair for a brief moment, thinking about the evening's events. How can Mel get away with this in this day and age? And how can we continue working together after his big come-on? I have to admit that I wasn't entirely surprised by his behaviour. So far in my career, I had grown accustomed to male clients staring at my legs while I delivered a presentation. Did I use it to my advantage? *Absolutely.* If a pair of stockings helps you crack open that very heavy glass ceiling, then why not? Was it an open invitation to ask for sex and touch me? *Definitely not.*

Still cringing at the thought of Mel's hands on my body, I walk past Bonnie's office and notice that her door is ajar. A quick glance down reveals a discarded skirt and two pairs of feet intermingled on her office floor. Stunned, I tiptoe stealthily toward the elevators until the sound of Bonnie's voice in a breathy *Je-t'aime moi-non-plus* purr makes me stop dead in my tracks.

"Oh, Harry."

Chapter 14

"So, dah-ling, how did it go last night?" Rikash asks, standing in my office doorway with a Cheshire cat grin. "Did you meet anyone interesting?"

"Sure, if big pot-bellies and crass behaviour are a turn-on. I had a rough night, if you want to know the truth, but I don't want the entire office to know about it. Can you keep a secret?"

"Yesss I cannn," he whines like a four-year-old. "Come onnn, tell me."

"It was horrible. Mel had his fat greasy fingers all over me the whole evening."

"Oh no."

"Oh yes. And I'm sure that won't be the end of it. You watch."

I turn on my computer and, sure enough, there isn't one but two emails from Mel Johnson in my inbox with my name as the subject line. The first one is addressed to Scott and Antoine.

Dear Sirs,

It is with much regret that I must advise you of an unfortunate incident that occurred last evening.

One of your associates, Catherine Lambert, engaged in inappropriate behaviour in my presence. She attended the Annual St. Matthew's Society Charity Ball and became intoxicated to the point of embarrassing me and several colleagues and their wives. As a result of her conduct, I see no other alternative but to consider sending my company's legal work elsewhere.

Her actions have seriously tarnished the reputation of

your firm, and I hope you will take the necessary action
to prevent such behaviour from reoccurring in the future.

Sincerely,
Mel S. Johnson
Managing Director
PLC Partners

The second one is addressed only to me:

Dear Catherine,
Too bad you didn't exercise your good judgment last night . . .

You've got to be kidding me. This is a nightmare! The
toxic stench of sexual politics is so strong that it's as nauseating as too much Azzaro aftershave. I march down the hallway toward Scott's office, hell-bent on clearing my name.

"He's already with someone," Roxanne says as I
approach.

"I'll wait."

"He doesn't like it when people stand in his doorway."

I stare at her defiantly. "Like I said, I'll wait."

I hear Antoine's voice through the door.

"I can't believe she would do something like that. It seems so out of character."

My heart sinks.

I knock, enter, and shut the door behind me.

"Scott, Mel's email is a complete lie." I can't read the expression on his face at all.

"That's a pretty strong statement, Catherine. What happened?"

My face turns beet red and my hands start trembling while Antoine stares at me sternly.

"He came on to me last night and he's frustrated because I turned him down."

There's a long pause while the two of them glance at each other. "Those are very serious allegations, Catherine. Are you sure? There are usually two sides to every story," Antoine throws out.

I'm holding back tears. I thought we were on the road to becoming friends, not preparing to throw each other under the bus.

"I swear to you that's what happened. I thought we were all part of the same team here." One of the longest moments of my life passes in silence. When I attempt to bring up Mel's second email message, Antoine cuts me off.

"Mel does have the reputation of being a skirt chaser."
I look at him gratefully.

"But he's a major client and we'll lose a big chunk of billables." Scott looks like he's really weighing his options. How could he even consider siding with Mel? "So I'm not sure that we can afford to sever the relationship. I need to think about this."

Merde! I storm out of Scott's office to take refuge in mine. I want to kick myself for being naïve enough to think that the firm would take my side on this. Money clearly takes precedence over employee respect. Could waging a war for more clients be going to Scott's head to the point of losing all sense of decency?

After a few minutes, I open my door and try to regain my composure. I'm pissed off because I should have seen it coming, but am I going to let this man's email get in the way of my career? No way. The question is, what will I do now? I decide to keep Mel's second email to myself while I speak to Lisa. I want her legal opinion about my options if I decide to file a sexual harrassment claim. God, I hope it doesn't come to that. But with Scott's reaction, who knows?

"Rough night last night?" Maria asks as she walks past my office.

"How d'you guess?"

"You told me you were going out with Mel Johnson. Everyone knows he's a real lech."

"What do you mean?"

"Honey, he's done it before to other female lawyers from this office. You're not the first one he puts his dirty little paws on."

Flabbergasted, my mind starts to spin. I thought I had earned Maria's respect when she came into my office to apologize after her big blow-up.

"Why didn't you tell me before I left for dinner?"

"It's not my place to gossip about firm clients."

"I would have expected you to at least give me a heads-up, Maria."

"You're a big girl, you can handle your predators like a lady, or so I thought." She turns around abruptly and leaves my office.

I stare out the window in disbelief. Is everyone in this place ganging up on me?

"Rikash, can you come in here?"

He walks in hurriedly.

"Shut the door."

"What's the matter?"

"Mel sent Scott an email saying that I got drunk and embarrassed him last night and that he's sending his work elsewhere."

"What an asshole."

"He even sent me an email saying *I* had poor judgment to refuse his advances. Can you believe this jerk?"

"Whatever you do, don't delete the message."

"I won't. I'm just not sure what to do about it yet."

"I have an idea."

"I'm not sure I like the sound of this. I'm already in enough hot water as it is."

"Don't worry. Rikash has it all under control."

"And there's another thing; I think Maria and Roxanne arc ganging up on me. Do they talk behind my back?"

"Dah-ling, don't act so surprised. They're bitches on wheels, I told you."

"Okay, that's it. This is war."

Chapter 15

There's a silver lining to every cloud. Just as I was seriously considering putting myself on the next Air France flight back to Paris and abandoning my legal career to wait on tables at my stepfather's bistro, Lisa calls with an exciting proposition.

"How about sneaking out for your client's sample sale?"

"Client?"

"Yes, Dior. It's practically research."

"Where? When?"

"It's in the ballroom at the St. Regis. Now!"

"This is perfect timing, I need to talk to you. I'll be right there."

I jump from my chair and start making my way to the exit; Dior at eighty-five percent off will definitely lift my spirits.

As I walk past Rikash's cubicle, he picks up my line. "It's Antoine. He needs to speak with you urgently."

"Tell him that I'll call him back later. I'm on my way to a client meeting."

"What meeting?"

"I can't say. Just cover for me."

"What if Scott or Bonnie is looking for you?"

"Just tell them I'll be back in an hour. Put everyone into my voicemail. I have my cell if the building is on fire, but otherwise it can wait."

I take the long way out through the other side of the elevator banks to avoid walking past Bonnie's office. No one can disrupt my shopping plans, not now.

I arrive out of breath. The last time I ran so quickly to get anywhere was in law school when I was late for a final exam. Outside the building, a long lineup of impeccably dressed women extends for more than two blocks. Lisa is wearing a black suit and waves at me from the entrance. "Over here. You can cut the line."

She greets me with a warm hug. "I'm so glad you could make it. There's a lot of fabulous stuff here, and it's all so inexpensive!"

I take a look around and I feel my pulse skyrocketing: exquisitely tailored ensembles are carefully hung on racks throughout the room, half-opened boxes of gorgeous shoes are piled high along the side of the wall, and hats and costume jewellery are meticulously displayed in glass counters. Clearly, there are no cheap fake copies here. Before we attack the discounted merchandise, I'm reminded of Rikash's sample sale shopping technique: just tell someone who is trying on an item you desperately want, *It's too bad they don't have that in your size!*

"I don't really *need* anything," I respond, trying to sound sincere. Who am I kidding? I had friends in Paris who attended these sales, but I never managed to get invited. And I was always desperately jealous.

"What did you want to talk about?" Lisa asks while perusing the costume jewellery. "I assume it's about last night? How did it end with the client?"

"Horribly. After I shot him down, he sent a nasty email to my boss and accused me of getting drunk and embarrassing him."

"You've got to be kidding me." She picks up a black crystal brooch.

"I know, can you believe that man? He even sent me a second email telling me I had poor judgment to turn him down. And when I tried to give my side of the story to Scott, he took the client's side."

"Bingo. You've got your case right there. If things turn sour, you could always discuss it with someone at my firm. There's a woman in our litigation department who specializes in harassment cases."

"Thanks, Lisa, I might take you up on that. I just hope that Scott will come to his senses."

"Good luck with that."

"At least Antoine seemed to be on my side."

"Good. He sounds like a decent one. Is he cute?" She walks toward the prêt-à-porter section.

"Yes, but very unpredictable. One day he's yelling at me about work and the next he's joking around and asking me to be his main contact in New York after he leaves for Paris. I just don't get it."

"Maybe he likes you."

I mentally dismiss her statement for two reasons. First, it's irrelevant—he's moving to Paris. Two, if that were true, then why would he ignore me after our flirtatious email exchange?

"I don't think so. He's seeing someone." A pale blue chiffon blouse catches my eye.

"Men are always seeing someone, Cat. It doesn't mean it's serious."

"He's leaving for Paris in a few weeks so I'm sure that's not it. Besides he has too much of a temper for my taste. You should have seen the screaming match he had with one of the secretaries. *Pretty scary.*"

"He's under a lot of pressure. You know how it is."

"Let's change the subject. Why don't we discuss the fact that Bonnie and the head of our litigation group were having sex in her office last night. *Quel scandale!*"

"What?"

"Yup, caught them right in the act. They didn't see me, but I heard them."

"Wow."

"Rikash had hinted that she was seeing someone in the office, but I never would have guessed it was Harry Traum."

"Power is a strong aphrodisiac. Besides, that stuff happens everywhere. Here, you should try this. It would look great on you." She adds a stunning turquoise cashmere sweater to my load. I follow her to the back of the room where complete strangers stand side by side in various states of undress in front of tall mirrors.

"I wonder if she's the reason behind Harry's divorce. Anyway, the less I know about it, the better. Enough about *moi*. How is Charles?" I slip into the tweed dress.

"Great. We're going away for the weekend to the Bahamas. He arranged it, not me," she says, admiring the cut of her ensemble in the mirror. "I love this. I'm getting these pants."

"How do you like it?" I ask after I've added a black patent studded belt to the dress. "It's the New Look *revisité*."

"Wow! That looks stunning, Cat! You look like Marion Cotillard in the Lady Dior ads! You have such a great eye. You should work in fashion, not in law!"

I go back to discussing her romantic life. "I totally misjudged him. He seems to be treating you like the queen you are, *ma chérie*. I can't wait to meet Charles."

"Don't worry, you will. I just hope I'm not wasting my time dating him. I'm looking for commitment."

"Then what you need to do is create some mystery. Deneuve put it perfectly: I like the idea of mystery, it's the pleasure of being a woman."

"Thanks for the tip. I'll try to create some mystery while we're on vacation," she says jokingly.

"Trust me, the best way to hold on to a man is to keep him guessing."

I try on a light pink wool coat Lisa had picked out for me. As I stand in front of the mirrors, several women in the room start cooing, "Oooh, that looks gorgeous, you have to get it."

A quick glance at the tag reveals the original price: $2,500. But hey, it's eighty-five percent off.

"They're practically giving it away," a woman next to me comments.

"That's a classic and you'll have it *forever*," Lisa raves.

"But that's just the problem. I'm not into monogamous relationships with my coats."

She ignores my comment. "Try on the navy suit. Every woman needs one."

"I already own a navy suit. I really shouldn't buy another one."

"But is it a *Dior*?"

"Well, no." I've always dreamt of owning one but couldn't bring myself to pay full price.

"Okay, so you *don't* really own one. Just try it on! Don't forget the evening dress and these black patent-leather shoes. You can't leave without them. They're the last pair in your size."

After I finish trying on all the items, we make our way to the exit and I get hit with a wall of financial guilt.

"Lisa, I really shouldn't be buying all this. I need to furnish my apartment."

She stares at me in disbelief.

"Listen, these are bargain basement prices. Besides, it's never a bad time to buy something you'll have for the rest of your life. And, honestly, when are you ever in your apartment?"

I hand my credit card to the cashier. As she swipes it, I cringe, knowing this will put a dent in my budget.

"Aren't you excited? You picked out such great stuff!"

"I am. The retail therapy was just what I needed. I'm just not used to spending this much money on clothes—I've been spoiled by vintage! I just need some time to digest."

"Don't think about it too much! I've got to get back to the office for a meeting. I'll call you later." She air-kisses me on both cheeks and disappears into the bustling streets with three large bags.

On my way back to the office, a strong feeling of buyer's remorse comes over me. Did I really just blow off Antoine to go shopping? Although my BlackBerry didn't go off, so whatever it was that he wanted couldn't have been *that* important. Lambert, for once and for all, get your priorities straight. But first, get back to the office without getting caught. Holding two huge white shopping bags, I tiptoe through the back door, hoping that no one will see me. Luckily, Nathan has his door shut and Rikash is out of sight. Attempting to make a run for it, I dash up the hallway and abruptly come face to face with Roxanne.

"A bit of shopping?" she remarks, staring at my bags disapprovingly.

"Yes, um, it's my mother's birthday. It's a big milestone, she's turning sixty. You know how it is."

"No, I really don't." She sneers.

Ah, merde.

I stash the bags behind my office door and return to my desk to check my voicemail.

You have seven new messages in your voicemail. Double

merde. Panicked, I check my silent BlackBerry—battery is dead. *Triple merde.*

"It's Phil Purcell from American Bank in San Francisco, this is urgent. Please call me back as soon as possible."

"Catherine, it's Antoine, please come by my office when you have a moment. I need to discuss a file before I leave."

"It's Antoine again; where are you?"

"Bonjour, Catherine, *c'est Maman,* just calling to say hello."

"Catherine, it's Phil again. I expect a quick call back, okay? We're not paying your exorbitant hourly rates for nothing. And I hope you're not billing your time while listening to all of my messages."

"Catherine, it's Scott. Phil Purcell just called me saying that he's been trying to reach you all morning. Are you not familiar with our fifteen-minute client call-back policy? Oh, and by the way, don't forget to bill your time listening to all of his messages."

"Catherine, it's Rikash. Where are you? I tried your cell but it's off. Scott is looking for you and he doesn't seem to buy the client meeting alibi, not sure what else to tell him. Please call me if you pick up your messages."

Ouh! I'm in major trouble now. I pick up the phone to return my calls when Rikash suddenly bursts into my office doorway. "Where have you been? Everybody's been looking for you, including your mother."

"I engaged in a little retail therapy. I was a bit depressed about the Mel episode."

He walks into the office and looks behind the door where my giant bags are overflowing with shoe boxes, clothing hangers, suits, and sequins.

"I'm afraid that this is more than a little therapy. This looks like an entire psychoanalysis. Oh my god, Christian Dior? Look at all this stuff. Did you win the lottery?"

"Rikash, shut the door. I was invited to a sample sale, I didn't pay full price for it."

"Why didn't you tell me?" He goes into a pout. "Did they have anything for men?"

I cross my fingers behind my back before I answer his question; I wouldn't want to be the victim of Rikash's nasty sample sale retaliation tactics.

"Nothing, I checked."

"This is gorgeous," he says as he picks up a black lace cocktail dress delicately embroidered with tiny black pearls. "Try it on. I want to see this on you."

"Rikash, I'm not going to change in front of you in my office."

"Why not? I'm gay, who cares?"

"What if someone walks in?"

"They're all out for lunch."

"I need to call Phil Purcell back before he sends one of his men over."

"Come on, try it on. It'll only take a second."

I slip behind my door and put on the dress.

"Okay. What do you think?"

"Sweetie, it's absolutely ravishing."

I strut before him, pretending I'm on the catwalk.

"When will you wear it?"

"Not sure. I have an important client event coming up."

"With who? Mr. Browser?"

I answer with a nod.

"You have to wear it. Let me feel the fabric."

I'm standing on a pile of files in my bare feet while Rikash sits on my desk holding up the bottom of my dress when Scott opens my office door. He stares at us for a moment and shakes his head with a look of exasperation.

That's it, I'll *never* become partner.

"Sorry to interrupt the fashion show. Catherine, Phil

has been looking for you, did you call him back? And can you please come to my office?"

"Sure, I'll be right there."

Ooh la la. What have I done? I feel like a complete idiot. I should have stayed in my office and got the jump on that Browser file instead. This is the last thing I needed after the whole Mel incident; I just hope I still have a job after our meeting. I throw a blazer over my shoulders and follow Scott down the hall.

"Listen, Catherine, I really don't care what you do in your spare time, but shopping while your client's calls go unanswered is a bit much, don't you think? We're completely swamped and not paying you to be out gallivanting on Madison Avenue."

Embarrassed and ashamed, I squirm in my seat, simultaneously cursing myself and trying to make the dress cover my thighs. This shopping excursion could cost me my future at the firm. I want to kill Roxanne for ratting me out.

"At least carry your cell phone so that we can reach you."

"I'm terribly sorry about all this," I answer, my voice shaking.

He changes the subject. "I just received a call from Jeff

Richardson. He wants to meet with us to discuss the prospectus next week when he's back in town."

"Yes, of course. No problem."

"I understand he called and gave you the details for their event at Cargenie Hall?"

"Yes, he did."

"Good, that's all for now." He goes back to his computer.

Relieved, I exit Scott's office as Roxanne smirks while typing away at her computer.

Rikash was right. *She. Is. Nasty.*

Chapter 16

There are two types of people that work in law firms: those who get stomach ulcers and those who give them. As Rikash hands me a memo I prepared for Bonnie yesterday, it's obvious that she falls into the latter category. Scribbled on the front page is a handwritten note:

This is NOT what I was looking for. It needs a LOT more work. Please see me to discuss.

An entire afternoon and evening of legal research and drafting wasted. Rikash was obviously right that Bonnie was extremely difficult about reviewing associates' legal research. She had won some writing competition in law school, was the co-editor in chief of the *Columbia Business Law Review,* and graduated in the top five percent of her class. She prided herself on her ability to dictate a faultless memo in record time and was quick to provide painfully detailed criticism of everyone else's legal writing. I wonder whether she engages in this type of critique with Harry behind bedroom doors?

Just as I was fantasizing about throwing her note into my wastebasket, the phone rings.

"Catherine, when can I expect your revised memo?"

I take a deep breath. I had been hoping to leave the office early to change before meeting Jeffrey for dinner but was clearly having a delusional moment.

"I'm working on a few deadlines for the Browser deal. Can it wait until tomorrow?"

I'm not sure why I even bothered asking since I already knew the answer to the question.

"No, I need this now."

"Right."

"And when I say now, I mean right now so you better get on it. This is a major antitrust case involving one of my biggest clients."

I dash to the firm library to ask for help locating a few books that were missing from the library shelves yesterday.

"Sorry, Catherine, they're still out," the librarian shrugs.

This must be karmic payback for the time I hid a treatise on Maritime law from a colleague who was desperately searching for it at two in the morning because he had badmouthed me to my boss. I immediately dispatch a paralegal to search every lawyer's office for the books I need for Bonnie's memo, and I ask her to start in Nathan's office.

The plaintiff is a large maker of computer hardware parts that believes our client secretly agreed with others in that industry to raise prices in violation of competition laws. I jump onto the LexisNexis and Westlaw research services to find additional precedents for similar cases. After printing out every commission decision, statute, press release, and article ever written on the subject of antitrust violations, I sprawl myself out over three tables, pull my hair into a messy bun, and kick off my heels. I index each document with Post-it Notes to classify my research. My motto: *Fail to prepare and prepare to fail.*

I concentrate for at least five hours without taking any breaks. I quickly synthesize my findings and furiously scribble notes in the margins of the first memo so that I can delegate the typing of my revisions while I continue doing some final research.

By the time I've finished reading all the precedents and rewriting the memo, Bonnie struts into the library.

"Catherine, are you still working on that memo?"

"Of course."

"Didn't you hear the news? We settled right after lunch."

I want to throw my stack of research in her face but storm out of the library shoeless instead.

"So where's he taking you for dinner?" Rikash asks as he hands me some new files.

"Per Se."

"How very sophisticated. It's one of the best restaurants in the city."

"Promise me you'll keep my dinner plans quiet. Even though it's a client event that Scott asked me to attend and even though the dinner is billable, I don't want anyone in the office to know that I'm going out, given the Mel Johnson incident."

"Of course, dah-ling, your secret is safe with me."

❖

At four thirty, I make a mental checklist of the things that need to get done before I go: call the printers, contact the SEC to make sure they received the draft Browser documents, return phone calls. I quickly work through my list and prepare to leave the office.

At five thirty, the phone rings. Rikash picks up and buzzes me on the intercom: "It's Phil calling from California, he sounds very agitated. Do you want to take it?"

"Sure, put him through." I take the call, assuming it's my last task of the day.

"Catherine, it's Phil Purcell from American Bank. We're at the printers and we need the document tonight."

"Hi, Phil, the document is almost ready, but you told me that you weren't going to print until tomorrow. Can I send it to you first thing in the morning?"

"No, I need it now."

"But—"

"No buts, Catherine, we need it tonight. We've been cooped up in here for the last forty-eight hours, and this is the last piece before we can go to print and go home."

Crap. What do I do? I don't want to seem like I'm blowing off work, but I can't exactly ditch my biggest client either. I hesitate for a moment before rushing out of my office and down the hallway to see if someone can cover for me. "Where's Antoine?"

"He's out at a client meeting."

Every other lawyer in the office is either on the phone or has their door shut.

"Ah, merde! I'm going to be late!"

Rikash walks into my office. "What's wrong? Can I help?"

"I have to leave right away otherwise I'll be late and I need to send a document to the printer in San Francisco."

"Is it ready? I can send it for you."

Given my recent run-in with Antoine about delegating work to secretaries, I hesitate for a moment before handing over the file to Rikash. If I prepare and review everything in advance, nothing can go wrong, right? Besides, I trust Rikash. I quickly make some final changes and email him the file along with the working group list, a detailed compilation of everyone's contact information.

"Okay, I'm leaving—you're sure you're on top of it?"

"Oooh, I love it when you talk dirty. Go on, muffin, have a blast."

After repeating my detailed instructions twenty-three times, and double-checking my BlackBerry battery, I dash out the door.

"Catherine!" A voice calls out from the bar.

"Jeffrey, hi. So sorry about being late. A client called at the last minute."

"No problem. Shall we sit and have a bite?"

He points to a cozy table next to a roaring fireplace with breathtaking views of Central Park.

"Hope you like my choice," he says as we take our seats.

I raise my eyebrows exaggeratedly in response.

"Are you kidding? This is one of the best restaurants in the city."

"It's one of my favourites," he responds while putting his Boss suit jacket on the back of his chair.

"So you eat here regularly?"

"Yes. The chef is known for his Napa Valley restaurant and I used to take clients there when I lived in California."

"And apparently his butter-poached lobster is to die for."

"How did you know?"

"You don't expect to take a lawyer out for dinner without her doing a bit of research in advance, do you?"

"No, of course not. Especially a newly transferred lawyer from the Paris office of Edwards."

"How d'you know?"

"You don't expect to have dinner with a CFO whose company is about to go public without him doing some research on the lawyer he's just hired, do you?"

"Touché. Of course not."

"We better order right away—the tasting menus run several courses."

"I'll let you pick since you're the regular."

"A lawyer giving up decision-making power. I'm really flattered." He signals the waiter to our table.

"We'll have the chef's tasting menu with a bottle of that red I had last week. It was outstanding."

The waiter nods, geisha-like, and gracefully takes our menus away.

"I hope they're serving the peach Melba tonight. It's really incredible. Foie gras with pickled white peaches in a sauce that—"

I start to giggle before he finishes his sentence.

"What's wrong? Please don't tell me you don't like foie gras or that you're a vegetarian, I'll cry."

"No, it's actually my favourite. It just makes me laugh that Americans love it so much. It just seems like you can find more foie gras in New York than in all of Paris."

"And I hope it stays that way." He smiles warmly and places his serviette on his lap. "So how are you enjoying New York so far?"

"I love it. It's so exciting. The energy here is really intoxicating."

"It really is, although some of the excitement will eventually wear off."

"I have a hard time believing that. There's so much going on in this city. I wish I had more free time."

"You're a corporate lawyer in New York. What do you expect? I'm lucky Scott let you out tonight."

"He didn't really let me out. He forced me out!" I joke.

"Ah, I see. Well, good for me then."

"Seriously, I was delighted when he asked me to join you. I haven't seen a concert in ages and I'm dying to hear some live music."

"So you like music, huh?"

"Yes, love it."

"What kind?"

"All kinds, really. I like to unwind to classical music after work, but jazz is my favourite."

His face brightens.

"Really? You like jazz?"

"Yes, *j'adore*."

The waiter brings our first course, a cappuccino of forest mushrooms.

"*Bon appétit.*"

"*Bon appétit,*" he responds after loosening the knot of his tie and flipping it over his shoulder. "Who's your favourite musician?"

"I have several, but Wynton and Ella are my favourites."

"You're definitely in the right building then."

"How so?"

"The Jazz at Lincoln Center Concert Hall is right here in the Time Warner building and this is Mr. Marsalis's home base."

"I'd love to see him play in New York. The last time I saw him play live was at the Montreal Jazz Festival. I was lucky enough to meet him backstage because of a close friend who knows him. He gave us a private concert. I'll remember it forever."

"That must have been amazing! I'm assuming you've been to the Marciac festival then?"

"Of course, it's fantastic."

"I'd love to go, especially in the company of a beautiful French woman."

Slightly taken aback, I continue our conversation like nothing happened. After all, it seems like harmless flirting. And it's billable.

"So you like jazz too?"

"Love it."

"Who's your favourite musician?"

"Miles. I think he's the greatest musician of our time. I'm also a big fan of Dave Holland and Charlie Mingus."

Pleasantly surprised by his level of musical appreciation, I smile before responding. "I just finished reading Miles's biography. He led a really tragic life."

"Didn't they all? When do you find the time to read with such a busy legal practice?"

"Mostly on weekends, but I try to read before I go to sleep every night. Although I haven't read anything other than the Securities Act these past few weeks."

"You mean that brick that sits on a shelf in my office? I don't think I've opened it more than twice."

"Lucky you," I say jokingly.

"Lucky me for having someone like you to read it for me." He smiles in a way that emphasizes his dimples.

I feel my cheeks becoming as deep a red as our wine. Although it's getting more difficult by the second, I try to keep the conversation purely professional. Reminding myself of what just happened with Mel helps. A bit.

"I can't wait to read something non-legal, but I guess it won't be for a while, given this IPO."

"No, we won't be reading novels anytime soon. Too much of that legal mumbo jumbo to get through. I get so exhausted after reading that stuff. It puts me right to sleep."

"I know what you mean."

"But this is what you do for a living. Don't you get tired of it?"

"It can be exhausting. That's why I keep a membership at Starbucks. I have my espresso injected intravenously."

"Don't tell me a French woman buys her coffee at Starbucks? Isn't that a bit sacrilegious?"

"It is. But there's one downstairs from my office. I guess I'm becoming a real New Yorker. I put convenience first!"

"I know a place in Midtown that makes great coffee. We should meet there next time. I need my jolt of coffee too these days; I'm travelling too much, and it's getting tiring."

"You travel a lot?"

"Back and forth between New York and San Francisco every week but now that the office has moved here, it should get better."

"Travelling for business isn't what it used to be. Those security lineups are ridiculous."

"Tell me about it. I got stuck in security at an airport in Arizona for at least an hour last week."

"Try getting through security in high heels with a French passport."

"No thanks, not interested. At least not in the heels. I wouldn't mind the French passport though."

"Oh?" I wonder why he would say something so odd.

"Because I could follow you back to France in case you decide to leave the country."

I sit up nervously, unsure how to react. He clearly has moved into full-blown pickup mode. Not wanting to be caught in another Mel Johnson–type situation, I try bringing the conversation back to the IPO.

"The public offering is looking very exciting, isn't it?"

"It is. I hope it isn't making your workload too heavy?"

"Don't worry, I'll manage."

"Are there any developments I should be aware of?" he asks after the waiter serves us our second course.

"Everything is on track so far. We filed the necessary paperwork with the SEC on Friday and we're on target for the start of the due diligence process."

"What about the directed share program? Is everything okay on that front?" he asks with intensity. "We have a lot of key business partners who we want to offer shares to, so I want everything to go smoothly."

I'm a bit surprised he wants to get into this much detail—but then, this is a working dinner. A directed share program allows company officers, employees, and their customers and vendors to purchase shares as part of the public offering. My mind races through the quantities of stocks we've set aside for their partners and buyers, and the paperwork that has been filed with regulators.

"It's looking good. Everything's with the SEC."

"Good to hear. I'll be travelling again early next week and I don't want any hiccups."

"Leave it with me. There won't be any problems," I say, trying to appear confident and in control.

"So, Catherine, what made you decide to become a lawyer?" he asks after our final course arrives.

"I love to analyze things, and I take pleasure in simplifying complicated issues and explaining them to people in understandable terms."

He smiles. "I'll enjoy working with you then. I don't like spending hours trying to decode complicated legal details. I'm into numbers."

"Sounds like we've both ended up in the right field. How did you become involved with Browser?"

"I studied accounting in college and then got involved with a few start-ups in Silicon Valley. One of the investors in my previous company lured me away to join Browser. It wasn't a sure thing at the time, but I'm really glad I did it. Things have gone really well since I've started. And look at us now, ready to go public."

He remains silent for a moment and smiles tenderly while gazing into my eyes.

"So did you leave some poor guy back in Paris to move to New York?"

Here we go again, back into slippery non-work territory. I need to steer the conversation back into professional mode with the grace and strategy of Mary Pierce playing against one of the Williams sisters at the U.S. Open.

"No, I've found it nearly impossible to mix personal relationships with the demands of my career." *(15–love)*

"I can't believe a girl like you is alone in the big city." *(15–all)*

"My job is my priority at the moment." *(30–15)*

"All work and no play makes Catherine a dull *laday.*" *(Ouch! 30–all)*

"You'll be glad work is my priority when you try to reach me at two in the morning to discuss your prospectus." *(Good shot! 40–30)*

"When I call you at two in the morning, you can definitely assume that it won't be to discuss the IPO." *(Wow, impressive backhand stroke! Deuce.)*

"As a lawyer, I never assume anything. I rely solely on facts." *(Okay, pretty strong return, advantage Lambert.)*

"And I would just love to learn every little fact about you, Mademoiselle Lambert."

My cheeks go from Shiraz red to Port burgundy as I stare down at my empty dessert plate. Sensing my uneasiness, he waves at the waiter to bring us the bill and hands over his credit card with the satisfied smirk of victory.

Game. Set. Match.

At Carnegie Hall, I put my BlackBerry on vibrate. *Just in case.*

After Jeffrey introduces me to the entire Browser executive team, we take our seats.

"I hope you'll enjoy this. It's a spectacular lineup tonight." He hands me a copy of the program and I flip to the concert details: Beethoven's Piano Concerto No. 4 in G Major.

As the orchestra begins, it transports me into another world. I'm in the most exciting city in the world, in a concert hall that gives me goosebumps, listening to some of the world's best musicians in the company of a gentleman—I mean, fantastic client. What else could a woman ask for? I'm basking in the moment when my left leg begins to vibrate: my BlackBerry is flashing with an email from Antoine.

I have a choice: ignore it for fear of being rude—*and risk becoming unemployed*—or read it quickly (after all, I can do it discreetly).

As I take a few seconds to consider my options, my BlackBerry vibrates a second time.

Then a *third*.

And a *fourth*.

All this vibration is strong enough to cause a micro-seism in the parquet and lower-tier sections of the concert hall. We're so close to the orchestra pit that I'm convinced I just heard BlackBerry interference come through the speaker system. I fumble to switch it to silent mode as I open the messages.

The first email reads:
Catherine, are you there?
A.

The second:
Where are you? I have an angry managing director from
American Bank on the line; he says you sent him the
wrong document. Please call ASAP.
A.

The third:
I'm in the middle of a conference call with a client. Where
the hell are you?

The fourth:
CATHERINE, PICK UP THE FUCKING PHONE WHER-
EVER YOU ARE AND CALL THE OFFICE NOW.

I'm in deep caca.

I count the number of seats between mine and the
end of the row: six. That's really not that bad, is it? I lean
in toward Jeffrey. "I'm terribly sorry, but I need to excuse
myself for a moment. I'll be right back." He looks puzzled as

I awkwardly scramble over the knees of the entire Browser executive team and run to the back.

"Antoine, it's Catherine. What's going on?"

"Where the hell have you been?"

"I'm at a client event at Carnegie Hall."

"What?"

I stay silent.

"That's just fuckin' great, Catherine. You're out at some concert while the rest of us are slaving over here at the office."

"Scott asked me to fill in for him at a Browser function, okay? I read your message about the document. Is Rikash around?"

"No, he left for the day."

"I don't understand what happened. I gave Rikash the document before I left so that he could send it to Phil."

"Haven't we gone over this before? How many times do I need to tell you? You shouldn't be delegating your work to a secretary."

My pulse starts to race and beads of sweat trickle down the back of my dress. Catherine, how could you have let this happen, *again*?

"I didn't delegate the actual drafting, just the sending.

If I tell you where the document is located in our database, can you send it to Phil?"

"Jesus, I don't have time to handle this. I'm working on a huge deal and I'm in the middle of a call with a client. Just come back to the office and take care of it."

I stand dumbfounded in the middle of the empty lobby. Did he just tell me to go back to the office in the middle of a Beethoven concerto? How can I explain this to Jeffrey? The team player and new-kid-on-the-block side of me responds: "Okay, I'll be there in ten minutes."

I look around and walk toward an older gentleman who appears to be an usher. I ask him if he could slip a note to Jeffrey. *Please?* Seeing the desperate look on my face, he agrees. I scribble a message on a piece of paper, show him my ticket so he knows exactly where Jeffrey's sitting, and run outside to catch a cab.

On my way back to the office, my feelings waver from anger to fear. I hope I don't get fired over this; I'm sure I gave Rikash the correct information. And if I didn't, I'll be completely mortified.

I rush past Antoine's office and shut my door. As I sit down in front of the computer, I only have one thing on my mind: getting back to Carnegie Hall. I try to compose myself before dialling Phil's extension at the printer's.

"Phil, it's Catherine from Edwards and White. What's wrong with the document we sent you earlier?"

"We received it, but it didn't have the revised offering price on the cover page and the company logo is missing."

"Can't you guys add the price and logo from over there? The printer has the graphics and all that information."

"We could have, but Antoine told us that you would take care of it. You guys need to get your act together."

Furious, I add the share price and the logo and send off the draft prospectus. Why did he make me come back to the office for something he could have done in two seconds flat? As I'm about to leave, Antoine looms in my office doorway.

"Listen, not to be overly critical, but I don't think you're taking your role here very seriously. You need to get your hands dirty like the rest of us if you want to get ahead in this place."

"I'm sorry you feel that way, but I've been working extremely hard and putting in long hours. I'm doing the best I can—I have big shoes to fill, you know." I throw that last bit in there, hoping that a little flattery will go a long way.

He crosses his arms. "I'm concerned about your future

at the firm. You don't want to be perceived as someone who's more interested in glamour and shopping than in doing the legal work. I handed you the Dior file so that you can impress them with your legal skills, not to attend their sample sales. The client has expectations and so do I."

"Have you seen the hours I've billed so far? I've been doing my share of legal work."

"I have. Your hours are acceptable but, frankly, aren't enough. We require your full commitment in order to make this relationship work."

Great, now he sounds like one of my ex-boyfriends. Is he truly concerned or is he jealous that Scott asked me to attend client events while he stays here getting paper cuts?

"Catherine, you really need to focus on your career if you want to be considered for partnership."

He knowingly hits my weak spot and I get a knot in the pit of my stomach.

"Listen, Antoine, I'm really giving it my all here. I've been working day and night. I'm not sure what else you want from me. I'm sorry about the shopping incident, but I apologized for that already."

"It's not just that."

"What is it then?"

He stares at me in silence and his lips form a tight pucker.

"What?"

He responds with a shrug and stares at his shoes. I wonder whether this has anything to do with the email I had sent him the other night. This is no time to bring that up. Keep it professional, Catherine.

"What is it?"

He remains silent.

"The Mel Johnson thing?"

He replies with a blank stare and a nod.

"Scott asked me to attend that stupid gala so I shouldn't have to justify going," I respond, fuming. "I already explained what happened and, frankly, I'm really upset that Scott hasn't sided with me on this. I could file a harassment claim against the firm for putting me through this."

"You could have handled it differently."

Differently? How? By sleeping with Mel? I can feel tears of frustration welling up and I want to scream.

"Is that so? How?"

"By not going."

"I didn't have a choice, Scott asked me to go, I already told you."

"We all have choices, Catherine. You don't have to attend every single party or concert you're invited to."

"Are you suggesting I should've said no to our boss?"

"All I'm saying is that you need to keep your eyes open. Don't you see what's going on around here? Things are about to change and I don't think that you should trust that anyone's looking out for anything but their own interests."

"Then why should I trust you?"

His face turns a deep shade of red. I can see him take a deep breath.

"It's quite simple really. If you look good, I look good. You have a lot of work on your plate, deadlines to meet, and I'm counting on you to help make my transition to Paris go smoothly. Got that?"

So this is all about saving *his* reputation, not mine. I'm humiliated that I didn't see it earlier—god, and to think that I flirted with him. I start past him to signal that our conversation is over. He remains planted in the doorway.

"What? Is there anything else you'd like to criticize?"

"It's just—"

"Just what? Tell me," I plead, my face inches from his and my heart racing.

"Never mind."

He walks back to his office and slams his door.

"Best of luck to you in Paris," I murmur as I leave the office, flustered.

Back at the concert hall, I anxiously wait for the intermission to find Jeffrey. I catch a glimpse of him and wave.

"Sorry for the disappearing act."

"I figured you either got kidnapped or you went back to Per Se for more foie gras!"

"Sorry, I got an urgent call from the office."

"Don't worry about it, I got the note. How about a glass of wine to help you relax?"

Relieved that I haven't ruined the evening, I smile back and nod.

"Fabulous idea. What about your colleagues?"

"I see them often enough as it is. Let's go to the bar."

We sip our wine while strolling through the Rose Museum, reading about Carnegie Hall's history, and gazing at treasures collected from famous performances.

"I hope I wasn't being too forward at dinner."

"Maybe just a bit, but it's nothing I can't handle," I say in jest.

"I rarely meet women who are as captivating and who smell as good as you do," he says while staring at a picture of Andrew Carnegie.

"Thank you. As for the scent, you can thank Mr. Dior."

"I'll make sure to send him an email first thing in the morning." He smiles as he gestures for us to walk back toward the main entrance.

We slip back into our seats and enjoy the second half of the concert. This time, as I turn *off* my BlackBerry, the lady sitting next to me gives me a dirty look.

"That was fantastic, wasn't it?" he asks as we head toward the exit.

"It was."

Outside, the smell of spring fills the air.

"Shall we walk? It's such a beautiful evening."

"Absolutely."

We stroll along majestic Fifth Avenue and turn right on 68th until we finally reach my doorstep.

"Thank you for a wonderful evening. I'm really sorry about the call from the office."

"Don't worry about it. It's part of the drill."

He leans forward and gives me a quick peck on the cheek. The heart of his lips seems to burn itself onto my skin. Keep it professional!

"*Bonsoir*, Mademoiselle Lambert."

"*Bonsoir*. Thanks again for the great evening."

He walks toward the street and waves goodbye as I enter the building.

"Don't worry, I won't call you at two in the morning just yet," he shouts. "Unless you want me to." He smiles, both hands in his suit pockets.

I wave good night to signal that our evening is over.

"Good night, Catherine."

As soon as the door is safely shut behind me, my head starts to spin. My god, this guy is so perfect. I need to call Lisa for a quick debrief.

"I have a 6:30 a.m. conference call with a European client. This better be important."

I recount my evening in excruciating detail and wait for her response.

"So what's the problem?"

"I'm attracted to a client, but I shouldn't be. I'd like to date him, but I can't and I won't."

"Okay, Mom. I guess you've already solved your big dilemma."

"You think I'm being old-fashioned?"

"Maybe. I mean, how often do you get a chance to meet somebody you really connect with? Just keep your options open."

"I'm worried about my reputation at the firm."

"Why? You can date whomever you want. Attorney rules of conduct don't prohibit it. Only lawyers involved in family law and divorce are forbidden from having personal relationships because of the weak emotional state of their clients." She pauses for a moment. "Unless you use undue influence or coercion to obtain physical favours . . . but that could be kind of fun, don't you think?" she adds jokingly.

"Very droll, *mon amie*. I don't like the idea of mixing my personal life with work; I want to be taken seriously. I'm already on thin ice."

"Just because this Antoine guy is a head case doesn't mean you're on thin ice. And you're working on a deal with Jeffrey so you'll see him again. You don't have to decide right this minute. You could always wait until the deal's done to get involved. Listen, kiddo, I'm going to bed."

"Good night, Lisa. Thanks for being a good listener."

I lie in bed analyzing every word that Jeffrey and I said during our evening alternately from the point of view of professional Catherine and crushing Catherine.

I finally fall asleep, exhausted like a tennis pro after winning a grand slam.

Chapter 17

"Lucky you to have someone watching out for you," Scott remarks as soon as I set foot in the office the next morning.

"Excuse me?"

He throws a printed copy of Mel's second email on my desk.

Ah, merde! Rikash sent the email to Scott without my consent. How could he?

"Listen, Catherine, I want to apologize. I should have believed you and told this bozo to f-off in the first place."

I sigh with relief; Scott does have moral backbone after all.

"Why didn't *you* forward me this message? I would have resolved it immediately."

"I don't know. I guess I was upset and wanted to think about it before reacting. I have my own way of handling things."

"You can say that again." He nods toward Rikash's cubicle.

"He can be rather unpredictable."

"That's an interesting way to describe him." He winks. "He's clearly looking out for your best interests. That's a rare commodity in this place nowadays . . ." His voice trails off. "I just want you to know that you're a valued member of the team."

Ahhh, I feel like a weight has been lifted. I'm not naïve enough to think that Scott is complimenting me out of the kindness of his heart; I'm working (and docketing) long hours on his Browser deal and I'm helping him keep the client happy. And this gives him an edge in the mighty battle of the warlords. Antoine may be right about Scott using me, but at least he's taking care of me, too.

"We're going to meet some prospective banking clients at the Met Bank for a sales call. Care to join us? I think they would really enjoy meeting you since they have plans to expand in Europe."

"Who's we?"

"Bonnie, Nathan, and I."

"Sounds good, thanks for thinking of me."

"Great. I have a car waiting for us. We'll meet you downstairs in five."

"A car? It's only a few blocks away."

"I know. Bonnie doesn't like to walk. It ruins her shoes." Scott pulls a face—and I smile too, thinking of the time Rikash "forgot" to get her a car.

Nathan, Scott, and I sit in the cramped back seat of the Town Car for thirty minutes before Bonnie makes her grand appearance in a skin-tight powder blue power suit.

Scott stares at her disapprovingly.

"What? Is there a problem?"

She throws her briefcase on the front seat and nearly knocks the driver out of his.

"You're *very* late," Scott hisses.

"I was on a call. As usual, a client wouldn't let me go."

"A bit on the short side, don't you think?" He glares at her suit.

"Are you kidding? It's *Geevenchee*."

"Whatever," he mumbles under his breath while shaking his head.

At the Met Bank offices, we're greeted by an energetic woman and three men dressed in business casual.

"Hey, Scott, glad you could come meet us."

"Sorry about being late, Amy, we hit some traffic."

"No problem. Let's have a seat in the boardroom. We'll be more comfortable in there."

"Amy, you know Bonnie and Nathan, but I'd like you to meet Catherine Lambert, who worked in our Paris office for six years before joining our New York group. She has significant banking experience and she's been an excellent addition to the team."

Bonnie and Nathan discreetly roll their eyes.

"Amy Lee. I'm the Director of Legal and Compliance here. Lovely to meet you. Would you like some coffee or anything to drink?" she asks.

"That would be lovely," Bonnie answers, sprawling herself out at the head of the table before anyone else has taken a seat. "You wouldn't happen to have a cappuccino machine, would you? I'm always in the mood for some *good* coffee."

Scott gives her an evil stare.

"I'm afraid not," Amy replies with a frown.

"Okay, then I'll have a Diet Coke."

As soon as everyone is seated, Bonnie cracks open her can of soda, throws her feet up on an empty chair, and launches haughtily into a soliloquy about her achievements and the firm's accomplishments.

"You've probably read articles in the *Journal* about Edwards and White being lead counsel on that Blue Crest deal. We're also at the top of the league tables in the IPO category and we represent most of the top-tier banks."

Halfway through her speech, she drops her head and whips out her BlackBerry.

"So sorry," she says while rolling the trackball. "There's a reason they call these little things CrackBerrys, they're so addictive."

Oh mon dieu, she's really lost her marbles now. I sit at the opposite end of the table shell-shocked. How is it that this woman became a partner? Shouldn't she be focusing on the client's needs rather than going on about our firm?

"The only problem with these little babies is that if you use them too much, you develop a BlackBerry *thumb*. It's killed my squash game."

Scott is now a deep shade of violet. Trying to save face, he interrupts Bonnie and mumbles something about an article in today's *Times* about Met Bank's positive financial earnings. Uninterested in Scott's spiel, the four in-house lawyers sit transfixed, gazing at Bonnie as if she were medusa. The male attorney to Amy's right seems particularly interested in the length of her skirt.

Actually, this is kind of fun. All of a sudden, I'm humming the words to ZZ Top's "Legs" in my head, a song I used to dance to with Lisa back in law school.

"So what are your biggest challenges these days?" Bonnie asks nonchalantly. "I'm assuming it must be difficult for you to keep track of all the new banking regulations and exceptions under Regulation R of the Gramm Leach Bliley Act?" she continues before Amy or anyone else can respond.

The four lawyers nod in agreement.

"While keeping your outside counsel fees low?"

They again nod in tandem.

"I've found that some of my clients save time and money using an electronic banking regulation service. If you're interested, you can use our access free of charge for a few weeks. Also, you shouldn't worry too much, since Regulation R includes a delayed compliance date—you're safe until the first day of the first fiscal year end after next September. Which for you means February 1st *next* year. And I definitely think your activities fall in one of the bank registration exemptions. If you want, I'll send you a memo I drafted last week on the subject."

"That would be fantastic!" Amy responds, her eyes wide with excitement. "And we'd love to try out that service."

"That would be really great!" the lawyer to the right of Amy tells Bonnie's calves.

"I'll have Catherine send you the memo and a link to the service," she finishes before standing, ready to leave.

Now I get why Bonnie gets away with her outlandish behaviour: she's a damn good lawyer. With a performance like that, it's easy to see why she's one of the top-rated corporate attorneys in the city and I can see how clients feel that she truly understands their business needs and genuinely respect her for it. I glance over to see storm clouds gathering on Scott's face—this clearly isn't going to be *his* client any longer.

"I assume you have final say on retaining external counsel?" Bonnie asks Amy while reaching for her briefcase. "If not, we should probably be meeting with someone at the bank who *does*."

"Yes, yes, of course," Amy answers. "I do."

"Great. We look forward to working with you then. This was a very productive meeting, don't you think?" She extends her slim Verdura-cuffed arm to shake Amy's hand.

"Yes, very." The three men concur while rising to catch a better glimpse of her cleavage.

A perplexed Nathan, an angry Scott, and an amused *moi* follow in the waft of her heavy perfume.

Back on the twenty-eighth floor, I notice that Antoine's office is empty.

"He packed all his stuff overnight," Mimi remarks as she sees me peering into the vacant space. "I guess he was in a rush to get to Paris."

"I thought he was leaving at the end of the month? No goodbyes, no going-away party?" I ask, stunned.

"Nope." She shakes her head. "You know Antoine, he's all work and no play."

I feel a pinch in the pit of my stomach. How could he leave without saying goodbye? A mixture of sadness and disillusionment comes over me. I had thought that we might've eventually become friends after he asked me to be his main contact in New York, but our last conversation ended any hopes of that happening.

"So how was it?" Rikash asks as I walk by his cubicle.

"Fascinating. I've never seen someone land a client that way."

"Not the meeting, silly girl. Your date with Mr. Browser. Did you get lucky?"

"First of all, it wasn't a date, and even if it was I would never do that on the first date. Don't you know that men never call you back if you do?"

"That's exactly *why* I do it. Anyway, do tell me about your evening."

"Not bad."

"Really? I would've guessed otherwise, given what's sitting on your desk."

A box wrapped in silver paper with a big red bow is sitting on top of numerous files and documents. A little card reads, *"Thanks for a fantastic evening. Enjoy. A très bientôt, Jeffrey."*

I open the box to find an Ella Fitzgerald CD box set and a bottle of J'adore. Although I'm touched by his gesture, it feels awkward receiving such a personal gift from a client. In the harsh light of day, I feel as though keeping it strictly professional is the right decision. I've learned my Mel lesson.

"It looks like you had a pretty great evening to me."

I raise my shoulders in response.

"What happened?"

"Nothing."

"Come on, don't be such a sourpuss, tell me! We're all one big dysfunctional family, you know. We don't keep secrets from each other."

"Let's just say we had a major interruption that kind of ruined the evening."

"What kind of interruption? The jealous wife kind?"

"Antoine vibrated me out of Carnegie Hall because there was a problem with that document for American Bank."

"Oh, crap. I hope it wasn't my fault? I sent the document the way you asked me to."

"It had nothing to do with you. Antoine made me come back to the office for no reason other than to ruin my night."

"What's up with him? One day he's got your back and the next he can be such a toad."

"You can say that again. I'll be fine if I never I have to deal with him again. Good riddance."

I sit in front of my computer and an email entitled "PRIVILEGED AND CONFIDENTIAL" from Jeffrey is waiting for me in my inbox.

To the Browser IPO team,
Please clear your agendas for Monday morning. The SEC is inquiring about an interview conducted by *Business Magazine* with the senior management of Browser and is threatening to delay the offering. This could potentially throw off our timetable and affect pricing of the deal.

My secretary will send meeting details under separate cover. Your immediate attention to this matter is greatly appreciated.

Thanks. Jeff Richardson.

I press reply and write him a formal thank-you email for his gift and he responds partly in French:

Avec plaisir, ma chère Catherine.
Have a wonderful weekend. See you on Monday.

As I stare at the gift box on my desk, my mind spins. Normally, I would be leery of such clichéd pursuit tactics. But for some reason, he's getting under my skin. Why couldn't I have met him at a jazz club instead?

Chapter 18

As Oscar Wilde put it, the only way to get rid of temptation is to yield to it. But it's not always the best idea to take advice from a man who died heartbroken, exiled, and penniless. As Jeffrey gets ready to address the crowd gathered at Browser's headquarters, I feel grateful that Scott is seated next to me and keeps me focused on work.

"I'm getting really worried about timing," Jeffrey announces, standing at the front of the room with his shirt sleeves rolled up. (And looking really handsome. Catherine, cut it out!) "The CEO granted an interview to *Business*

Magazine just before we filed the Registration Statement and *Business* is planning to print the article just before we price the deal. The SEC wants to impose a cooling off period before we go live."

"So what happens now?" one of the bankers throws to the crowd of legal professionals.

"I think we have a major regulatory concern," a prominent lawyer and former SEC staff member who represents the underwriters declares. "The SEC can force Browser to delay the offering. They've done it several times before."

I'm fumbling through my memory. The interview could delay Browser's offering because securities regulators restrict what company executives can say publicly while preparing to sell stock for the first time. Is there a way out of this, though?

My heart racing, I somehow gather the courage to throw in my two cents.

"I disagree."

About twenty-two pairs of eyes turn scornfully toward me. I catch a few of them glaring at my black patent stilettos. My stomach drops and I begin to sweat. I can feel Scott's eyes on me.

"Oh?" Jeffrey responds.

"I think a valid argument can be made that Browser's IPO has already been extensively covered in the press and the article doesn't add anything new."

"I think that's pretty weak," the ex-SEC official counters. Scott throws me a stern look.

"I've argued this point before and it worked."

"I don't mean to burst your bubble, missy, but I've been at this for far longer than you have."

"I'm not disputing that, sir, but isn't your job to represent your client's best interests? I don't think allowing the SEC to delay this offering is in any of our best interests."

"I agree," Jeffrey concurs.

Humiliated, the former SEC lawyer squirms in his chair.

"Catherine, can you please call the regulators to discuss this point? I'd like you to take the lead on this," Scott announces proudly.

"Sure, happy to."

At the end of the meeting, while Scott is caught up in a conversation with another lawyer, Jeffrey rushes toward me.

"Wow, you don't suffer fools, do you? I was impressed back there. How about grabbing a quick coffee?"

"Don't have time. I need to make an important call to the SEC, remember?"

"Lunch?"

"You'll need to check with Rikash, my assistant. My lunch schedule is quite full these days. Maybe I can squeeze you in on Wednesday."

"So you want to squeeze me, do you? Wednesday it is then."

He walks out of the room with a large satisfied grin. I exit with a look of victory on my face. Bravo, Catherine!

Chapter 19

"I heard you kicked some serious butt at the Browser meeting yesterday. Way to go," Rikash annouces as I get in the next morning.

"I was just doing my job."

"That's what I like about you, Catherine, you have a tiny ego. In fact, it's the smallest in this firm's history. They should put a bronze plate next to your office door that says so."

"I needed to speak up. It was in the client's best interest."

"I'm sure Jeffrey liked it." He winks. "A self-assured

French woman would be catnip for Mr. Numbers. I bet he was all over that."

"Shhh. Stop it."

"Oh come on, stop being so prissy, you're French, for god's sake. You're supposed to flirt in your sleep."

"Well I don't, okay?"

"As Mae West put it, 'Don't keep a man guessing too long, he's sure to find the answer somewhere else.'"

"Thanks, I'll keep that in mind."

I shut my door to get some work done. I try to concentrate on my numerous files and upcoming deadlines but have trouble getting Jeffrey out of my mind. Rikash is probably right. Who am I trying to fool? I'm seriously falling for this man. I play a silly game and try to imagine Jeffrey as being married with six kids, sporting a large pot-belly, terrible breath, and worse table manners to convince myself that he's all wrong. In short, I mentally paste his face on Mel Johnson's body. It works for an entire thirty minutes.

But that half-hour buys me enough time to prepare SEC documents for Scott. He had asked me to help a client with its 10K and F-1 filings. As I fill in the blanks, I wonder how on earth the SEC came up with these form titles. Even though I've been doing this for years, in my mind, 10K refers exclusively to gold jewellery and F-1 to car racing. At least I can fill them out at F-1 speed now. Once completed, I email the documents to Rikash with instructions to create a new file before emailing them to Roxanne.

I overhear her voice coming through on his phone.

"Who the fuck does she think she is? She can't email them to me herself?"

Furious, I storm out of my office and make a beeline down the hallway in her direction.

"Uh-oh, be careful, sweetie, she can bite and she has rabies," Rikash calls after me.

I arrive out of breath in front of her desk and she stares innocently at me as though nothing happened.

"Can I help you?"

"Yes, you can. For starters, you could wash your mouth with soap and treat your co-workers with some respect."

She laughs in my face. "Wash my mouth with soap? Ha! Who are you? My mother?"

"Thank god, not. Working with you is bad enough, I wouldn't want to be related to you in any way."

She sticks out her tongue in response. Forget it—this is infantile.

I want to run into Scott's office and tell him about her

behaviour but decide against rattling on his prized little assistant. I'll have my day, I just know it.

"I was impressed with the way you defended your argument the other day. I can't believe you had the guts to stand up to one of the top regulatory lawyers in the city."

I had caved in and accepted Jeffrey's lunch invitation because Scott had asked me to update him on my conversation with the regulators. Who am I kidding—I was going to find a good reason to say yes. I've barely thought of anything but Jeffrey in the last two days or slept more than a few hours, tossing and turning until dawn, debating with myself whether to keep our relationship professional.

He had made reservations at Fleur de Sel, a quiet restaurant with exposed brick, pressed white tablecloths, and a fabulous menu.

"I thought you might like it here. The food is terrific and it's cozy."

"It's lovely. The name reminds me of my summer vacations on L'Ile de Ré, where they harvest sea salt."

"Phew!" he says playfully. "I'm relieved that you like my choice. Now let's order lunch, I'm starving!"

He chooses the veal confit and I order the goat cheese ravioli. We chitchat a bit, and then the conversation turns to our last meeting.

"You really gave that former SEC lawyer a run for his money. Did you see the look on the poor guy's face?"

"I guess I can't help myself. I hope he wasn't too offended. My father taught me to speak up when I believe in something."

"He's a wise man."

"He *was* a wise man. He died several years ago." I look down. This is always a painful topic for me.

"I'm sorry to hear that. I know what it's like to lose someone. My sister died of cancer two years ago," he responds, with a look of genuine tenderness and compassion.

"I'm so sorry. Was it sudden?"

"Yes, very. She died of lung cancer even though she'd never smoked a day in her life."

We pause briefly as the waiter serves out lunch.

"How old was she? Did she have any children?"

"She was young, thirty-nine. She had a son, a ten-year-old named Adam. He's a great kid. He comes to New York regularly to visit me."

As I listen to him and see the emotion plain as daylight

on his face, my heart melts. My reservations about dating a client are beginning to disappear as quickly as the ravioli on my plate.

"Listen, Catherine, I know that you'd prefer to keep our relationship professional, and I respect that. But I want you to know that I'm really attracted to you and not just physically. I think you're a brilliant lawyer and lovely woman and sometimes in life you need to take a chance. I mean, at the end of the day it's just a job."

My stomach drops. My face flushes. I'm at a loss for words. Although I wasn't willing to admit it to myself, I was secretly hoping that he would break the ice and raise the issue. Still on the fence about getting involved with him, I consider my answer carefully as the waiter brings us our desserts.

"Just a job? It's more like a life sentence!"

He laughs and then reaches tentatively for my hand. I stop nibbling at my crème brûlée.

"Any way I could make you change your mind?"

I stare at my plate and look away before answering. My mind says *non*, but my heart says *oui*. This is like a textbook romance; but could it be too good to be true? I've played out dozens of different scenarios in my head a thousand times in the last few days, trying to find the right solution that doesn't compromise my career. Maybe the best way to handle it is to ask Nathan to take my place on the Browser deal and explain my situation to Scott. Not good for my billables, but good for *me*.

"I have an idea," I respond tentatively.

"Shoot. I'm all ears."

"I could ask that another lawyer take my place on the IPO. Then it would be a non-issue, wouldn't it? One of my colleagues is dying to—"

"Absolutely not." His tone changes abruptly.

I'm stunned. Why would he react so violently to my suggestion? I pull my hand away and he reads my face.

His tone softens again. "Especially after that stunning performance at the meeting on Monday. You're the best person at your firm for the transaction. This deal is your chance to prove yourself."

I consider his words. It's true, this is my big break. What was I thinking? I must really be falling hard.

"You're probably right. Well, that was my big idea."

"I know it sounds like I want it all, and the reality is, I do. I want you to represent my company and I want you to go out with me Saturday night. I have two tickets for a

Wynton Marsalis concert," he adds with a huge grin.

"You really can't take no for an answer, can you?"

He shakes his head.

"I'm not sure about this, Jeffrey. I need some more time."

"How about we walk up to Union Square?"

"I was thinking more like a few weeks, not a few minutes," I laugh.

We walk along Broadway—it's a beautiful afternoon. I feel totally relaxed in his company, as though I can talk about anything. Why does life need to be so complicated?

"It's great to actually see a bit of blue sky; I haven't seen much of the sun in the last while."

"Time flies when all you do is work."

"Yes, it does."

We arrive at Union Square and he guides me to the closest bench. The setting is romantic and would be the perfect place for a first kiss. *Stop it!* Catherine, what are you thinking?

"Do you miss France?"

"Yes and no. I miss seeing my mother and going out with my friends in Paris. But I really love New York. This is the place to be for my career."

"I would miss it if I were you. It's such a beautiful country."

He talks about his nephew's next trip to the city and I lose track of time in his presence. The conversation flows so easily that I could talk for hours.

At two thirty he looks at his watch.

"Before I forget, how's the directed share program coming along?"

Surprised that he abruptly switches back to business, I hesitate for a moment before answering. "Um, very well. We're on target with the regulators."

"Perfect. Glad to hear." His shoulders seem to drop with relief.

"So are we on for Wynton's benefit concert on Saturday?"

"It's a benefit?"

"Yes, *madame*, and it's a tribute to the great ladies of jazz. Come on, it will be amazing!"

"*D'accord*, you win," I say with an air of defeat.

Like the great jazz musicians of our time, I'll need to go along and improvise.

Chapter 20

"CATHERINE!" Harry Traum's deep voice bursts out of my speakerphone as soon as I get back to my desk. "My office. Immediately!"

Terrified and clueless as to why he wants to see me, I tiptoe slowly toward his corner office, trying to make the least possible noise. A large gold plate with the inscription GEN. HAROLD J. TRAUM, ESQ. rests against the doorframe. This is my very first time going to see Harry Traum. After witnessing his terrifying U.S. geography lesson on my first day at Edwards & White, I've avoided him like the plague.

I am met by a closed door.

I knock gently, but there's no response. Could he be in there with Bonnie? I certainly hope not! I knock again with a bit more forcefulness and as his voice bursts out, it creates a minor typhoon in the hallway.

"COME IN!"

He is sitting in his large leather chair in the centre of the room while a dark-haired lady in a tight black skirt cuts his hair.

"Catherine, this is Juanita."

His office is littered with trophies, military paraphernalia, and pictures of countless children and grandchildren on numerous vacations by the sea. There are three large wooden signs hung above his desk that read, *This We'll Defend, Victory Starts Here,* and *Equal Justice Under Law.* From what I can see, it looks as though Harry is the better prepared partner for war at the firm.

"There's something important I need to discuss with you, Miss Lambert," he says sombrely with his arms crossed while Juanita hovers around his giant head.

"Oh?"

"Are you familiar with a lawyer's duty of confidentiality?" he asks gravely.

"Of course."

"Really? So what would you do if I told you that Antoine had a serious drinking problem? Would you tell anyone?"

Caught off guard by his question, I fumble for an answer.

"Um, no, of course not."

"Now what if I told you that Scott was a *homo*"—he takes a deep breath—"*sexual?* Would you tell someone about that?"

Mon dieu, what is this line of questioning leading to? I feel beads of sweat rolling down by back.

"Of course not."

"And what if you were working on the high-profile merger of a public company? Would you tell any of your boyfriends?" he asks, his voice getting increasingly louder and more intimidating.

"No. I wouldn't. Mr. Traum, may, um, may I ask what this is regarding?" I stutter.

"If you are familiar with your duty of confidentiality, young lady, and you wouldn't tell anyone about any of this, explain to me, Catherine, WHY YOU TOLD A GODDAMN SECRETARY, A SECRETARY FOR CHRISSAKES, THAT I WAS GETTING A DIVORCE? NOW EVERYBODY IN THIS FUCKING PLACE WILL KNOW ABOUT IT!"

As he shouts, drops of spit fly across Juanita's face and bosom. She backs away for an instant while the colour in his face goes from scarlet red to a lighter shade of rouge. My mind is racing . . . I didn't tell a secretary, a secretary told *me*. I am completely *sous le choc*. I can't believe Rikash would do this to me; there has to be another explanation. I decide it's better just to take responsibility than to throw Rikash under the bus.

"I didn't—I didn't mean to, it just slipped out. It was an accident. I'm sorry."

"Edwards and White associates don't have accidents, got that? I was expecting a lot more from you, Catherine, and, frankly, I'm very disappointed. We have very high standards here and if you can't meet them, we'll have to revisit your future here, understand?"

I feel weak in the knees and my entire six years at the firm flash in front of my eyes. Again. I was already feeling down and out after my fight with Antoine and walking a tightrope with Scott because of my midday shopping expedition, but this might be the nail in the coffin. Could all those gruelling billable hours I've docketed over the years be wasted over a divorce rumour that I had no part in?

"Yes sir, I do."

"So how did you find out I was getting divorced?" The colour of his face has now returned to its normal dark pink shade.

I get a sudden lump in my throat. "I don't remember."

"You don't remember?"

"No."

He shakes his head, sighs loudly, and glances at Juanita.

"Well, when your little brain does remember, you damn well better let me know. I'd like to make an example out of that big mouth and fire somebody."

"Mmm-hmm, will do."

I walk out of Harry's office feeling like a ten-year-old who's been reprimanded by the school principal. Could Rikash have betrayed me? Could I have been wrong to trust him so quickly? As soon as I exit Harry's office, Scott rushes in and slams the door. What is going on around here?

"Rikash, in my office right now!"

"What is it? You look perturbed."

"Perturbed doesn't begin to do justice to how furious I am. Harry Traum just gave me an earful because he thinks I've told you and everybody else at the firm about his divorce. How did that happen?"

"I have no idea, but it wasn't me, I swear!"

"Then who told him? My job is on the line because of this. I won't let some ridiculous gossiping ruin my career."

"Dah-ling, you need to trust me on this. I watch your back every second you're in the office, I swear. Just as I know that you watch mine."

After the anger and humiliation slowly dissipate from my body, hallucinatory visions of treacherous firm secretaries come to mind. They are lounging languorously atop the firm's main boardroom table, dressed in Roman toga garb holding pitchforks and are feasting on the finest caviar and champagne while laughing demonically at the head on a silver platter that rests at the centre of the table: *mine*.

"Of course. Sorry, Rikash."

Chapter 21

They say that youth is unduly busy pampering the outer person. That may be so, but given the amount of time I've spent in the office lately, a bit of pampering is definitely in order. Saturday afternoon I drop by the hair salon at Bergdorf's to get a *brushing* as well as a manicure and pedicure. It took some serious detective work to finally get Lisa to share the names of her beauty specialists in the city, but it was well worth the effort.

Although Parisian women are known for enjoying lavish beauty rituals and treatments (Michel Perry, one of my favourite boutiques in Paris, offers nail lacquers that match the shades of the shoe designer's creations), like everyone else in New York, Lisa treats her beauty regimen like a business; the return on investment carefully calculated with every appointment she makes. She must spend several hundred dollars a week keeping up her appearance. The mani/pedi is a must (her favourite nail colours: Your place or mine? by Essie), she wouldn't dream of going anywhere without first getting her hair blown out, and she relies on countless massages, rub downs, and other therapies to help her cope with her job. I'm not sure how she does it—her practice is as busy as mine. Although I love to splurge on facials, waxing, and spa treatments, I barely have enough energy after work these days to take care of basic maintenance.

After I get home, I lounge about reading the *The New York Times* and turn to the Wedding Announcements page. I love these; they remind me of the M&A pages of the deal. com where companies boast their most recent acquisitions. As I read about the new Mr. and Mrs. Ron Smithenhower, I find the whole thing deliciously pretentious. Isn't marriage supposed to be about love? Not about sending your shares soaring on the social stock exchange?

I flip to the Business section and spot a brief mention

of the Browser offering. The press is referring to it as the most highly anticipated IPO this year. Part of me can't believe that I'm having dinner with the man orchestrating this whole deal. Another part of me can't believe that I'm the lawyer behind it. This is exactly why I came to New York. I put on my new Dior dress and a pair of snakeskin sandals with patent leather ankle straps and spray on some J'adore before I dash out onto the street. At seven o'clock sharp, Jeffrey's cab pulls up in front of my building.

"Are you ready to swing?"

"I am!"

"You look gorgeous." He kisses me on the cheek.

"Thank you."

"I think in France you kiss on both cheeks, don't you?" He reaches for the other side of my face and brushes my lips. Our eyes lock for a long moment and I feel dizzy.

The concert begins and Dee Dee Bridgewater sings "Misty," one of my favourite jazz standards. I find myself thinking that the lyrics sum up my feelings about Jeffrey, especially the part about wanting him to lead me on. Is it really what I want him to do?

During the concert intermission, we head for the bar for a glass of champagne.

"Wow!" Jeffrey looks like he's trying to wrap his head around what we've just seen.

"I know—it was amazing! Did Diana Ross actually just make a surprise appearance? I couldn't believe it when she walked on stage in that shimmering white dress." My heart flutters with excitement as we clink our glasses. "Thank you for inviting me."

"I know this may sound a bit corny, but I feel totally relaxed when I'm with you, Catherine. You have a very calming effect on me."

"I'll take that as a compliment."

"You should. I haven't felt like this in a very long time."

I try to focus on my professional self, which is reminding me that I'm about to dive deep into the choppy waters of being romantically involved with a client. This might be a terrible mistake, one that I might regret for a long time. But Jeffrey is nothing like Mel. Still, I pull out the Black-Berry from my evening bag nonchalantly to signal that this soirée is really all about business. He shakes his head, laughing, confiscates the electronic device, and puts it in his suit jacket. He grabs my arm, pulls me in closer, and we kiss.

I let go of the buoy and feel myself drifting out to sea.

Chapter 22

"Good morning, gorgeous," I say to Rikash as I walk by his cubicle. "Love the shirt. How about a cappuccino? It's on me today."

"Dah-ling, you're glowing. What happened to *you* over the weekend?"

I answer his question with a mischievous smile.

"Oh!" he blurts out, his eyes big as saucers. "No way . . . Jeffrey?"

I nod, grinning.

"You naughty girl you."

"Shhh, keep it down."

"I want all the details!" he exclaims as he follows me into my office and closes the door as I sway toward my chair.

"Promise me you won't tell anyone about this. I'm already walking a thin line here after what happened with Mel Johnson and Harry Traum."

"I promise, I promise."

"Okay, he took me out to this fantastic jazz concert. We had an amazing time. He kissed me. It was magic."

"Damn. I knew he was a good catch."

"Hey, you know what? Let's skip Starbucks today and order coffee from Fred's at Barneys. I'm in the mood to celebrate." I pull out some money from my wallet. "That should cover it. Order yourself a treat and get something for Mimi."

He leaves my office whistling "La Vie en Rose" and struts back in about ten minutes later with a tray overflowing with coffee and danishes.

"There are studies that show that the smell of cinnamon buns increases penile blood flow, so I hope you won't mind that I picked up a few."

He drops off my latte with a big smile.

"You should shag more often, sweetie. It makes mornings a lot more fun for the rest of us."

"Rikash, I didn't."

"Really? If this is pre-shag behaviour, I can't wait to see what we'll be ordering for breakfast when you *do* do it."

Maria and Roxanne watch from their cubicles as Rikash, Mimi, and I dive into our fabulous breakfast.

"Mimi, haven't you noticed something different about Catherine today?" Rikash asks, his mouth covered with powdered cinnamon.

"She looks radiant."

"I know, she's in lust," Rikash says with a wiggle of his hips.

I give Rikash a look to make sure he doesn't cross the line.

"*Goawd*, I wish I was your age again," Mimi says with a sigh. "Lust is the greatest thing for your complexion."

"Some people really like to show off," Roxanne remarks loudly so we can hear her.

"What's up with her? I've never met anyone so frustrated in my life," I say after a sip of my latte.

"That's nothin', hon," Mimi says, waving her gold bangles in the air while sipping her cappuccino, "you should have met some of the other secretaries we've had in this *oaffice*, somethin' straight out of a Hitchcock movie. Real scary."

"Really?"

"Oh yeah. We found a butcher knife once in one of the girls' desk drawers. We had to call the police and sent her away in handcuffs."

"No way!" Rikash and I exclaim in unison.

We sit in my office indulging in pastries and gossiping until Scott breaks up the tea party.

"Mimi, I need you to take care of the accounts receivable, not chat over coffee." She follows him back to the reception area, sulking.

"It's Roxanne. She's such a tattletale. She can't tolerate that anyone else would have a bit of fun in the office," Rikash murmurs, visibly upset that Mimi should bear the brunt of our fun.

"All she and Maria do all day is talk about everybody else in the office behind their backs. You should hear what they say about Scott and Bonnie during their lunches in the boardroom: so nasty. They would definitely get fired for it."

"Is that right?"

"Dah-ling, believe me. I can hear them when I cover the phones at reception."

After Rikash settles back at his desk, I pull out of my drawer every lawyer's best friend: the old Dictaphone. If it records legal documents for transcription, why couldn't it also record bitchy secretaries who love to cause trouble for everyone else?

Around noon, before Maria and Roxanne come back to the boardroom with their pizzas from Famiglia, I surreptitiously place my Dictaphone at the opposite end of the boardroom table under a nondescript piece of paper and let it rip. Pleased with my plan, I run out to pick up a sandwich; I can't wait to hear the scathing gossip on that tape. An hour or so later, I casually make my way back to the boardroom, retrieve my dear friend from under the piece of paper, settle back into my office, and let the good times roll.

"Oh god, this pizza's so good, I could have it every day," Maria starts.

"You do," Roxanne replies.

"Oh yeah, you're right," Maria answers with her mouth full. "But it's not from *Barneys*," she says, putting on a hoity-toity accent. "Can you believe she ordered coffee from Barneys and she didn't even offer us any. She hates our guts." She continues chewing.

"It's reciprocal," Roxanne answers. "I can't fucking stand her. She thinks she's some prima donna or someting."

I chuckle to myself. *Now this is getting* très *interesting.*

"And Rikash kisses her butt all day long. He's such a kiss

ass. He tries to be nice to her so she doesn't find out he's actually asleep all day after raving in the clubs all night," Maria replies. "And I'm so glad Antoine finally moved to Paris," she continues between bites. "I was about to tear his head off. He thought he was somethin' special. Thank god I don't ever have to stare at his scary face again."

They both laugh hysterically.

"Want to hear the latest?" Maria asks. "I walked into Harry Traum's office last week and found draft divorce papers on his desk. I guess his wife finally found out about his long lunches with Bonnie," she says, updating Roxanne on the gossip front. "That might be why he's thinking of leaving the firm; he likes to screw her but can't stand working with her."

So it's Harry who might be leaving! This is proving more useful than I expected.

"I can't say I blame him. She's such a bitch. Anyway, you won't believe what I did. I told him Catherine was spreading rumours at the firm about his divorce! Oh my god, you should have seen his face, he was so pissed."

"You did not!" Roxanne yelps.

"Believe it, sista, but promise me you'll never tell a soul."

"Don't worry. It'll be our little secret 'cause I sure

wouldn't want him to be pissed at me. I wouldn't want to be cut off from the car service; I used it the other night to get to my hairdresser in Queens. It's way more comfortable than the subway," she admits, chuckling.

"And to go shopping at the outlet mall. Can you believe we actually got away with using the office car for that?" Maria retorts.

Bingo. I have the goods. Proud of my investigative skills, I turn off my Dictaphone. The next time either of them pulls anything nasty on me, it will be *checkmate, ladies.*

Chapter 23

"There's an Amy calling from the Mct Bank. She sounds like she's totally stressed out."

"Thanks, Rikash, put her through."

"Hi, Amy, I'm sorry I haven't sent that memo Bonnie drafted, I'll get it to you right away."

"That's not the reason for my call." I suddenly register the note of panic in her voice. "We've just received notice that we're under regulatory investigation, and Bonnie suggested I call you. I understand you've dealt with these types of issues for a French bank when you worked in Paris."

"Um, yes I have."

"Great. We're hoping that you're the best person to handle this."

"What's the investigation about?"

"One of our traders hid millions of dollars of trading losses from his manager and committed fraud in client accounts."

Oh, this is serious. My mind spins through similar matters I've worked on in the past and I put on my regulatory hat.

"How did you find out?"

"He came clean after one of the clients complained. I hope we're not in any major trouble"—her voice shakes— "I guess we could be subject to massive fines."

"Not if you have adequate supervisory procedures in place to detect this type of behaviour."

She remains silent. Uh-oh.

"You do have supervisory procedures and controls in place, don't you?" They must. Everyone does these days.

"Yes . . . but I'm not sure they're adequate. The Feds notified us last year that our procedures were faulty." I can hear her breaths becoming shorter and faster. And I'm starting to understand why.

"Did you update them?" I ask with a sinking feeling that I already know the answer.

"Not yet. We're understaffed and haven't had the time to get to it."

"Oh." *Merde.* I try to keep my voice calm despite what she's just told me. I don't want to create unnecessary drama, but I now realize that Amy and her bank have a really serious problem.

"What's the highest fine we can get? A few hundred thousand dollars?"

"It can actually be in the millions, but I wouldn't go that far just yet."

"Oh my god, I'll lose my job!" she exclaims, now 100 percent panicked. "I'm the head of the legal and compliance departments; could I go to jail for this?"

I take a deep breath.

"It's *extremely* unlikely unless there was intent on your part to commit fraud. But recent scandals and the climate of the last few years have changed the regulatory landscape so both regulators and prosecutors are aggressively pursuing any improprieties. So the answer, I'm afraid, to your question is that *yes,* it's a possibility."

She begins to sob. This is the rare occasion when I hate

my job, when I'm the bearer of bad news. Do what you do best, Catherine, stay calm and remain optimistic.

"Listen, Amy, you need to keep your cool right now. Everything will be okay. Just do exactly what I tell you and nobody will go to jail."

"Okay." Her sobbing stops.

Good job, Catherine, stay strong and guide her confidently through this. You've done it before.

"Can you start by sending me a copy of the letter you received from the regulators?"

"Sure."

"After that you should write a letter to your clients saying that you're looking into this matter. Then you need to lock down any relevant background information, including emails and phone records. After that, you should decide whether to suspend the trader, but I strongly recommend that you do. Please remember to document all your actions. I also think that you should take a collaborative approach with the regulator, so I would contact the investigator and tell him or her that this is your intention; cooperation will surely have a salutary effect."

"We'll get on it right away."

"Good. Let's talk again later today."

"Thanks, Catherine, I knew you were the right person to call."

As soon as I hang up with Amy, Bonnie's voice erupts through the speakerphone.

"Did Amy call you?"

"Yes, she just did."

"What did you tell her?"

"That she should collaborate with the regulators and that she needs to begin prepping to do that right away."

"Not that, about her going to jail. I hope you told her that it's not even a possibility."

"I can't say that; there's always a remote possibility," I answer, perturbed that she would suggest I lie to a client.

"What the fuck are you talking about? The client needs *reassurance* right now," she shouts into the phone. "I think they should fight this. Jesus, I shouldn't have sent her to you. What kind of a lawyer are you?"

"I'm an honest lawyer. I don't like lying or giving people false hopes."

"It is *not* lying to a client to say that she's not going to jail when that's what the case law says, got it?" Her voice has trailed up to high-pitched soprano vocals. "That's what you are paid to do, Catherine, to advise clients on the law, not to raise unlikely scenarios and act like the grim reaper."

Oh zut! Maybe she's right. The case law does make it really unlikely. So far in my career, I've operated under the principle that, when asked by a client, it's best to be honest and give the best- and worst-case scenarios. But I'm now questioning whether that is a realistic way to practise law—especially here in New York.

"Perhaps Amy would be better served by the litigation group?"

"Out of the question. We're handling it, Amy's *my* client."

I'm right in the middle of another battle of the warlords. *Fantastique.*

"And you better change that negative attitude or you'll be drafting dry cleaning memos ten years from now." She abruptly hangs up the phone.

"I'd much prefer to be pressing shirts at Madame Paulette's than having to deal with you," I mutter into the phone.

"We're going to the Waverley Inn for drinks, want to come?" I had actually cringed when my phone rang right after my run-in with Bonnie, but I'm thrilled to hear Lisa's voice.

"Who is 'we'?"

I know she's referring to the obnoxious trio but ask her anyway and then accept the invitation. *I need a drink.*

"Sounds great. I'll meet you guys there."

"Perfect, we'll see you at eight. Don't be late, we don't want to lose our table, it's really hard to get a rezy."

I arrive at seven forty-five and the bar is completely packed. The tiny room, which has dim lighting and low ceilings, is filled with fashion types, writers sporting the ubiquitous tweed jacket, and professionals in suits alongside the usual party crowd. I take a deep breath and can actually feel my shoulders start to relax back to their normal position.

Amanda waves from the far end of the bar and gives me one of her best Julia Roberts smiles.

"Catherine, how aaare you? You want a glass of Veuve?" Oops, there go my shoulders back up.

"No thanks."

In no mood to engage in mindless chatter, I make my way around her to sit next to Lisa, who recognizes my *I need to talk* expression and orders me a glass of red wine.

"What's up? You look awful."

"Bonnie."

"Again? What happened now?"

"She told me I was a bad lawyer."

"What? Why?"

"Because I told a client the truth. She thinks that's giving bad advice."

"What do you mean? What happened?"

"It's a long story, but a client asked me if it was a possibility that she could be fined or go to jail and, even though it's extremely unlikely, I told her that yes, it was a remote possibility. Bonnie got really pissed with me."

As I recount the heated conversation, I feel even more dejected. I've been putting in long hours to earn partners' respect and what do I get in return? Being told that I don't know how to practise, in operalike fashion.

"I don't understand why everyone just puts up with her abusive behaviour."

"Don't worry about it, she's a bitch. Why don't you join us for a long weekend in Ireland to forget about it?" Lisa asks while handing me a glass of Beaujolais.

Ireland? With these three divas? I'd rather spend the weekend at a camp for troubled teenagers.

"We're staying at Philip Treacy's G hotel, it's totally fab!" Beverley gushes.

"But not as great as the newly revamped Hotel du Petit

Moulin, the Christian Lacroix hotel in Paris; a real jewel!"
Amanda interjects.

As I sit half-listening to another shallow conversation, my BlackBerry buzzes with an incoming email. Worried about finding a nasty message from Bonnie, my first reaction is to turn it off and get so sloshed that I completely embarrass the three hedonistas. But my professional self gets the better of me and I take a look.

From: Amy Lee
To: Catherine Lambert
CC: Bonnie Clark; Scott Robertson
Re: Thank You
Dear Catherine,
I just wanted to give you an update on our conversation.
I followed your advice and contacted the regulators to demonstrate a willingness to cooperate. They were quite receptive to our approach and have confirmed they will keep this in mind should there be any penalties imposed on the firm. Also, I think it's safe to say that I won't be going to jail for this—although I don't think the same can be said for our trader.

Thank you very much for being forthright with me today and not just telling me what I wanted to hear. I appreciate your honesty. You are a great lawyer, Catherine, and I'm delighted that you'll be working with us on this matter.

I'll call you tomorrow to discuss this further.
Kind Regards,
Amy

I'm on top of the world. The fact that she copied Bonnie and Scott on her note makes me want to burst with happiness. Just as I'm about to start screaming with joy, I receive a text message from Jeffrey that makes my heart flutter and puts me over the moon.

I miss u. Can't wait 2 c u. R u free 4 lunch 2moro?

"Ladies, the next round is on me."

Chapter 24

"You need a break from all that hard work," Jeffrey says, sitting across from me at Café des Artistes.

I look around the room to admire the art-covered walls. I feel like I'm in a Woody Allen movie.

"I know I do, but I'm stuck working on this annoying IPO with a super-demanding client," I tease.

"Okay, okay, it's all my fault."

He stares at me hesitatingly before he continues.

"If I'm the one keeping you in the office, then I should be the one getting you out of it." He gives me a mischievous look.

I feel my palms getting sweaty, as I suspect he's about to propose something that I might not be ready for.

"I've got something to ask you," he says, staring into his glass of Chardonnay.

"Sure."

"I hope it isn't too soon to ask, but how about spending the weekend in Bridgehampton? One of my friends owns a house out there and he's invited me out for the weekend."

The weekend? *Ooh la la* . . . Am I ready for this? Although my strong physical attraction to Jeffrey is coaxing me to accept on the spot, the professional side of me is riddled with worry. Spending the weekend means that we will inevitably sleep together and this might put me in a hot seat professionally. If I accept, there'll be no going back.

He reads the expression on my face. "You don't have to answer right away."

"It's not that I don't want to. I'm just a bit concerned about how this might affect my reputation at the firm. I know this seems like just another job to you, but I've been sweating it out at this firm for more than six years. I want to make partner."

"I understand." His hand softly brushes my cheek. "There's no doubt in my mind that you'll make it." Resolve melting . . . pull it together, Lambert!

"Let me think about it."

"Okay, you have until dessert." He reaches for my hand. "I'm sure you would really enjoy meeting my friends. They can't wait to meet you."

"I'm sure I would—it's just that I have a lot going on at the office." I throw a bit of work in there in case I decide against it.

"I'm the client, remember? Doesn't the client always come first?"

"Yes, but you're not my only client. That's the problem."

"Don't you know that all problems are opportunities in disguise?" He winks and signals for the waiter to bring the cheque.

During the days that follow our lunch, Jeffrey sends me emails such as *"S'il vous plaît, Catherine! Dites oui!"* Like a good lawyer, I sit in my office listing the pros and cons of going away with him for the weekend:

Pros

— Salty Atlantic Ocean air is far more appealing than the office building's ventilation system;

— Fresh lobster beats cold boardroom food;

—Bathing in salt water helps to reduce appearance of cellulite;

— Sharing common interests with Jeffrey will surely make the weekend memorable (My Nina Simone greatest hits CD is already in my bag!);

— Will spend the night with one very attractive male . . . *(Ouf, Catherine, try to beat that one!)*

Cons

— BlackBerry reception may be spotty on the beach;

— Difficulty to maintain confidentiality of getaway;

— Open to office gossip if spotted out there by a colleague;

— Might fall behind (slightly) in the Dior file and other matters.

Somehow by magic, in my opinion, the pros outweigh the cons, so I cave in and accept his invitation. Now I need help with the important stuff. I call Rikash into my office.

"Jeffrey invited me to go the Hamptons for the weekend."

"Lucky you. At least one of us will be getting some."

"Stop it! I'm already anxious enough as it is."

"Don't worry. I'm sure he'll find a way to take away that anxiety."

"Enough already! I didn't call you in here to torture me, I need some wardrobe guidance."

"No you don't. You have more style than anybody I know."

"Flattery will get you everywhere. I'd really like some insider expertise."

"In that case, you've come to the right place."

"Perfect—I want this to go well—I'm really looking forward to a quiet weekend away from this place."

He gives me a puzzled look.

"Quiet? You really *do* need some help."

"Why?"

He raises his perfect eyebrows. "The Hamptons has a scene that makes Saint-Tropez look like a sleepy town. You know that, right?"

I had read about it in a few travel magazines but had no idea as to what awaited me there.

"Okay, so what do I need to bring?"

"Anything that shows some skin."

"But I'm as pale as Marie Antoinette right now—bare skin won't be pretty."

"Dah-ling, don't worry about the tan, you can buy that in a bottle. But you definitely need some revealing outfits." He pauses for a moment. "And some strength training."

"Excuse me?"

"You should firm up if you're going to get naked. Black-Berrying isn't exactly the most body-enhancing workout."

"I only have three days left before I leave."

"With enough resistance training, you can change your body in forty-eight hours. Trust me, I do it all the time. You need to see Angel, my personal trainer. He'll work wonders. Let me call him now to see whether he can take you right away for an emergency consultation."

He struts out of my office with the satisfied look he gets from enlightening me about fashion, beauty, or the city. What would I do without him?

He buzzes me on the intercom.

"Okay, you're in for five sharp. He'll be waiting for you at the Reebok Sports Club."

"Rikash, I don't have any workout clothes with me and I'm swamped. I have a ream of papers to sort through for the Met Bank file. What if Bonnie calls looking for me?"

"Honey, Bonnie is out getting botoxed and shopping for her Crème de la Mer, so don't worry about a thing, I've got it all covered."

Being the jock that I am, I show up at the Reebok Sports Club on the Upper West in four-inch heels, a body-skimming dress, and pearls. I feel as though I've just flown in from outer space: the combination of sweat, grunting, muscle flexing, and pheromones flying around makes me dizzy. I take a seat as two men with enormous bulging chest muscles walk by me in the tightest Spandex I've ever seen. One of them stares at me lasciviously.

"New member?"

"Um, yes kind of."

"See ya around then." He winks.

What on earth am I doing here? I desperately want to run back to the office and hide under my desk. Maybe I should skip the workout and go for an espresso and a croque monsieur at the club café instead? As I pull out my BlackBerry to check my e-mail, a tall blond man wearing skin-tight black yoga pants and a black V-neck sweater enters the reception area.

"Catherine?"

"Angel?"

"Lovely to meet you, sweetie." He kisses me twice. "Any friend of Rikash's is a friend of mine."

"Did he tell you, I don't have any workout clothes?"

"No problem, sweetness, I have some for you in the women's locker room. Here's the key. Meet you back here in five."

I quickly change into head-to-toe Lycra and futuristic sneakers and rush back to the waiting area.

He checks my body out for several minutes. I feel like a prize heifer at the country fair.

"Okay, I've identified the problem areas."

Problem areas? Ouch, somehow, I already feel the pain he's about to inflict on my body. The sauna is looking pretty good to me right now.

With a look of pity, Angel struts toward me and grabs my arm, nearly asphyxiating me with his Acqua Di Gio cologne.

"Let's go, honey, there's no time to waste. You need a serious workout."

We enter a fishbowl of a room with equipment that could be in a James Bond movie. Catherine Deneuve once said that as a woman gets older, she needs to choose between maintaining her face and her fanny. By the looks of what awaits me, I'd rather save my face; facials are a lot less scary.

"Let's start with some Pilates."

He points to a contraption that looks like something out of a Chinese torture chamber.

"This is a Reformer. It will strengthen your core muscles and focus on the whole body rather than individual body parts."

I nod apprehensively. Looking at this machine, I expect to be leaving the gym in several parts. I climb on and Angel makes me do resistance exercises until my face turns blue. After fifteen minutes, I try to escape by bringing up work.

"Angel, I need to go to the locker room to check my email. I'm working on an important transaction at the moment and—"

He shakes his head, not buying it.

"Not on my time you don't. Come on, girl, give me twenty more! We need to burn those French food–induced calories."

He starts his stopwatch and crosses his arms like a drill sergeant. As soon as I finish torturing myself, he approaches.

"Before I forget, could I call you about a personal legal matter? My insurance company is giving me a hard time."

I'm not even remotely surprised by his request; lawyers are always being asked for free advice. Given that I'm upside down and totally at his mercy, I acquiesce.

Once we get out of the torture chamber, he makes me jump rope for twenty minutes. I try to alert him to the fact that I can feel a heart attack coming on, but there isn't enough air in my lungs to do so.

"Okay, now the medicine ball exercises."

He fetches an enormous red ball and makes me do a squatlike walk while holding the ball over my head.

"That's great for your tushy, so keep doing this for at least fifteen minutes."

I walk around the room looking like a retarded penguin and feel totally ridiculous. To make matters worse, Mr. Muscles is checking me out through the glass window while sweat is pouring down my face and I can't stop worrying about all the work that is awaiting me back at the office. After an hour and a half of sweating and inflicting pain on my body, I throw in the towel.

"Angel, it's been a real pleasure, but I need to run. Thank you so much for everything. I feel revitalized."

"Good luck with the Hamptons." He pats me on the back. "Rikash told me about your weekend."

"Thanks."

"I'll call you next week about my insurance question."

"No problem."

"See you again soon!"

That's as likely to happen as me drinking red wine from a cardboard box.

Back at the office, Rikash stares at me as I wobble past his cubicle with a traumatized look on my face.

"I don't want to talk about it."

He sees from my pained expression that I'm dead serious. He turns back to his computer and continues typing.

My entire body feels like Jell-O; I have trouble sitting down and can barely lift my arms to keyboard level, so I try to think about my upcoming weekend with Jeffrey to make myself feel better. I get back to finalizing the memo on U.S. copyright laws for Dior, despite the pain emanating from my inner thighs.

Chapter 25

"Let's go shopping at lunch. We need to get you something that'll show some cleavage."

"Rikash, in case you haven't noticed, I don't have any cleavage. And when exactly am I supposed to have time to go shopping? Look at my desk."

"Put your phone on call forward. I've been going out to the Hamptons film festival for years. Trust me, sweetheart, you need something really sexy."

Rikash is making the scene out there sound like a Victoria's Secret model convention and this is making me more nervous by the minute.

"How about at one o'clock?"

At one sharp, Rikash stands in my doorway making melodramatic gestures as I walk Amy through an SEC demand letter on the phone. I nod and give him the five minutes signal.

At two o'clock, while I'm still on the call, he again points to his watch and I nod but can't move.

At three o'clock, he walks by and waves but I'm forced to ignore him—Scott and I are reviewing the draft Browser prospectus.

At four o'clock, Rikash once again attempts to lure me away by faking an emergency call while Nathan sits in one of my chairs. His attempt wields no reaction from Nathan, who prolongs his stay by asking more questions about the Browser IPO, when I plan to leave the corner office, and the status of my billable hours.

Five o'clock rolls around and I haven't yet made it out of my chair. Rikash drops by on his way out.

"What happened to our shopping date? I'm going home now."

"I know, I know, sorry. I had to put out a few fires. I'll probably be here 'til midnight. Can we do it tomorrow?" I follow him as he makes his way toward the elevators.

"Sure, but you can't put this off any longer. You're leaving tomorrow," he says, shaking his head, visibly concerned about my cleavage-minimal wardrobe. "You need to channel your inner Brigitte Bardot this weekend. It's time to bring sexy back."

Friday morning turns out to be even more chaotic than I'd expected. I'm bombarded by the bankers and lawyers working on the Browser IPO and am under a tight deadline to send the memo on U.S. copyright laws to Pierre Le Furet at Dior. At eleven thirty, I look up from a conference call to see that Rikash has planted himself right beside me with my bag in his hands.

"We're going *now*. I'm not leaving your office until you follow me," he whispers loudly. "I'm doing this for your own good. Come on."

I gesture for him to hold on. As soon as the call ends, I send the memo off to Dior's Paris headquarters and we rush out the door and make our way to Barneys for a sprint shopping session. He's practically beaming as we push through the revolving door, while I'm trying to ignore the sharp pains coming from every muscle in my body.

"This will be good for my spirits. I can't stand the negative atmosphere around the office these days."

"You think office morale is lower than normal?"

"Low? Muffin, it's downright in the dumps. All the political bull and the increase in billable hours seem to be taking its toll on everyone's mood."

"You're probably right."

"I heard that even the partner in charge of the Intellectual Property department might be leaving. And he's been with the firm longer than some of the antiques in the reception area."

"Really? How did you find out?"

"Everybody's been talking about it. If he leaves, I bet he takes some important clients with him. I hope it won't affect our jobs."

"I doubt it. Have you seen the workload on our desks?"

"Of course, I'm the one who manages your in-tray, remember? I guess we just need to do what we can to keep up appearances and lay low until the storm blows over."

"Is that why you're wearing a tie on a Friday?"

"I'm doing what I can to play the game. Besides, you know I can't stand casual Fridays. Have you seen how most people dress? It's bloody awful." He waves his hand in the air disdainfully. "I think I'm going to propose casual-sex Fridays instead at our next staff meeting. It would do wonders for the office morale."

"Great idea. I'm sure Bonnie will buy into it."

We make our way to Barneys Co-Op floor where they keep some of the trendiest collections; not my normal first stop. The first thing Rikash picks out is a bright fuchsia see-through top with tiny sequined butterflies that are positioned to strategically cover your nipples.

"This is hot."

"Are you kidding? I can't wear something like that, too see-through."

"Come on, you'll look great." He stops to pick out a pair of skin-tight white jeans with sequined pockets. "These are amazing together!" he exclaims.

Despite my better judgment, I head to the changing rooms with an outfit straight out of *Boogie Nights*, complaining the whole way.

"I can't believe you're making me try this on. It's so not me, you know that. I could never leave the house wearing this." I come out of my dressing room clutching my chest to take a closer look at my outrageous accoutrement in the mirrors and try to stand tall in front of the mirrors despite the pain in my legs caused by too many squats.

"Doesn't she look fabulous?" he asks two women standing next to the change rooms' entrance.

"Gorgeous," one woman sighs wistfully. "I wish I could still wear stuff like that. My best friend had a top like that back in the days of Studio 54."

Okay, now that gives me even less comfort. My assistant is about to send me off to a romantic weekend dressed in head-to-toe disco.

"I'll take the white jeans," I say, caving in to one of his choices to avoid a tantrum, "but let me find another top that isn't so transparent. Save the nipple scandal for Indian Fashion Week."

"You're so prissy! Why don't you get yourself a muu-muu to wear at the beach? That would be a real turn-on." Frustrated, he takes the pasties disguised as a shirt back to the racks.

"Now this is more like me." I pick out a backless pink silk chiffon halter top sprinkled with dainty white flowers.

"You need matching shoes."

"I need a new pair of shoes like Paris needs more traffic. I already have sandals that I picked up on the Côte d'Azur that will look amazing."

"Oooh, perfect!" he gushes.

"I still can't believe I'm going away with Jeffrey. I need to pinch myself!"

"I'll take care of that for you." He squeezes my right arm. "Oh, I feel some muscle there. Angel really made you work."

"Work? He nearly killed me!"

He frowns as we head toward the elevators.

"Wait! What about a bathing suit?" he asks. "Do you have anything indecent?"

"I bought a new bikini last year."

He stares at me with a baffled look.

"You need to get a super sexy one to make a big impression on the beach. Come on, hurry up." He walks so quickly that I have a hard time keeping up. Looking around, it's obvious that New York glamour girls with lots to spend and little to hide come here for of-the-moment bikinis. Rikash rattles off all the trendiest bathing suit designers and hands me five suits, each fit for a Brazilian bathing diva.

To his mild chagrin, I pick out a classic black two-piece that covers my so-called problem areas and head for the change rooms. I catch a glimpse of my naked body in the mirror and this reminds me that Jeffrey's about to see me *au naturel*. Feeling insecure about my lack of *bronzage* and still slightly conflicted about my decision to spend the weekend with a client, I rush out of the change rooms.

Rikash approaches the counter as I pull out my wallet. "You're not going to like what I'm about to say, buttercup, but have you done a bit of background research on Jeffrey?"

"What do you mean?"

"Into his past. I just want to make sure he isn't another one of those players you find in the Hamptons. There's more out there by the square foot than privet hedges."

Catching me off guard, my back goes up. Why would Rikash say something like that a few hours before I leave?

"Rikash, this is no time to plant any doubts in my mind, I'm already nervous enough about the weekend as it is. Do you know something I don't?"

"I just don't want to see you get hurt."

My shoulders relax. "Thanks for looking out for me." I pat him on the back. "It's time to go back to the office before Roxanne catches me shopping again."

"No kidding. Miss Killjoy would love to catch you with those bags, wouldn't she?"

"Mmm-hmm. Let's not have her ruin our fabulous day, shall we." I change the subject. "I hope you aren't too disappointed with my bikini selection?"

"Diana Vreeland once said that you should never fear being vulgar, just boring." He squeezes my shoulder tenderly.

"Are you calling me boring?"

"Of course not, dah-ling. I wouldn't be caught dead in public with you if you were."

Chapter 26

Those who think that getting away to the Hamptons for the weekend is a relaxing experience must be totally off their *bergère*. Traffic on Highway 27 crawls at a snail's pace and keeps you wondering whether you will ever get anywhere. I stare out the window—we're surrounded by bumper-to-bumper large luxury SUVs and convertibles. Luckily, the time flies as Jeffrey holds my hand during the drive up, shares stories about his years spent in California, and teases me about the French.

"The traffic is worse than in Paris. But at least we don't have to deal with the Parisians!"

"Ha! If your cars weren't so huge and didn't take up half the highway, we would've arrived hours ago."

"I feel like driving over some of these bozos! Maybe we'll get our own plane after the IPO."

"Not too fast, *monsieur*, we're not there yet." This reminds me that I should check my BlackBerry; I pull it out of my handbag and quickly peruse the fifty or so messages already filling up my inbox. There's one from Pierre at Dior congratulating me for the memo I drafted on copyright laws: this puts a huge smile on my face. The next one is from Bonnie, who is strongly recommending that I stop "wasting my time" on frivolous intellectual property matters for French clients: this one's a real downer.

I'm about to turn my BlackBerry off to prevent a major mood swing when Jeffrey interjects. "I know I said no shoptalk, but since you're checking your messages, how's our prospectus coming along?"

"I spoke to the regulators yesterday and the approval process is moving forward nicely."

"Thanks for putting in the extra hours, I really appreciate it. Keep up the good work and we'll be celebrating big-time when it's over."

During the rest of the drive, he plays with my hair and

kisses my hand, and I quickly forget about the office. This is pure bliss.

We arrive in Bridgehampton around ten o'clock and pull into a long, narrow driveway. The house is a large shingled Cape Cod–style home with a five-car garage and has a parking area filled with Porsches and other expensive convertibles I can't even name. I can hear a loud thump of dance music coming from the backyard.

"Hey, Jeff, welcome."

A tall, hefty man greets us in his dripping swim trunks. He gives Jeffrey a high-five. "Hello, Catherine. I'm Charlie. Please make yourselves comfortable. I have some champagne on ice and a warm hot tub waiting for you guys in the backyard. You can take the larger room upstairs. All the others are taken."

We make our way upstairs to drop off our bags. This isn't a room—we have a whole wing to ourselves. I am awestruck by the sheer opulence and size of everything. Forget inviting fifty of your closest friends, you could host a ball in here.

As soon as we put down our bags, Jeffrey kisses me on the forehead and pulls out his swim trunks enthusiastically.

"Come on, gorgeous, hop into your bathing suit, let's hit the hot tub."

I reach into my bag for my new bikini and find a copy of the *Kama Sutra* hidden at the bottom. As I open the cover, a note from Rikash spills out:

> *Here's to adding a little Indian spice to your weekend.*
> *Put it to good use. Just remember that the Sanskrit*
> *word for the male organ, the lingam, means* "Wand of
> Light." *Need I say more?*
>
> *Big hug.*
> *Rikash*

Still giggling, I come out of the washroom a few minutes later wearing my new bathing suit. Looking at Jeffrey's face, I'm glad (for the thousandth time) that I listened to Rikash. We walk hand in hand to the backyard where a group of people are frolicking in the pool and in the hot tub.

"Come have some champagne," a man with a tan that would make George Hamilton jealous calls out from the hot tub. "Charlie bought some Dom Perignon."

"You've gotta get in here, the water's delicious," a blonde

woman with very large breasts and not much to cover them shouts. "I'm Rebecca, nice to meet you."

"Catherine, lovely to meet you."

"Catherine, how did you meet our Jeffrey?"

"Um, we met through a colleague of mine—I'm a lawyer," I answer, wiggling my way out of telling her he's a client.

"Isn't that sweet."

"So, Rebecca, what do you do?" I ask.

"I'm in the beauty business. I run a spa downtown."

"Are you guys coming with us to the polo match tomorrow afternoon? We're going there after the beach," George Hamilton asks, smoking a cigarillo.

"That sounds great. Doesn't it, Catherine?"

I nod.

"We'd love to," Jeffrey answers enthusiastically.

After thirty minutes of soaking in bubbles—and drinking them—I begin to relax, although my skin is now shrivelled up like a prune. We make our way upstairs and before we enter the room, Jeffrey grabs my arm and kisses me.

"I'm so happy you could come. You're making my weekend very memorable. Why don't you open the door?"

I look at him hesitatingly.

I turn the handle and the scent of fresh flowers hits me

immediately. As the door swings open, I see bouquets of white calla lilies and peonies are scattered on the dresser and bedside tables. My heart stops and I feel weak in the knees.

Jeffrey turns me around and starts kissing me tenderly on the nape of my neck. His delicate kisses make their way to my shoulders and back, and his hands slowly make their way down to my hips. He lifts me into the air and carries me across the room, where we both fall on the edge of the bed. The salty sea air breezes through the room and I lose all self-restraint. We kiss passionately for what seems like an hour before he caresses my thighs and whispers, "I want you so badly." A mental warning sign pops up in my mind that I've just crossed the line with a firm client, but it disappears as quickly as the strings of my bikini.

They say you know you're in love when you can't fall asleep because reality is finally better than your dreams. It must be true, since I haven't slept a wink. Exhausted and exhilarated, I can barely believe my luck as I gaze out to the oceanview.

A smiling face and full mane of delicious bedhead turns to face me the next morning. *Quel bonheur!*

"I picked up a little something for you." He hands me a tiny box with the inscription *Chaumet, Paris*.

"Jeffrey, what did you do?"

"Come on, open it!" he exclaims, kissing my forehead.

I pop open the small box and suddenly feel a little dizzy. It's a dainty white-gold heart-shaped pendant.

"It's gorgeous, but this is way too much." Despite my protest, he takes it from my hands, places it around my neck, and attaches the clasp.

"Just like you."

I reach for his tanned forearm and pull him back toward the bed. He falls over me and I slide one hand up his back while the other pulls his white T-shirt over his head. He lifts me from under his warm body and positions me kneeling over his dark chest. As I look into his eyes before we have another passionate round, lightning hits my veins.

Later, I lie on my stomach as he kisses me tenderly and plays with my hair. "Let's grab breakfast in town, check out the shops, and then go to the beach for a while before heading to the polo match. Sound good?"

Now that's one full schedule for a Saturday. It rivals my

typical day at the office. And I thought people came out here to relax. Yet somehow I mean it when I say:

"It sounds perfect."

After a quick shower, I go downstairs and walk into a scene that feels like a cross between *The Great Gatsby* and *Animal House*. Tanned women are romping around in their bikinis, sipping margaritas, while men dressed in tennis whites are heading off for a game. I sneak in a quick peek at my BlackBerry to ensure there are no fires to put out before breakfast: nothing looks urgent. There's an email from Lisa asking whether I want to meet her and Charles later at the Surf Lodge in Montauk for drinks. I reply that unfortunately my schedule is booked more solidly than if I was working on a takeover bid.

"We're going to town for breakfast," Rebecca announces, pulling up her backless (and almost frontless) halter top.

Yes, I can see that you're definitely going to town.

"Okay, see you there."

"I'm starving. Let's hit the road," Jeffrey announces.

En route to Southampton, I sit in his convertible with the summer breeze flowing through my hair. I breathe in the fresh air and revel in the luxurious feel of this seaside retreat. With my silk scarf delicately tied around my neck, I feel like one of those happy models in the J. Crew catalogues.

"What are you thinking about, sweetheart?"

"Hmm?"

"You look deep in thought."

"I'm just enjoying the scenery. I haven't been out of the office in a while. And it's all your fault." I poke him playfully.

"Yes, it is." He kisses my hand.

His cell phone rings and his face turns serious as he looks at his call display.

"Yes?" he answers abruptly. "What do you mean the numbers don't add up?" he yells into his Bluetooth. "I told you the number of shares outstanding. Can't you count properly?" He screeches the car to a halt at a fruit stand, slams the door, and starts a one-sided screaming match on the side of the road while annoyed shoppers shake their heads.

Surprised to see this new side of him, I can't help but stare. Is this what he's *really* like? This is a side of him I haven't seen. So far, he's seemed so collected and in control. After pacing for more than fifteen minutes, he comes back to the car. His face is flushed and he looks perturbed.

"I can't believe these goddamn bankers, they're so incompetent. We're paying them a fortune in fees. I have to do everything for this fucking deal!"

"Is there anything I can do?"

"No, it's an accounting issue."

"Okay, let me know if there is."

"I'm afraid we need to head back to New York first thing tomorrow morning. I'm sorry, Catherine."

"Don't worry about it. I'm also involved in this transaction, remember?"

He stares out his side window for a moment and sighs before responding.

"Listen, I'm really sorry I lost my temper like that. I'm feeling a bit fried these days."

"I understand. You're under a lot of stress. But don't feel like you need to carry the entire load by yourself."

He looks at me tenderly. "Thanks, you're the best."

We park in front of Sant Ambroeus on Southampton's main street.

"They serve the best espresso in town, just for you, *madame*."

"Perfect!"

While we wait to be seated, Jeffrey chats up the maître d' in broken Italian and I recognize a familiar voice behind me. I turn and find myself face to face with Leanne, one of Lisa's three musketeers.

"Hi, Catherine, looks like you finally made it out here."

"Yes, I guess so. Leanne, this is Jeffrey."

She stares at our interlaced fingers and I recognize the same look of envy that she had when our waiter offered me chocolates at Daniel. She clearly wishes she were in my shoes, and, standing tall in my Tropeziennes sandals, I can't say that I blame her.

"Nice to meet you." She looks at Jeffrey, intrigued. "I think I've seen you here before."

"Hi, Leanne, nice to meet you. Aren't I a lucky man?"

The maître d' gestures for us to follow him to the back of the room. I wave goodbye to Leanne as we take our seats, *tête-à-tête*. He plays with my fingers while gazing into my eyes and right at this moment I'm feeling quite good about my decision to accept his invitation.

After a delicious brunch and a bit of browsing in the shops, we head back to Charlie's house to change for the polo match. Since my whirlwind shopping excursion with Rikash hasn't equipped me with anything specifically horse country-ish, I put on my new outfit and top it off with a white cloche hat that I picked up at a vintage shop in Saint Germain.

We arrive at the polo grounds and it's a sea of champagne, caviar, and oyster stands all set up under a large white tent. A glitzy fashion show is underway, with models competing with the horses for the attention of the attendees. The tent is full of the *jeunesse dorée* of Manhattan.

We take a stroll on the grounds and I notice that Amanda, one of the mistresses of the universe, is standing in one corner of the tent, so I walk over to say hello. Jeffrey follows.

"Jeffrey! So nice to see you again," she exclaims, ignoring me.

"Hi, Amanda, have you met Catherine?"

"We have. Hi, Catherine. Nice hat, it's so . . . *different.*"

"The two of you know each other?" Jeffrey asks dumbfounded. "What a small world this is. Amanda participated in one of our early rounds of financing."

"Is that right?" I reply unenthusiastically. I provided her with a recent round myself; I paid for her dinner at Daniel. "That's great."

"Are you two here together?"

"Yes we are." He answers proudly and gives me a peck on the cheek.

"Really?" She looks shocked. "I heard you guys are going

public. Congratulations," she says, giving him sweet eyes.

"Yes, we're almost there. Catherine is working hard to keep the IPO on schedule."

Okay, it's now out in the open that I'm seeing a client. Come on, Catherine, you need to get over it!

"Good for you," she adds condescendingly.

"We're both a bit tired and looking forward to finishing off this deal."

"God, I know what you mean." She puts her hand on his shoulder. "I'm working so hard right now, you have no idea. Before I forget, I ran into Tina last week at the gym. She looks really great."

"Who's Tina?" I ask.

"Oh," says Amanda with not a small amount of glee in her voice. "Jeffrey's ex-wife."

An ex-wife? I suddenly feel a sharp pain in the pit of my stomach, but I try to maintain my composure. How could he not tell me he had been married? What else is he hiding from me?

Jeffrey stares at me with a look of panic and sees from my reaction that I'm not thrilled with the discovery. He pulls me away after we say goodbye and as soon as we set foot in his car, I let her rip.

"Why didn't you tell me you were married?"

"Catherine, I'm sorry. I wanted to wait before I told you. I was worried you wouldn't want to be with me."

"That is pretty important information. I can't help but wonder if there's anything else you're keeping from me."

"There isn't, I promise. We got divorced two years ago. We're just friends now."

"I'm not sure about this, Jeffrey." I turn my face away and look out to the polo grounds. "Maybe I should stay at a hotel tonight."

He takes my hand. "Come on, Catherine. Please don't be like that. I'm sorry I kept this from you."

I stay silent for a few seconds before turning toward him and looking deep into his eyes to find out if he really means it.

"I don't want you to stay in a hotel, babe. I want you to stay with me."

After he pleads one more time and kisses me tenderly on the cheek, I give in.

"Okay, but no more surprises."

"I promise."

In his convertible, we leisurely drive through Water Mill and Sagaponack. As we pass by a quaint general store and lovely clapboard houses, it feels like being in a Ralph Lauren ad. The lawns are so green and manicured; I want to tell him to stop the car so I can roll around on them.

He taps me on the head and whispers, "I love your hat; it's so you."

We drive around in these breathtaking hamlets, but I can't shake that uneasy feeling about him hiding his ex-wife from me. Why wouldn't he say anything about it? Could they still be seeing each other? I try to get rid of any negative thoughts as he pulls the car over near the dunes on Gibson Beach. I'm amazed that there's hardly anyone to be seen on this gorgeous stretch of white sand.

"Wow, this is a great beach. Where is everybody?"

"I don't know and I don't care." He peels off his T-shirt and linen pants. "Just another hard day at the office!" He runs into the ocean in his boxer shorts. "Come on, get in here, now!"

I roll up my white jeans and meet him in the surf. He picks me up in his arms to carry me over some waves and pretends to throw me into the ocean. We splash around and I feel like Helena Christensen frolicking about in Chris Isaak's "Wicked Game" video (minus the glamazon physique and deep tan, but hey, this is no time to burst my bubble).

After we dry off, he runs to the car and returns with a picnic basket filled with lobster salad, cheese, and white wine.

"When did you find the time to get this?"

"Keep all the questions for the legal stuff, babe. Just enjoy." He playfully taps his finger on my nose and digs into the salad.

I tense up again after he says this and I wish that he'd stop referring to work. I take a sip of my wine and listen to the sound of the surf; we watch the sun set below the crashing waves and I quickly forget any misgivings I had about his ex-wife and dating a firm client when he kisses my cheek.

When we get back to Charlie's house, there's a major party going on in the backyard: hip hop is blaring from the speakers, men in muscle shirts are dancing on the tennis court, a group of people are standing on the back steps pouring vodka shots down their throats, and couples are sprawled out on the white couches.

A sudden cheer comes from the pool area. Rebecca has taken off her top and is about to jump into the water. A group of men are clapping and egging her on.

"Come on, baby, you can do it!"

She throws herself into the water and a man follows her in, fully clothed. Afterward, a fight breaks out on the lawn between two men.

"I asked her to dance first."

"No, I did."

"She's mine. I slept with her last night."

"So did I, you son of a bitch."

After one of them trips the other, they begin a slow rolling descent toward the swimming pool in their navy blazers and blue-and-white seersucker pants. Where am I?

"Can you believe those two guys are bankers who graduated from Ivy League schools?" Jeffrey asks.

"And they probably majored in accounting in college."

"Not all accounting majors are like that, okay? Let's get out of here."

Jeffrey laughs, tickles me, and we kiss. We walk back to the house, where a man approaches me with a large camera.

"Cheese!"

I embrace Victoria Beckham's no-teeth policy and give him a smirk instead.

"I guess that means you'll be on the Internet."

"What?"

"That's Sal. He has a blog where he posts party pictures after every weekend."

Oh wonderful, that's all I need, to be exposed online at a wild party with Jeffrey. That will do wonders for the old career. I hope nobody at the office knows about the blog.

"Let's go."

"Alone at last," I say with a sigh as we head back to our room.

"A bit much, isn't it?"

"*Mon dieu*, it's a real jungle out here."

"You haven't seen half of it. It can get much worse. I'm so not into that crazy scene anymore. It's become old. *Real old*."

He turns out the lights and, as far as I'm concerned, right at this moment things can only get *real* good.

The next morning we get up at six thirty sharp to hit the road. We tiptoe out of the house, making as little noise as possible, drop our bags in the back seat of his car, and try to silently head out of the long driveway. As we do so, a convertible Maserati swooshes by us. Rebecca is sitting in the passenger seat and a man with a deep tan and salt-and-pepper hair has one hand on the steering wheel and one hand up her skirt. Proudly doing the "drive of shame," she is only now coming home.

"Bye, you guys, see you soon!" she screams at the top of her lungs, probably waking up everybody in Charlie's house and in the same breath letting everyone know she's just been shagged.

Feeling light-headed, I take in the last of the Hamptons scenery before we hit the highway. My BlackBerry buzzes as soon as we hit the on-ramp; I have several emails from Antoine that quickly bring me back to reality. I start by reading the last one:

Dear Catherine,
I needed your assistance on a conference call with Dior this morning, but I guess you were busy with the Browser deal and unavailable. I have asked someone here in Paris to take over this file going forward. It will be easier for you and the client. Laurence will contact you this week to transfer the file here. Thanks.
A.
P.S. Please remember the old maxim: Trust, but verify.

What? I can't believe this. Devastated that he would

take the Dior file away from me and still reeling from our heated conversation before he left, I want to delete his message and throw my BlackBerry on the side of the road. And *trust, but verify*? What is that supposed to mean? Isn't that what Ronald Reagan said about the Soviets during the Cold War? Is this another one of his metaphors for warlords and battles for territory?

"What's the matter, Catherine? You look preoccupied."

"I'm not preoccupied, I'm seriously pissed off."

I refrain from telling Jeffrey about the Dior file being taken away; he might think that I have less interest in working on his deal than on cracking down on fake bags, although I must admit that, professionally speaking, I do prefer working for the French luxury house. You can take a French woman out of Paris but you can't take Paris out of the French woman.

"Why?"

"More work. That's all."

He smiles tenderly. "So I'm not the only one who thinks highly of your legal skills."

"Hmm."

I quickly say *au revoir* to peace and tranquility and *bonjour* to a major headache.

Chapter 27

"How was the weekend?" Rikash asks as soon as I set foot in the office Monday morning.

"Sensational. The outfit we picked out together was a major hit. I received so many compliments."

"Really?" he asks, grinning proudly. "What about Jeffrey? Did he like it?" He's fishing for more information.

"He definitely did. And thanks for your little note of encouragement."

"Did it work?"

"It sure did." I give him a knowing smile.

"Fantastic! But I hope he's treating you like the princess you are."

"I'll fill you in later. I have a few fires to put out."

"Oh dear, reality has already reared its ugly head."

"You can say that again. I received an email from Antoine, Mr. Buzz Kill."

"Oh no! Did he make you cut the weekend short?"

"No, Jeffrey had to come back to the city for an emergency meeting."

"What did he want, then?"

"To tell me that he's transferring the Dior file to Paris. He thinks I have too much on my plate. I'm really upset about this, Rikash."

"I'm sorry, sweetie, but you are quite *busy* with Mr. Browser."

"I know, but it's my favourite file. The legal aspects are fascinating and I don't need to tell you how I feel about their products. And there goes my lifelong dream of attending the shows at Paris fashion week."

"Don't worry, sweetie pie, you don't need Dior for that. I can get you into the shows at Bryant Park in a flash."

"Thanks, Rikash, you always know how to make me feel better."

I arrive in my office with renewed enthusiasm. A tall pile of green books with the inscription *Barbri* towers over my desk. From where I stand I can decipher the word *Multistate* on the cover page of the top one.

"Is that what I think it is?" I ask, panic-stricken.

Barbri offers preparatory courses for those unfortunate souls braving one of life's true tortures: the New York bar exam. Given my membership to the Paris bar, I thought I could avoid being plagued with the New York course for at least another year, but it looks like my fate has clearly been decided.

"Looks like your summer is being cut short," Maria comments as she walks past.

Rikash stares at me with a look of pity. "I didn't put them there, dah-ling, I swear. Must be Roxanne."

A few minutes later, Bonnie drops by. "Catherine, can I speak to you?"

"Sure."

"Everyone who works in the New York office has to take the New York bar exam. You need to get it done *ASAP*. It's imperative for your career."

"When is it?" I ask in a panic.

"End of July."

"What?"

"I passed it years ago and only studied a week for it. You have more than enough time."

I want to tell her, *One day I'd like to be like you*, but think better of it; she might think I want to take her place and become even more difficult.

"I guess I have no choice in the matter."

"No."

Looking at the number of books in front of me, I estimate my chances at holding up my workload while maintaining a relationship with anything but my desk to be pretty much nil.

"Lisa, do you have time to meet me for a coffee?"

"Hi to you too! How did the weekend go?"

"Forget the weekend. I've got a major crisis."

"This sounds serious. I have a better idea. I'll meet you at Kirna Zabête in Soho at noon."

After answering all my emails and returning urgent calls, I jump in a cab and head downtown; I'm feeling dizzy at the thought of studying on top of such a heavy workload.

I try to temporarily put this out of my mind. Arriving at the store, I spot a large Plexiglas sign with big red letters hanging next to the entrance: *So many designers, so little time.* And that pretty much sums up my life.

I've read about this boutique in fashion magazines and have been dying to stop in. While I wait for Lisa I peruse the racks stocked with up-and-coming designers. I'm gravitating toward a divine Pierre Hardy turquoise clutch when she arrives.

"So what's the big crisis?" Lisa asks, her heels clicking as they hit the stairs. She gives me a warm hug.

"I'm in big trouble. They want me to take the bar exam this summer on top of keeping up my billable hours. How will I manage that?"

"Why didn't they tell you sooner?" she asks, fingering a silk Balmain blouse.

"I'm not sure. I guess they just woke up."

"Well, you *do* need to pass it to practise law in New York. You might as well get it over with now."

I imagine myself studying day and night in my tiny apartment in the sweltering heat, gasping for air while Jeffrey frolics on the beach with Amanda and Leanne.

"Jeffrey will forget about me," I whimper.

"Jeffrey's in the middle of a major transaction." She picks up a gorgeous electric blue silk dress. "He's stuck in his office just like you. Tell me about your weekend. I'm assuming it went well if you're worrying about him so much?"

"It was pretty amazing. I think I'm falling for him."

"That's great, you deserve someone special, Cat."

"I'm still a bit concerned about dating a client. I don't want this to affect my career."

"Why would it?"

"What if something goes wrong with our relationship? It's always a possibility, isn't it? It would put me in a precarious position at the firm."

"Stop being so pessimistic."

"It's not that simple. I still need to prove myself."

"Not for long. Come on, Cat, why do you think they transferred you here? To make you a partner. Why else?"

"I hope you're right."

"Case closed. I'm going to try this dress on." She walks to the change rooms.

"Wait, you didn't tell me about your weekend with Charles."

"It was fantastic. You guys need to check into the Surf Lodge for a weekend. It's the coolest place."

"So things are good between you two?"

"They're fantastic. He asked me to move in with him."

"And what did you say?"

"No, of course."

"What?"

"I told him that I need to think about it because I was considering moving to Europe."

"You said what?"

"I followed your advice and created some mystery."

I stand in front of the change rooms, speechless. It's the first time since I've known her that she's followed any of my advice.

"Wow, I'm shocked."

"And you know what? It worked. He's been texting me non-stop saying he doesn't want to lose me and is dying for me to move in. I have a feeling he'll commit."

She walks out looking like a dream. "Lisa, you look amazing!"

"I'm invited to a senior partner's wedding. This is perfect." She goes back to the change room and I to the subject of the bar exam.

"Bonnie thinks that studying for the New York bar exam is a piece of cake. I've heard so many horror stories:

apparently someone was taken out on a stretcher after hyperventilating in the Javits Center. And one of the summer associates even has a sign in his office that reads, 'When Sartre said that hell was other people, he obviously hadn't taken the NY bar exam.'"

"Enough whining. If I passed it, so can you," she scolds. "You were the one with better grades in law school, so stop worrying, okay?"

"Okay, okay. If you followed some of my advice, I have no choice but to follow yours. After all, you're the one on partnership track."

I pick up a bag of gummy bears from the boutique's candy display; if I'm not satisfying my craving for fashion, at least I'll be getting a sugar fix. It immediately lifts my spirits and helps me get past the whole exam drama. Like everyone else who has faced this daunting challenge, I need to hit the books.

C'est la vie.

A voicemail from Jeffrey is waiting for me when I get back.

"Hi, sweetheart, it's me, please call me back as soon as

possible." Assuming that the call is work-related, I return it right away.

"That was a great weekend, wasn't it?"

"Amazing. Thank you so much for everything."

"The pleasure was all mine, Mademoiselle Lambert. And guess what? You're officially on the Net."

"On the where?"

"On the party blog I told you about, remember?"

"What's it called again? I hope the picture looks half-decent."

"It's called partyworld. You're the first person you see on the site next to the words *Charlie Benson's pool party*. You look terrific."

Ah, merde. I nervously make my way to the blog to check.things out for myself.

"Charlie really liked you. We can go back whenever we want."

"That's sweet, but I don't think I'll be making it out there for a long while. I just found out I need to take the bar exam in a couple of weeks."

"What? What about the IPO?" His voice turns from tender to harsh.

"I guess I'll need some help in getting this done. Some of my colleagues can help out."

"That's completely unacceptable, Catherine. I want you to be the person in charge. I trust you. I don't want to babysit other lawyers from your firm," he says, his voice getting even louder. "I'm going to call Scott and tell him that I need you on the IPO, not studying for some exam. It's non-negotiable."

I know that Jeffrey wants me to lead the transaction, but why is he getting so hot under the collar over this? Other lawyers at my firm are more than capable of handling the file.

"It's required by the rules of practice. I don't think you can make them change their minds."

"Oh yeah? Just watch me."

After I hang up, I stare out my window and get a bit nervous about Jeffery calling Scott. I hope this doesn't make things even more complicated for me. I attempt to review a forty-page shareholders agreement for Bonnie but, given the state of my nerves, I have trouble focusing.

I grab my yellow highlighter and start flipping the pages when Nathan walks into my office. For once, I actually welcome the distraction.

"Hey, what's that you're looking at?"

Merde. I absent-mindedly left the party blog on my screen and a large close-up of Rebecca swimming topless in Charlie's pool is flashing on my computer.

"Nothing. I was, um, doing some research on Lexis-Nexis and accidentally came across this site." I roll my chair over to my computer, trying to disguise my conspicuous non-work-related browsing.

"Wow, who's that?" he asks, mesmerized.

"Well, um, I don't really know her."

"What site is this?"

"I'm really not that familiar with it. It's some party blog. It's by this guy who takes pictures at parties. People are so vain," I say, trying to fake an air of disgust.

A look of envy comes across Nathan's face as he stares at the screen. He then takes over my mouse and clicks furiously away, ogling the photos.

"Hey, isn't that you?"

"Hmm, I guess it is. I was at a party over the weekend."

"I'm impressed. Man, I'd sure love to have this guy's life," he muses after I pry his fingers off my mouse. He leaves my office and a few minutes later, I hear him shut his office door.

"Nathan, there's a call for you from the Securities Commission," I can hear Maria saying on the intercom.

"Take a message. I'm in the middle of an important file."

I chuckle to myself. He's not working on anything, he's browsing the blog.

I go back to reviewing the shareholders agreement when Scott walks in.

"Jeffrey Richardson just called. You told him about the bar exam?"

"Um, I may have mentioned something, yes," I mumble awkwardly.

"He's asked me to reconsider the firm's decision of making you take the exam this summer because of his IPO."

Look innocent. Look innocent.

"Really?"

"He told me that if you stop working on the file, he'll take his business elsewhere after the deal is done." Scott stares at me sternly with his arms crossed. "I talked it over with Bonnie. This is a major transaction and we don't want to lose the business, so I told him that you won't have any problems handling both. The exam really isn't that difficult."

I nod with a fake smile as I hold back tears.

Chapter 28

"That was some party you attended, sweetie," Rikash comments as he drops mail into my in-tray. "I'm just disappointed that there were no nude photographs of the bouncer. He has a nice backyard."

"Excuse me?"

"Don't kid yourself, everyone in the office has seen those Hamptons pictures."

"What?"

"Nathan has showed them to everybody in the department and I'm surprised he hasn't added them on our intranet. He seems fascinated by that blogger's lifestyle. Must be feeling like he's missing out on real life or something."

I drop into my chair, mortified. That means everyone here now knows that I'm seeing Jeffrey. This is the last thing I need right now. Why am I always getting into trouble these days? Is someone trying to send me a message?

"Don't worry, Jeffrey isn't on any of the pictures . . . Just you in that killer outfit I picked out." He winks.

Scott is next to drop by, with a "Great shot, Catherine. You should be in *Page Six Magazine*."

I want to crawl under my desk. Thank god I didn't buy that see-through top at Barneys, I'd never live that down.

"Thanks. I received a last-minute invitation I couldn't refuse."

"No kidding."

A few minutes later, Bonnie storms into my office and slams the door. My office feels like it's located at the foot of the Arc de Triomphe at the height of morning rush hour. If this traffic keeps up, I will either post a sign on my door that reads ON STRIKE or engage in the French driving manoeuvre of lifting my middle finger in the air while screaming, "*Vas te faire . . .*"

"Women like you make the rest of us look bad. Catherine, you're a professional and we expect you to carry yourself that way."

"*Pardon?*"

"All those pictures on the Net," she snarls. "I can't believe you would stoop that low. Don't you know that it takes a lifetime to build a reputation and only a few minutes to ruin it?"

"I do. But unlike some people around here, I don't think I've done anything to tarnish my reputation."

"What are you trying to say, Catherine?" she shouts. Her face is now as red as her Valentino suit jacket.

"Nothing other than what I just said."

"How dare you?" she hisses. "You think you know it all, don't you? You have no idea what some of us have gone through. I'm not going to let some junior talk down to me, so you better watch your mouth, young lady. I certainly didn't get where I am today by spending my weekends at degenerate parties in the Hamptons."

"I didn't realize I couldn't have a social life when I joined the firm."

"You should work on having an *appropriate* social life. You're an ambassador of Edwards and White. You carry the firm's reputation wherever you go, including to bordellos."

Bordellos? I'm blown away. Why would *she* be upset by my appearance on some party website? Is it out of genuine concern for my reputation or just plain jealousy?

"There's no easy way to the top, Catherine. Just remember that. And while we're on the subject, you need to bring in some clients if you're ever going to be considered for partnership. Spending your weekends at cheesy share houses isn't where you're going to drum up some lucrative business for the firm."

Easy way to the top? If this is easy, I'd hate to see the hard way. I decide against telling her that I was the guest of one of the firm's most important clients but decide to defend my rain making record instead.

"For your information, I've already brought in some business."

"Is that right? Who?"

"The Reebok Sports Club."

She looks stunned by my response.

"I didn't see them in our client database."

"That's because I haven't added them yet. I'm working on something for one of their fitness directors." To make it sound important, I decide to exaggerate the truth.

"Pfff. Amateur stuff. You're not even close to the big leagues, my dear," she scoffs.

Even though it isn't what I want to hear, I know Bonnie is giving me valuable advice; bringing in clients is a necessary step toward partnership. I wonder whether Madame Paulette Dry Cleaners would count as new business. They've asked me to represent them on a small claims court matter since I've sent them many new customers.

"One more thing," she throws out at rapid-fire speed. "If you want to get ahead, you should get yourself a red suit."

"A red suit?"

"Yes, all the powerful women on Capitol Hill wear red. It symbolizes power, passion, and prestige."

This is the first time someone has told me how I should dress and I'm seriously offended. I'm dying to tell her that she should browse corporette.com for help in selecting a less provocative work attire, but I bite my tongue and go with:

"Yes, apparently red can bring out the fire in some people. I'll think about it. Thanks."

Annoyed that Nathan would show my pictures to everyone in our group, I make my way to his office for a strongly worded chat. I barge into his office without knocking and recoil. He is perched above a small mirror with a fine line of white powder traced along its centre. As he turns toward me, I see a dusting of white on the tip of his nose.

"God, um, sorry."

"Wait, Catherine, I can explain."

"No thanks." I shut the door as quickly as I opened it.

Chapter 29

"**B**onjour, *ma chérie*."

Ah, the familiar voice of home. I hadn't taken the time to reach out to her recently, so I'm happy she takes the initiative to call.

"*Bonjour, Maman.*"

"How are you doing? I hope that they don't have you working as hard these days."

"No, of course not." *Liar.*

"I hope you're taking good care of yourself. Have you been eating properly?"

I can't bring myself to admit to her that I've been living on Gatorade, dosas, and bad coffee.

"*Mais oui.* How about you? How are things back home?" Not that it's apparent, but I really do hate lying to my mother.

"Things are great. Christophe and I have been gardening and sailing every day. It's been really wonderful."

Sailing every day? The only "fresh" air I'll inhale for the next while is the lemon-scented spritzer in the ladies room.

"Actually, I'm calling because we thought we'd surprise you and come to New York for a short visit. Christophe wants to visit his son—you remember, he's attending summer classes at NYU."

Oh god, her timing couldn't be worse. But how can I manage to tell her that?

"Are you sure you want to come right now? It's really not the best time of year to come to New York. The heat is really starting to get stifling. And I know how much you hate the muggy weather."

"It's okay, I really don't mind."

"I'd love to see you, but things are hectic with an important file right now and I may not be able to spend much time with you."

"Don't worry. It's New York. There are plenty of things to do. I'm dying to do some shopping."

Major panic attack. My mother coming to town means no time to study, a massive setback in my billables, and, more to the point, no Jeffrey. Given the ups and downs of my dating history, I haven't told my mother about him. Why get her all excited too early in the process? More often than not, she's ended up seeming more disappointed than I was when things didn't work out with one of my boyfriends. I always thought it was best to wait until things were more serious. But given the amount of time Jeffrey and I have been spending together and that Jeffrey seems completely smitten, I decide to break the news.

"*Maman?*"

"Yes, *ma chérie?*"

"I've been wanting to tell you. I'm seeing someone new. He's really amazing."

She lets out a shriek that I'm sure dogs in Central Park were able to hear. "I'm so happy to hear that there is someone to watch out for my angel! You know how I get worried about you living alone in New York. What's his name?"

"Jeffrey."

"Jeff-ree, what a beautiful name." I can practically see

her doing a romantic little dance to the syllables of his name. "I can't wait to meet him."

Zut! I didn't think this through; of course she wants to meet him. Not sure that he'll feel the same way, though; girlfriends' mothers can be scary. My mother is like an Impressionist painting: she's really quite lovely but best appreciated at a distance.

"I don't know. He's as busy as I am with work these days."

"Tell him your mother is coming to town. I'm sure that he'll make the effort. We'll be arriving next Friday."

"You already booked your flight?"

"*Mais oui,* of course."

My fate is sealed; no work, no fun for a whole weekend. And plenty of extra hours to make up for it.

"Okay, but I'm warning you, my apartment is very small."

"*Pas de problème.* We don't take up much room. See you Friday."

I dialled the first five digits of his work number and hung up three times before I had the courage to actually call.

Nothing like a visit from your mother to turn you into an awkward teenager again.

"Jeffrey? Um, I hate to bother you with this but can we have dinner with my mother and her boyfriend sometime this weekend? They're coming to town for a few days."

"Babe, you know how busy things are right now. I'll do my best but can't promise you anything." *Merde*, this is really awkward. And I'll have to explain this to my mother. Double *merde*.

"I understand, let's see how the week goes."

He senses my disappointment and quickly backtracks.

"If I get out of the office early on Friday, I could have you over for dinner at my place—then I could cook for them."

"Really?"

"Yeah. You didn't know that I'm a real cordon bleu, did you?"

He's charming *and* knows how to cook. Could this get any better? My mother will just die. My father never cooked a meal in his life; now she had found herself a boyfriend who owned a restaurant and prepared three course meals like Alain Ducasse. She also made a point of reminding me that I needed to find a man who could at least make a decent coq au vin. A home-cooked meal by my new boy-friend will put her over the moon.

"My mother would be thrilled."

That following Friday afternoon turns out to be madness, as usual.

"Rikash, how are we doing with that memo? I need it ASAP."

"Whoa. Hold your horses, dah-ling. What do you think I am, a real secretary? Read my lips: *Re-lax*."

"I need to send it out this afternoon."

"Why don't you go for a walk around the block? I can't concentrate when people breathe down my neck."

"No. I'll just wait here." I stand next to his cubicle with my hands on my hips.

"What's the matter with you? If you don't mind me say-ing so, you're a tad frantic today."

I sigh. "My mother and her boyfriend are flying into town today."

"Ah, now that explains it. The parents, huh? Where is

Jeffrey going to sleep? Between *maman* and her *petit ami?*"

"*Très drôle.* Just keep typing, will you?"

About ten minutes later, my phone rings.

"*Bonjour,* Catherine, we're here. We're in a cab and on our way."

My neck stiffens and my palms get sweaty.

"I'm still at the office."

"That's no problem. We'll just meet you there. We know where it is. I have that business card you sent me. See you shortly." She hangs up before I can object.

"Rikash, my mother is on her way."

"What? Oooh, I can't wait to meet her."

"Never mind. Just finish the damn document."

The next thing I know, my mother is sauntering down the hall. She throws her arms open wide a good six feet before she gets to me, then hugs me in front of the entire support staff.

"So this is where you slave away all these long hours," she declares, winking at Rikash. "God, your office is fantastic. I love the views. And so spacious!"

"Thanks."

I decide not to mention that this is only a temporary

space and that I'll soon be relegated to a windowless cubbyhole. Or that my office is about twice the size of my apartment.

"Mom, Christophe, this is Rikash, my invaluable assistant."

"We've spoken a few times. *Bonjour, Maman!*" He walks toward my mother and gives her a hug. As he does, Christophe takes a quick step back to avoid his turn.

"I love what you're wearing," Rikash adds, staring at my mom. "God, you and Catherine could be sisters."

She giggles like a child. I remind myself for the thousandth time how good he is.

"Catherine, where are we having dinner?" my mother addresses the office. "I'm dying to try a restaurant I was reading about in *Vogue*."

I cut her off—this could go on for hours. "We're invited to someone's home for dinner."

"Really, whose?"

I stare at her with big eyes while shaking my head, hoping some sort of mystical mother-daughter bond gives her the message that she shouldn't say his name.

"Is it Jeff—"

I cut her off again. Bad manners, but desperate times . . .

"Mom, why don't you and Christophe drop your bags at my place and freshen up? I'll meet you there in an hour. I still have a bit of work to do before I can leave tonight." I pass her my keys.

"Make sure you leave shortly. It's Friday night," she says, as if that meant anything in this crazy place.

"Dah-ling, she's so sweet," Rikash comments after my mother has mercifully left the building.

"Don't be fooled. She can be a tad sour."

"Oh come on, don't be too hard on her, she's your mother."

"Which means she can stress me out like nobody else. Let's just finish the memo so I can go home."

"Are you having dinner at Jeffrey's tonight?"

I nod, putting my index finger to my lips.

"God, what a catch."

"Jeffrey, your soufflé is absolutely *parfait*," my mother gushes.

"Thank you, Mrs. Lambert. It's a family recipe."

"And ordering the bread from the Poilâne bakery just for me, *mon dieu,* I feel so honoured! Catherine, do you still cook on the weekends?"

"It hasn't exactly been at the top of my list—maybe soon."

In Paris—back when I had spare time—I used to go shopping on weekends at the neighbourhood *marché* and pull together mini-feasts. Hearing my mom bring it up gives me a pang for those simpler and less stressful days— total French clichés of slow food, good company, and great wine. I occasionally daydream of that being my life again— cooking like Julia Child, my bosom pressed against the bowl while I mix delicious cakes. My mother quickly snaps me out of my reverie.

"But you have no kitchen; that's a strange way to live, *ma chérie.*"

A buzzing sound interrupts our conversation.

"Catherine, it's your BlackBerry," Jeffrey points out.

"Excuse me, I'll go turn that thing off."

As I make my way down the hallway toward the bed-room, my phone rings again. I bet I know who it is.

"Catherine? It's Bonnie. I need you on a conference call in ten minutes."

"I'm in the middle of a dinner party. Can't we do this later?"

"No. The Met Bank is the target of a hostile takeover and I need you on the call."

I sit in Jeffrey's bedroom, stunned. It's eight o'clock on a Friday night and I'm about to participate in a conference call. What's wrong with this picture? If my mother finds out, she'll kill me. I casually make my way to the kitchen and signal to Jeffrey to follow me back down the hall into the bedroom.

"I need to hop on a conference call in ten minutes. Can you cover for me? I don't want my mother to find out. She'll rip my head off."

"No problem. Leave it with me."

I finish my soufflé and then before the main course is served, I sneak off to dial into the conference call.

"Who just joined?" a voice asks as soon as I click in.

"Catherine Lambert from Edwards and White," I answer in a hushed voice.

After about ten minutes of listening to senior management's dissertation on the proposed takeover, I tiptoe back to the dining room to take a few bites of my main course.

"Are you okay, Catherine?" Christophe asks as I take my seat.

"Of course."

Jeffrey bombards my mother with a million questions to keep her distracted. Five minutes later, I stand up again and make my way back to the bedroom. This time, my mother gives me one of her dirty looks.

"We believe that tendering our shares in this bid would be good for stockholders."

I want to scream, "Why don't all of you get a fucking life?" into the phone, but I bite my tongue given that I'm supposed to be an ambassador of the firm and presumably ambassadors don't yell obscenities in the middle of conference calls.

"Sorry, who's on the line from Edwards and White?" a voice asks. "We'll need some help with the due diligence process."

"We would be delighted to take on that mandate." I recognize Bonnie's best brown-nosing voice. "This is Bonnie Clark and I also have Catherine Lambert on the line. She worked on a recent regulatory inquiry with your legal department, so she'll be helping out. She's extremely knowledgeable about your industry and your company."

A compliment from Bonnie, now that's a first; I feel

all warm and fuzzy inside—and a little alarmed. She must really want this piece of business. I then realize what she just said, the part about me helping out. Don't I have enough on my plate at the moment?

"Great news, we're thrilled to have you on board, Catherine."

"I agree that Catherine is quite knowledgeable about your company."

I freeze as I hear Antoine's voice. I take a quick look at my watch. It's about two in the morning in Paris. Why is he involved in this deal?

"Catherine has most of the documentation in New York, but I'll coordinate some of the documentation review from Paris," he continues. "You still have the Met Bank files in your office, don't you, Catherine?"

As I'm about to answer the question, I feel my mother's Gallic glare eviscerating me from the bedroom doorway.

"What on earth are you doing, *bordel de merde*?" she barks loudly. I'm mortified at the thought of the entire deal team hearing my mother's voice—this expression needs no translation. I wave her back to the dining room.

"Yes, um, I believe they're still in my office."

My mother doesn't move. She remains planted in the doorway with her hands on her hips.

"*Franchement!*" she shouts.

"I hear some noise in the background," someone on the conference call comments. "It sounds like someone's watching a foreign film or something. Can whoever it is turn it down? It's a bit annoying."

I turn around to stare at the wall and, after a few long minutes during which I can feel her eyes boring holes in my spine, she finally leaves the room.

"As I was saying . . ."

The conference call ends and my phone rings again.

"Yes?"

"Catherine, it's Bonnie. Can you conference in Antoine, I'm at Le Bernardin and can't do it from here. This is important."

"I'm in the middle of dinner and I don't have his home number in Paris. Can we do this tomorrow?"

"No. Just call the local directory assistance."

After spending twenty minutes with the international operator trying to find Antoine's home number in France, I finally have my two esteemed colleagues together on the line.

"Antoine, just for the record, the takeover target is *my*

client, not yours. It was your lead but you left it behind when you left New York. *End. Of. Story*," she says before hanging up, leaving us both speechless. Huh. I guess Met Bank was Antoine's idea.

"Whatever," he says before the line goes dead.

Hmm . . . now that conversation was worth ruining my dinner as well as my relationship with my mother, wasn't it?

I slink back into the dining room and both my mother and Christophe ignore me. Jeffrey stares at me with raised eyebrows. Okay, I'm in big trouble now. Following a long awkward silence, my mother decides to go on a tirade.

"Catherine, you're so impolite. It's unbelievable! I did not raise you like this. Jeffrey cooks a wonderful meal and we come all the way to New York to visit and you hide in the bedroom talking on the phone. What's wrong with you?"

"*Maman*, it was an urgent phone call from the office. I had to take it."

As soon as I finish my sentence, Jeffrey's cell phone rings and he leaves the room to take the call.

"Not again!" she gasps. "Are all of your dinners inter-rupted this way?"

The truth is that we don't really have dinners like this. We usually eat takeout food from plastic containers while sitting in our offices, but I keep that to myself.

"It's Friday night, Catherine. Can't you just ignore it, *non*?"

"No, I can't."

Jeffrey comes back to the dining room and takes a seat at the table.

"Mom, we're both very busy right now. This is how people live in New York."

"Unfortunately, Catherine is right about that." Jeffrey tries to come to my rescue.

"Jeffrey, I'm sure that you mean well, but please stay out of this. My daughter is working way too hard and I don't like it one bit. She's heading toward a medical condition, just like her father. Look where he is now: six feet under!" she exclaims and dramatically points to the ground with her tanned, jewelled hand, momentarily blinding us with her Panthère de Cartier diamond ring as her finger catches the chandelier's shimmer.

"Can we change the subject?" I try to redirect the conversation. Both Jeffrey and Christophe look like deer caught in the headlights.

"I think you should change jobs. This is not a life for you," she declares matter-of-factly. "Your cousin Françoise just loves her new job at Chanel. She works hard, but she's home by six o'clock to take care of her children. Now that's an appropriate schedule."

Here we go again with the old "your perfect cousin found a dream job" spiel. As much as I hate to admit it, I'm jealous of her new Chanel gig. I again try to change the subject, but my mother just trammels right over me.

"Françoise apparently visited a famous psychic in Paris and she told her that she should leave her stressful job because she would find something amazing. A few weeks later, she accepted an offer from Chanel. I think you should try it."

"Try what? Seeing a psychic? I don't believe in that nonsense."

"Everything she predicted happened. *All of it.*"

"Come on, *Maman*, please."

"Catherine, I think you should go. I noticed they have them all over the city. You never know, *ma chérie*, she may divulge something about your career that you wished you had known."

I'm not sure I want to know any more than I already do: I fought the law and guess who won.

"I noticed an advertisement in the taxi today for a

Madame Simona. Why don't you call her?" She hands me a piece of paper with a scribbled phone number.

I'm suddenly reminded of a joke I heard on the radio about the Psychic Network: If they're psychics, why do they need a phone? But looking at my mother's face, this is clearly no laughing matter. I can't read minds but I understand that this is non-negotiable.

Chapter 30

"M adame Simona?"

"This is she."

"Hello, my name is Catherine. I heard about you through a close friend. She says you have great psychic powers and that I should definitely meet you."

Great, I just lied to a psychic.

"Yes, my child. When would you like to come?"

"When are you available?"

"Can you come tomorrow at seven?"

"How about seven thirty? It will be very difficult to leave the office before seven o'clock."

"That will be fine. Ah, and bring along a picture of your husband or boyfriend if you wish to discuss such matters."

"I'm not sure I have a picture of him."

"Okay then just bring something that belongs to him, anything, his socks. See you tomorrow, my child."

I arrive Monday evening at Simona's Lower East Side walkup at seven thirty sharp. Feeling both excited and apprehensive, I press her buzzer and wait a few minutes before she answers me.

"Hello?"

"Madame Simona, it's Catherine." Should I really need to tell her?

"Ah yes, come up, my child."

I walk up four flights of stairs in the excruciating heat and stand in front of her apartment for a brief moment before knocking. Banging noises emanate from the other side of the door. I knock and wait patiently until she unlocks the bolt.

"So sorry to keep you waiting. *Pleeeze* come in."

Simona is in her late fifties. She's wearing a long skirt and wool sweater in the middle of the New York summer, bulky wooden jewellery and large glasses that exaggerate her already wide-set eyes. She has a pale complexion, thick bangs, and frizzy grey hair and looks like a cross between Sonia Rykiel and Robin Williams in *Mrs. Doubtfire*. She stares at me inquisitively for a few seconds before she directs me to follow her. We only take a few steps in her long hallway before she signals for me to take a seat in one of the two chairs set up around a metal folding table. A lamp hanging above our heads is covered with a purple piece of cloth, presumably to give her hallway an air of mystery. The usual occult paraphernalia is carefully displayed on the small table: a crystal ball, multiple stacks of tarot cards, and unidentified vials of powder and crystals.

As soon as she sits down, she reaches for my arm.

"Give me your hand."

Taken aback, I decide to forego any resistance and hand her my palm.

"Ah yes, I see that you enjoy shopping."

I nod. Not exactly shockingly insightful; most women in the city are into the sport.

"You work in an office, don't you? You're a business woman. I see work, lots and lots of work."

Okay, I'm not too impressed so far. If my two-piece

Dior suit wasn't enough to give this away, I think I told her that on the phone.

"Yes, that's for sure."

"I see difficult people, lots of paper and computers. And I see books, lots of books."

Startled, she opens her eyes. "Oh my god, are you a lawyer?"

"Yes."

"Jesus, I forgot to have you sign my release form!" she exclaims. "I don't want any trouble."

She jumps from her chair, walks to the back of her apartment, and returns with a crumpled piece of paper. "Okay, sign here," she orders.

I take a look at her coffee-stained document; it's one of those standard disclaimer forms that can be found on the Internet. As soon as I release her from any and all liability, she grabs my hand again.

"I see people making fun of you behind your back, my child, nasty women."

Hmm, now this is a little more interesting. "Yes, I already know about them."

We're suddenly interrupted by the ring of my cell phone.

Visibly vexed, she opens her eyes and looks as though she's about to put me under some horrible spell.

"I'm sorry. Can you please excuse me for one second? It's my office calling."

She crosses her arms and shakes her head.

"Catherine Lambert."

"You're not in your office. Where are you?"

"Hi, Bonnie, I'm at a meeting at the printers' downtown," I lie.

"I'd like you to drop by Cravath's to pick up some documents on your way uptown."

"Of course, no problem."

"When will you be back at the office?"

"In about an hour."

"Can you also stop by Nobu for some takeout sushi?"

"I won't have the time to go to Nobu *and* go to Cravath's. I'm on the East side."

Annoyed, I turn off the phone.

"I'm terribly sorry for the interruption. That was one of the nasty women," I say, trying to lighten the mood, but she's not amused. Simona grabs my hand again and closes her eyes.

"I see lots of fighting, slammed doors, and gossiping at your office."

Okay, now she's starting to impress me. The rumours of partners leaving the firm as well as the backstabbing have reached new levels lately.

"Yes, you see correctly. There are lots of dirty office politics going on at work."

"It looks like you might get caught in the middle of it. Be careful, my child."

Wonderful, something else to worry about; I knew I should've ignored my mother's suggestion that I see a psychic.

"I also see dissatisfaction with your job." She shakes her head while still firmly gripping my hand.

Her statement throws me off balance. I've had my share of difficult moments and encountered some difficult people at the firm, but am I truly dissatisfied?

"You don't seem very happy."

"Hmm. Really?"

"Not what you wanted to do as a child, right?"

"Yes it was. I've always wanted to be a lawyer."

"But before that, you wanted to be an actress, a movie star, maybe a singer. I can see that very clearly."

"Maybe when I was ten years old, but I've changed aspirations since then."

"Really, but why? It's your destiny, my child; you can't change that. It will only bring you more heartache if you do."

"Really? You see that?" I ask. This is a little ridiculous—every little girl wants to be a movie star.

"I see more, I see more . . . Ah yes, you have great fashion flair, don't you? Why aren't you working in this area?" she asks in a loud, intimidating voice. "And you have contacts that could help you!"

"I think you may be wrong here," I reply delicately to avoid offending her. "I love fashion but not as a career. You're probably referring to my cousin Françoise. She studied fashion design in London and works at Chanel."

"*Do it! Do it!* You must do it before it's too late!" she shouts.

"Look, Simona, I have a good job and I've worked extremely hard to get where I am now, I'm not going to throw it all away. I want to become a partner of Edwards and White. And I can't even draw a straight line, so a career in fashion isn't going to pan out."

"Stop worrying about such petty matters, my child.

Your passion is waiting for your courage to catch up! Once you do what you really love, money will come pouring in, I guarantee it!" she exclaims, still holding my hand tightly. "When are you most happy at work?"

These days, when my office door is locked and no one can enter, I want to reply but try to find a better answer.

"When I'm helping someone solve a problem or when I explain complex legal issues in simple terms. It's like magic."

She gives me a blank stare, looking unconvinced.

"Not true, my child. You are happiest when handling artistic- or fashion-related matters!"

I think back to the different files I've worked on at Edwards & White. It's true that I was over the moon when Antoine first handed me the Dior file, but it's now been taken away. So much for dealing with fashion.

"That's true, but such matters are incidental to my job. I specialize in banking and securities law."

She sighs loudly and shakes her head. "What is stopping you? Fear?"

I open my mouth to protest, but she cuts me off before I can make a sound.

"Fear of what? You're so young, I don't understand. Perhaps a terrible curse was placed upon you."

A curse? I imagine Bonnie sitting at her desk with a voodoo doll version of me, taking great pleasure in poking pins into my arms and legs before throwing it out her office window.

"I see troubles with your family in your youth, your mother crying herself to sleep at night."

"Hmm." I stay silent as she triggers vivid memories of my mother curled up in her bedroom sobbing.

"A young widow stranded alone."

How on earth would she know that? I feel a shiver run down my spine.

"I see depression, severe depression. Was anyone in your family depressed?"

"My mother went through a depression after my father died."

"She's very beautiful, your mother."

"Yes, she is."

"This event seems to have scarred you, my child. You yearn for security. But you must let go! This is bringing you down! If you don't let go, you will suffer from a great depression yourself."

"You think so?"

Memories of my mother's depression still haunt me to

this day. I don't want even to think about the possibility of going down the same road she has.

"What do you mean, do you think so? I do not think, I see! I can see it!" she shouts. "We must do something to get rid of all the negativity."

A bit leery, I try to change the subject to my love life. At least that's pleasant.

"Do you see anything about a man?" I ask nervously.

"Did you bring something that belongs to him?"

"Yes, a tie." I rummage through my bag and pull out one of Jeffrey's ties.

"Perfect."

She grabs the tie, holds it with both hands, and closes her eyes.

"Oh, he's very good-looking, a bit stubborn, and used to getting his own way."

"Yes. Anything else?"

"I see money, lots and lots of money coming to him shortly."

"Hmm. Anything else?"

"I see a wedding."

"A wedding?"

"Yes, in a foreign country."

Wow, now that's unexpected. Although things are going smoothly with Jeffrey, marriage isn't something that I'm ready to consider.

"And there's another man who goes out a lot, to nightclubs, and who very much cares about you."

"That's my assistant. I'm not getting married to him. He's gay."

"I see . . . Oooh! Trouble for this man!" she shouts.

"Trouble? For Rikash?"

"Yes."

"Are you sure?" I ask, worried. "You must be mistaken, he has no troubles. He's as carefree as they come."

"Hmm," she adds pensively. "Oooh, I see the wedding again. It will be by the water."

"On the beach?"

"Maybe. And it will be beautiful."

"One last question: Will I pass the bar exam?"

"Ah, the bar exam, I don't know."

"What do you mean, you don't know?"

"I can only help you so much, my child—I can't guarantee miracles. You need to work for that one."

"Right."

"Okay, that will be two hundred and fifty dollars," she finishes suddenly.

"It's over?"

"Yes, I told you everything that I could see," she answers abruptly. "I have other clients waiting, you know. I'm very busy. I don't have all night!" She stands up from her chair.

This brings me back to reality and reminds me that I need to pick up Bonnie's documents on my way back to the office.

"Now before I forget, I want you to take warm baths in rose petals and vinegar."

"What for?"

"The roses attract happiness and the vinegar wards off evil spirits. Please do as I say, it's very important."

The next day, a bit shaken by Madame Simona's visions, I come back to the office with a few dozen roses and a bottle of balsamic I picked up at the corner deli during my lunch break. I can't believe I'm going to follow her instructions, but I'm feeling just off kilter enough to think, *better safe than sorry.*

"Oooh. More roses from loverboy?" Rikash sighs.

"No, these are from me to me, for my apartment. Rikash, have you ever, um, talked to a psychic before?"

"A psychic? I don't believe in that mumbo jumbo."

"You don't? I thought you would be into it. There are some people out there with incredible powers, you know. Aren't you a bit curious?"

"Not at all. You see, dah-ling, I really don't care to find out about my future ahead of time. I try to live in the moment. Besides, I don't believe in paying someone to tell me what I already know: that my life is a total mess."

"I went to see a psychic last night, Madame Simona. It was a little unnerving."

"Really? What did she tell you?" he asks, suddenly very interested.

"It was really thought-provoking." I hesitate—I don't want him to think I'm an idiot—but I could use some reassurance. "She told me that any dissatisfaction with my career probably stems from traumatic events in my childhood. She also saw that I was meant to work in fashion."

"Sweetie, every young woman living in Manhattan is dissatisfied with her job and aspires to work in fashion. Not impressed. Okay, what else?"

"She saw some pretty personal things about my family," I answer, trying to counter his doubtfulness. "And she saw that I'm getting married by the water in a foreign country. Isn't that romantic?"

"I expect an invitation. Maybe I could be one of your bridesmaids?"

"I can't picture you in a pink dress."

"Don't be so sure. I look fabulous in fuchsia taffeta. Did she see anything about me?"

"No, um, she didn't mention anything," I lie, not wanting to tell him about the trouble she mentioned.

"Too bad. I hope you didn't pay her more than fifty dollars."

"Hmm."

"How much? A hundred?"

"Higher."

"A hundred and fifty?"

I don't answer.

"More?"

"No, that's it."

"Are you nuts? She really took you for a ride, silly girl."

"I know, but it was worth it. I finally got my mother off my back."

"Whatever," he answers, shaking his head.

He doesn't need to know that I actually paid $250 for my visit. After all, it did make mother happy. And bathing in rose petals might do wonders for my tired complexion, while the vinegar might help keep the evil spirits at the office out of my way.

Chapter 31

"Oh my god, Rikash, if I lose this draft, I'll kill myself," I scream from my office.

"I'll kill you first. We've been working on this document for three days straight. If I have to spend one more day on it, I'll throw up."

It's getting closer to the bar exam and I've been burning the midnight oil for the last ten days to keep Browser's IPO on course while attending half-day exam preparation seminars. Jeffrey's mood has been roller-coasting from anxiety to euphoria on an hourly basis, and trying to find some time to spend together in the last few weeks has been challenging. We've been communicating mostly via email and cell phone, often late at night from our offices over takeout food.

At one thirty in the morning, Rikash and I are still at the office trying to finalize an important memo that needs to be sent to the SEC in only a few hours. The sixty-five-page brick has to get sent out to the attorneys representing the underwriters for their review. After three days of non-stop work, it's almost finished. I'm giving it one last proofread as Rikash listens to techno on his MP3 player while waiting for my final revisions. My computer suddenly freezes.

"I don't understand what's wrong with it. I was using the spell check and it just froze."

"Okay, let me have a look."

Rikash takes over the controls of my computer and I watch his long, dainty fingers move gracefully over the keyboard. He's technically savvy and understands computers more than anyone I know. Every time something goes wrong in the office, Rikash is called to the rescue. Still, my heart is pounding.

"Rikash, I'm really nervous. Will I lose the most recent version?"

"Come on, relax, dah-ling, relax. I'll have it unfrozen in no time. Do you think I actually want to sit around here all night and retype this ghastly thing? I have more important things to do. I'm meeting friends later."

"Later? It's one thirty in the morning. How do you do it?"

"You don't want to know."

"You're right, I don't."

He continues to fiddle with my computer.

"Where did you learn all this? I thought you were a filmmaker."

"I'm from India, remember?"

"What does that have to do with it?"

"Don't you know that some of the sharpest technological minds are from India?" He switches into his "I'm going to enlighten Catherine" tone. "In the 1960s, in an effort to make India a competitive and economically independent society, the Indian government created top-notch engineering schools, the Indian Institutes of Technology, and they quickly became very prestigious. It's very difficult to be admitted into one—you need extremely high scores on pre-screening exams. My younger brother just passed his entrance exams, so he'll start next year."

"Really? You never told me that."

"I'm so proud of him. I'm hoping to make some money by selling my documentary to help him get through it."

As he talks, I stare at him admiringly. He has a big heart and a lot more depth than he is willing to show.

"Is that how you learned your computer skills, through your brother?"

"I have a few cousins who attended thc IITs and all they talk about is bloody computers. I also temped at another firm before coming here and had no other choice but to brush up on my skills."

"I'm impressed. I'm sure your skills come in handy here. Most lawyers are technically challenged."

"Not all of them are. Some are actually pretty sharp. Antoine was really good with computers."

"Really?"

"Mmm-hmm. I know we complained about him, but I actually liked him. He's extremely smart. Did you know that he finished magna cum laude at Yale Law School?"

"No, I didn't. He was too busy burying me with work for us to swap resumés."

"He was always good to me. He even helped review the script for my most recent documentary."

Surprised, I let out a gasp. When did he find the time?

He seemed so caught up in his work. Did I misjudge him by thinking he was completely self-interested?

"Hmm. That was nice of him."

"He's totally into the arts."

I'm reminded of our early conversation about his pro bono work for the Harlem school and that he does have a big heart. It's too bad we left off on such bad terms.

"Anyway, how's the document? Do we need to spend the rest of the night here?"

"No, I have it."

"Thanks, Rikash, you're a saviour. How can I pay you back? A bottle of your favourite gin?"

"Nah, a big kiss will do just fine." He lifts his arms in the air and moves in for some air kisses. "Are you seeing Jeffrey tonight?"

"I'm supposed to give him a call before I leave the office. Shockingly, he's working late too."

I dial his cell and it's turned off. I call his office and a woman answers the line.

"Hello, is Jeffrey there?"

"No, he's not. He left a few hours ago."

"A few hours ago?" Hmm. That's odd. We usually speak before he leaves his office. "Did he say where he was going?"

"No," the woman answers abruptly, "he didn't."

I call his apartment and there is no answer. A bit worried, I leave a message.

"Jeffrey left his office and didn't even call me. We were supposed to get together tonight before he flies to San Francisco tomorrow." I sit in my chair, sulking.

"Don't worry about it. Something must have come up. I'm on my way to grab a drink at Tenjune. Why don't you join us?"

"It's too late and I need to study. And they probably wouldn't let me in dressed like this anyway."

"Are you kidding? You're with me, girl. And you'd love Chloe and Amber. They both work in the fashion industry and they're fabuloso."

"I really can't. Tomorrow's a big day and I need to study for the exam. Go ahead and have fun, and don't drink too much. We need to send the memo first thing in the morning."

As Rikash leaves the office, I sit at my desk staring at my email inbox. There are several notes from Jeffrey saying that he misses me and that he can't wait to see me. I kill time for a few minutes hoping that he'll call me back.

The phone rings and I pick up, relieved.

"Dah-ling, this is your last chance. Stop moping around the office like a big loser. You need a break from all those Barbri books. Hop in a cab and meet me in the Meatpacking District. I'll wait for you at the door."

I change my mind after hearing the L-word. If Jeffrey's going out tonight, then so am I.

I exit my cab in front of Tenjune and the doorman immediately lifts the velvet rope at the sight of Rikash kissing me on the cheek. We weave through the dance floor and Rikash waves at two attractive women sitting on a sleek leather couch sipping martinis.

"This is my boss, so behave, okay?" They both giggle and greet him with hugs.

"Catherine, meet my friends Chloe and Amber."

"Nice to meet you."

Chloe is a tall honey blonde with a dazzling smile and Amber is a petite light blonde with big blue eyes. Both are dressed in skin-tight jeans with gorgeous chiffon halter tops in pastel colours and are wearing towering stilettos. Do they go to work dressed like this? *Quelle chance!*

"Catherine, try the watermelon martini. It's amazing," Amber gushes.

Rikash waves at the waiter, who immediately recognizes

him and takes our order. "Sweetie, this one's on me."

"So what do you ladies do exactly? Rikash mentioned that you both work in the fashion industry."

"I'm a stylist for Armani," Chloe answers with a sweet Southern accent.

"And I'm a buyer for Bloomingdale's," Amber says, her head bopping to the loud music.

"That sounds so glamorous. I just spent the last three days drafting a sixty-five-page document and I've been studying like crazy for a hellish exam, so I haven't slept in weeks."

They both stare at me as if I have four heads.

"Oh god, I couldn't handle those hours," Amber comments. "It would totally kill my social life."

Rikash hands over the watermelon martinis.

"Here's to forgetting about work and your exam!" Chloe toasts.

I'll drink to that. I take a small sip of my martini and then finish the rest in one gulp. "These are delicious."

I signal to the bartender to bring us another round. After I've slurped down my second one at record speed, Rikash shakes his head.

"Pace yourself, you haven't had a decent night's sleep

in more than a week and you have a very long day ahead of you, remember?"

"Tomorrow? Who gives a shit about tomorrow? As far as I'm concerned, Jeffrey and his big deal can take a flying leap off my big fuckin' toe." Oh god, I'm slurring.

Rikash puts his arm around my shoulder. "Please calm down, sweetie. You're getting a bit carried away."

As Rikash debriefs Chloe and Amber on my relationship situation, I suddenly feel out of place in this noisy nightclub. I check my cell phone to see if Jeffrey called. How could he leave the office without calling me?

"I can totally relate," Chloe shouts. "Believe me, sister, if I were you, I'd be on the next plane outta here. I haven't had a real relationship in three years and some of my friends are going on four. All the men in this city have dirty dicks. They've slept with so many women that they've either been booed out of town or their dicks have fallen off. Go find yourself a nice French boy."

"Stop it," Amber shouts. "That's not true."

"Oh yeah? When was the last time you had a functional relationship?"

Amber stares back at Chloe in silence. "A very long time," she murmurs, her eyes watery.

"Amber, isn't that the guy you made out with last week?" Rikash points to a very hot, very drunk twenty-something across the room. "And check out the body on that guy with the red shirt, he's hot. God, I'd love to see him in a dhoti."

"In a what?" Amber asks, puzzled.

"You know, the skirt thingy Indian men wear over their crotch in the south. It's the male equivalent of cleavage."

All three ogle and giggle. The bartender comes back with another tray overflowing with martinis. Amber grabs one and struts toward her makeout partner. After three martinis, I'm starting to feel really good. The music is getting increasingly louder and, as far as I'm concerned, a lot better.

I take off my suit jacket, make my way toward the hot guy in the red shirt, and gyrate my hips in front of him. The next thing I know the two of us are getting down on the horseshoe-shaped dance floor; he follows the song's lyrics literally and loosens up my buttons. Both Rikash and Chloe give me the thumbs-up from atop a banquette where they're now perched.

Red Shirt is really getting into it and starts sucking on my ear. He's also playing with my hair and holding my hip so that we sway together to the sound of the beat. Wow, why haven't I been doing this every night? This is way more fun than doing research in the office library.

"Catherine, COME UP HERE AND JOIN US!" Chloe screams. "It's so much better up here!"

I pull away from a frustrated Red Shirt and make my way to the top of the banquette to join my posse.

"Watch it, lady!" a hipster shouts as I grip his shoulder trying to make my way to the top. Chloe is performing a perilous balancing act shaking her bottom while still holding her martini glass. From where I stand, I can see the entire club. The energy emanating from the crowd is intoxicating. I dance with Chloe as we shout the lyrics at the top of our lungs.

Rikash stares at me with a look of amusement. It's the first time he's seen me let my hair down and he's enjoying every minute of it. I decide to dial Jeffrey's number; I'll show him who's out on the town. I signal for Rikash to pass me my handbag from the other side of the banquette.

"WHAT?" He lifts his arms to emphasize the question. "DO YOU NEED MONEY?"

I shake my head and mimic a phone with my fingers. After he tosses it to me, I dial the number. As I lift the phone above my head so Jeffrey can hear the fun I'm having, it slips out of my hands and goes flying underneath the leather couch.

Quelle catastrophe!

I start pointing to the back of the banquette, and Amber and Rikash stand immobile, looking puzzled.

"I dropped my cell!"

"Huh?"

"I DROPPED MY PHONE UNDER THE COUCH!" I shout at the top of my lungs just as the music stops.

Rikash mobilizes the nightclub staff to search for my phone, and two huge bouncers arrive at the scene carrying flashlights.

"She's a very important person. She's an attorney working on a major IPO and she needs her phone," he says, trying to justify the brouhaha. The two bouncers move him out of the way and get on all fours trying to find my phone. This is why it's a good idea to take your assistant drinking with you.

A bald man hands it over. "Here it is, lady. Be more careful next time."

I turn my BlackBerry on to make sure it's working and the time pops up. It's four in the morning.

Oh mon dieu, this party is really *over*.

"It was nice meeting you, but I need to go home."

"Catherine, you can't go home now, we're going to Florent for a late-night snack," Chloe says plaintively.

"Sorry guys, but I need to be in my office in about three hours."

I say goodbye to my new friends, kiss Rikash on the cheek, and stumble into the street looking for a cab. I'll be paying for this in a few hours and will most likely fail the bar exam. Right now, it feels worth it. As I wait for the next taxi to pull up in front of the club, Red Shirt walks over.

"Hey, it was cool dancing with you earlier."

"Thanks. It was 'cool' dancing with you too," I reply awkwardly.

"We should get together some time. You know, hook up or somethin'."

"Yeah, that sounds fun." I jump into the cab and disappear into the early morning.

At home, I dive onto my bed and the room spins. As I stare at the ceiling, the phone rings. I move slowly to pick it up from my bedside table.

"Hello?" I'm still slurring.

"Hey, sweetheart, where were you? I think you hit the

dial button on your cell phone and called me by mistake. All I could hear was a lot of noise."

"I was out with Rikash, we went for a drink after work."

"It sounded like some drink."

"Where have you been? I tried calling you earlier."

"I had a meeting at our bankers' offices and then came home and crashed. Are you okay? You sound off. Where did you think I went?"

"Um, nowhere special."

"Listen, I'm really sorry about tonight, babe, I got stuck in meetings. I'll make it up to you on Friday when I get back from San Fran. I really miss you."

All doubts dissipate from my mind and I fall asleep on my bed fully clothed cuddling the phone.

Chapter 32

Whoever drafted the rule against perpetuities was either: a) sadistic, b) deranged, c) high on some really strong stuff, or d) most likely all of the above. As if learning the archaic vernacular of the law of real property wasn't enough fun, we're required to understand it. I've read it more than a hundred times, and I still don't understand what the hell it's about.

I spend the weekend locked up in my tiny apartment in the sweltering heat studying in my slip and brassiere. The only air in my self-made prison is coming from an old ceiling fan working at half its capacity. I make hourly trips to the Starbucks on the corner of Third and 66th for a double shot of espresso to prevent a complete shutdown of my nervous system. Jeffrey and I had agreed that it was best not to see each other until the following weekend, as I needed the little energy I had left to get through the exam. Since he didn't want me delegating work on the Browser deal on top of exam hell, I have to review emails and documents first thing in the morning or late at night before I go to sleep for a couple of hours.

I wake up the first day of the exam completely exhausted. I down two cans of Red Bull and half a banana for breakfast to survive the crazy day ahead. As I arrive at the Javits Center, thousands of people looking as tired as I feel are lined up like sheep waiting to be sent to the slaughterhouse. I join the line at the back and feel my pulse thundering like the Paris Metro. The doors open, revealing rows of tables and chairs that could fill a few football fields. I take a seat, set my pencils and bottle of water down, and wait for the start signal. The first day of exam is an intense six-hour marathon of multistate multiple-choice questions. After it's over, I stumble home and have alphabet soup anxiety dreams all night.

The following day is no better, with fifty New York State multiple-choice questions and three hours of essays. It's cruel for them to put the essays at the end. My head is pounding, my hair is filthy, and I have to answer this:

> Jack approached Peter, an undercover police officer, and asked if Peter had one pound of marijuana for sale. Peter replied that he could provide it to him at a price of $1,000, and they made arrangements for the sale. At the appointed time and place, Jack paid $1,000 to Peter, who instead delivered one pound of oregano to Jack. Peter then arrested Jack and charged him with criminal solicitation and attempted possession of marijuana. Question: Can Jack be arrested for buying oregano?

The question that comes to my mind is, doesn't the NYPD have more important things to do than sell oregano? And why isn't Jack suing Peter after getting screwed on the sale?

The entire bar exam experience, a closed-book nightmare on twenty-four different legal topics, will go down in my personal history as one of my most challenging experiences. I walk out of the two-day examination feeling like a total zombie, and I can barely remember which continent I'm on or my last name. I have no clue as to whether I passed and won't find out for several months. Right now, I don't care. I go straight home, turn off my BlackBerry and computer, and fall into a well-deserved deep sleep.

Chapter 33

*H*ow *about dinner Saturday night at Jean Georges?* is scribbled on a note attached to a bouquet of peonies from Jeffrey.

"I guess you guys made up," Rikash says, staring at the bouquet.

"It was a misunderstanding. All that stress has been going to my brain. I should trust him more and freak out less. He's been so good to me. He's taking me to Jean Georges tomorrow night."

"Wow, maybe he'll pop the question."

"Come on, we've only been dating seriously for a month."

"This is New York, dah-ling, anything is possible. Remember what that psychic told you."

"We're definitely not there yet."

He walks toward my desk and looks around to make sure no one is listening. "Catherine, I have to tell you what happened to me the other night after you left the club. I met someone extraordinary. I think I may be falling in love."

"What? *You* in *love*? I thought you didn't want to be tied down to just one person?"

"That was before Dimitri. He's the nicest guy I've met in a long time. We locked eyes as I was leaving Tenjune and he asked me if I wanted to join him for a coffee. We stayed up all night talking."

"That's great, Rikash! I'm so happy for you. You deserve to meet someone special."

"It's such an amazing feeling. We have so much in common. He's a freelance filmmaker and we're thinking of working together on a documentary. And oh—my phone is ringing." He practically skips back to his cubicle.

I look in my inbox to see an email entitled *Firm Retreat in California* waiting for me.

To all Edwards & White Attorneys,
In order to commemorate an outstanding year, Edwards & White will be holding a worldwide firm retreat in San Diego this fall. The agenda and list of activities will be circulated at a later date.

We look forward to seeing you there.
The Executive Committee

An outstanding year? For whom? The idea of travelling with my misfit colleagues so that we can waste a beautiful weekend on useless team-building exercises like paintball *(perhaps I could fill the balls with cement, let them harden, and shoot rocks instead?)* isn't my idea of fun, but I try to look at the bright side: it'll get me out of the office and will allow me to catch up with my Paris colleagues.

"Let's order champagne! I'm in the mood to celebrate." Jeffrey puts down his menu. "Your exam is over and the IPO road show went really well; we managed to gather a lot of interest from institutional investors," he adds with relief.

"That's great news. I'm really happy things are going

well, but I have to admit that I can't wait for it to be over."

"We should take a trip in the fall. How about St. Barts? A friend of mine runs a resort over there."

"Sounds perfect."

Jeffrey reaches for my hand and slowly caresses my fingers.

"I really missed you. You have no idea."

"So did I." As I lock eyes with him, his gaze gets more intense by the moment.

"I can't wait to take you home. You have the most beautiful, intense eyes. You're fuckin' gorgeous, babe."

I blush while sipping my wine. How perfect is this man?

"Every night after a long day of meetings I would lie in bed just thinking what a lucky guy I am, and I bought you a little something in San Francisco."

"Not again?"

He pulls out a tiny grey silk pouch. Inside is a ring from the Dior Gourmette collection with dainty flowers and butterflies. I try to be mature about it, but my eyes must be lighting up like a child entering FAO Schwartz for the first time. I've been drooling over this collection since before I left Paris.

"Oh my god, Jeffrey, it's stunning!"

"I know how much you and Mr. Dior get along."

"This is way too much."

"No, it's not. You totally deserve it."

I slip the ring onto my middle finger and feel on top of the world. This man is so kind and generous. How could I have ever hesitated to date him?

"Can we get the cheque, please?" He signals to our waiter.

"Certainly, sir."

"Before we go, I just have a small favour to ask you. I hope you won't mind?"

"Anything."

"It has to do with the directed share program you've been working on."

"Okay," I answer, assuming he wants to add a last-minute participant to the list of prospective shareholders.

"You know I was going to allocate a portion of the directed program shares to two Swiss business partners." He's staring into my eyes again with that ever increasing intensity, but this time it doesn't feel romantic.

"Yes."

"I've changed my mind."

"Right," I answer, getting more uneasy with the sudden change in the tone of his voice.

"I want to transfer those shares into an account I hold with a trust company in the Cayman Islands. You won't mind helping me out, will you, babe?"

I stare at him for a brief moment, completely shell-shocked. My entire body starts to tremble as I try to convince myself that this isn't happening. He can't be asking me to transfer shares from his own company to an offshore account; there must be another explanation. My legally trained mind is racing at frantic speed. Is he trying to get around those contractual lockup obligations? As a senior officer of the company, he is required to hold his IPO shares for a few months after Browser goes public before he can sell them. No matter what his intentions, what he's asking for is totally illegal. He guesses my apprehension from my prolonged silence.

"Don't worry, sweetheart, I'm not doing anything illegal. I just want to avoid paying taxes on some money I'll be making from selling some shares in the next few weeks. I've worked so hard for it, I don't want to give it all to the taxman. Understand?"

You're not supposed to be selling shares in the next few

weeks; that's the whole point of the lockup period. And more importantly, those shares don't belong to you. I'm appalled and mortified that he's asking me to do this. After he pays for our dinner, I excuse myself and run to the ladies room. I stare blankly in the mirror as tears slowly roll down my cheek; I wipe off the smudge caused by runny mascara and feel as used as the tissue I throw into the wastebasket. Nauseous, I hold my hands in front of my mouth to prevent my dinner from spewing over my new Dior dress. Be calm, Catherine, everything will be okay. This must be some bad dream. This can't be really happening. You'll soon wake up and everything will be fine.

I sit in silence in the taxi on our way back to his apartment, crestfallen. My hands grasp my evening bag tightly as I mentally recap some of the events leading to tonight and a flashback of several conversations about the IPO comes to mind: *the directed share program*. This has been a topic of conversation since we met and he was probably planning this all along. How could I've let this happen? Stupid, Catherine. Really stupid.

"When this deal is over, babe, I'll be able to afford a place in Bridgehampton and in St. Barts. I can have both. Can you imagine?" He becomes possessed by a crazed, eerie laugh. "Did you hear what I just said? We'll have both. We can have it all!" He hollers at the taxi driver and to passersby walking along Park Avenue. Funny, I feel like I've been left with nothing at all.

At Jeffrey's apartment, I lie on the edge of his low modern bed, silent. His hands caress my shoulders, but I remain paralyzed.

"Come on, baby. What's wrong?"

"I feel sick. Must be the champagne and the wine. I'm not good with mixing."

I run to the bathroom to vomit what feels like half of my body weight. I don't recognize the woman staring back at me in his oversized mirror, but I try to look back at her with comforting eyes. My mind backtracks to Jeffrey's outrageous request and I want to scream, but I hit the marble counter with my fist instead. How could I have been so naïve and put my career in jeopardy for this man? I've got to get out of here.

I tiptoe out of the bedroom as soon as Jeffrey has fallen asleep and make my way to his kitchen. I try to scribble something on a piece of paper. I want to write, *I will send you to jail for this, you son of a bitch* but keep my cool and opt for:

> *Dear Jeffrey,*
> *Sorry about last night. Wasn't feeling very well.*
> *Will call you later.*
> *Catherine*

It's better for me to pretend like nothing's wrong until I can figure out what to do. Maybe I'm totally blowing this out of proportion—I'm exhausted, after all. I walk aimlessly on the Upper East Side for a few hours trying to console myself by staring into shop windows before collapsing on a bench in tears. It was all an act, the flowers, the gifts, the dinners, and putting on a friendly face for my mother. And how could I not have seen the signs? *Merde!* My feelings of sadness turn into anger and then into guilt: Could my personal relationship with Jeffrey have clouded my professional judgment? How could I have been so stupid and fallen for such a smooth operator and put my career on the line for a scumbag? And how will I handle this mess at the office? I dial Lisa's number, but she doesn't pick up.

Later, I hole myself up in my apartment; everything seems dreary and cramped. I turn off the phone, close the curtains, crash on my bed, and turn on the DVD player to watch a movie that is quite à propos in the circumstances: *Bonjour Tristesse*.

"Lisa, it's me. Sorry to phone-stalk you on a Sunday night, but I really need to talk." After leaving about twenty messages on her voicemail, I finally get Lisa live.

"I want to die, Lisa. Jeffrey's been using me all along," I blurt into the phone before bursting into tears.

"Calm down, sweetie, what are you talking about?"

"Promise me you won't tell anybody. This is really horrible. Jeffrey asked me to help him steal from his company."

"What? You're joking. This is a joke, right?"

"No, it's not. Jeffrey had the nerve to ask me to illegally transfer Browser shares to an offshore account. He doesn't care about me, Lisa. The only thing he cares about are the millions he's about to make. I feel so gullible. I just want to go home."

"I can't believe it. What did you say to him?"

"Nothing, I felt so crushed. He completely silenced me. God, to think that I fell for his big charade and trusted him. What a sucker I am."

"No, you're not. You took a chance on love, which makes you brave. He's a total asshole. What are you going to do about it? Are you going to tell Scott? You can't just let him get away with this."

"I haven't thought about it yet," I answer after blowing my nose. "I keep hoping maybe I misunderstood him. That he wouldn't do this to me . . ."

"There's only one way to find out. Tell him you won't do it and see how he reacts."

Chapter 34

"Where's Rikash?" I ask Mimi first thing Monday.

"He called in sick today. He sounded horrible on the phone."

God, I wish I could confide in him right now. I cover my face with large reading glasses to hide the bags under my eyes. Sitting in my office, I stare at the Browser file and my first inclination is to rip it up into a million pieces and throw it out the window. Several frantic messages from Jeffrey are waiting in my voicemail, so I pick up the phone to dial his number.

Sooner rather than later, I need to confront *le démon*.

"Hi, Jeffrey, sorry for the disappearing act on Sunday morning. I was really sick. Must have been all that rich food I ate Saturday night."

"How are you feeling, babe? Are you okay?"

"Much better. Do you have a few minutes to chat?

"Of course."

My hands shaking, I try to gather the courage to confront him head-on: "Listen, I've thought about what you asked and I don't think I can do it. It falls outside the scope of my mandate."

"What? What the hell is that supposed to mean?" he replies, his tone now aggressive.

I pause before answering and brace myself for the worst.

"It means that you should ask someone else to take care of it for you."

"You can't be serious? I'm only asking you to do me a tiny favour; I'm not asking for a lot." His voice has now turned ice cold.

"I reread the provisions of the underwriting agreement

and the offshore transfer would violate its terms."

"What? What the fuck are you talking about? When did you suddenly turn into Little Miss Perfect?" he shouts into the phone. "Are you turning on me? Catherine, don't you dare do this to me. Not now."

Shocked and heartbroken by the way he is talking to me, I want to scream at the top of my lungs, *"Ô rage! Ô désespoir! Egoiste! Egoiste!"* like in the Chanel perfume ads.

"Jeffrey, calm down. All I'm saying is that I'm not entirely comfortable doing this, that's all."

He tries to put on his sweet voice. "Listen, babe, I already told you that it's nothing illegal. I'm doing this at the recommendation of my accountant, so it's all legit. You just transfer the shares into my secretary's name at an offshore account and we're good to go. Can you have dinner with me tonight? We could talk about it some more and I'll explain it to you. I've already made us a reservation at Chanterelle and had them put aside that bottle of Sauvignon Blanc you like from their private cellar."

How did I ever fall for this crap? I could lose my licence to practise law. And how greedy can someone get? He'll already be making millions of dollars legitimately next week, does he really need to make more pocket change at the expense of his reputation, his company's reputation, and, more importantly, our relationship? I thought we had such a great connection, a shared passion for music and the arts. Could he have made it all up to seduce me? My stomach sinks to my knees when I realize that my interests in jazz music, reading, and travel are listed in my profile on the firm's website and on Facebook. He played me like a fool.

"Not sure. I'm swamped over here. I'll call you back."

"I miss you," he adds before I hang up the phone.

I sit in my chair, dejected. *Que faire?*

"Mind if I join?"

"No, please go ahead."

It's lunch and I'm sitting in the corporate library sifting through newspapers to take a break from Bonnie's endless demands and avoid reading my emails since I can't get through more than a few lines without thinking of Jeffrey. I'm totally useless and bummed out—to the point where I'm actually pleased to be interrupted by Nathan walking in with his lunch from Fresco on the Go.

"Here, Catherine, I brought you an espresso. I know how much you like it."

I look up from my paper, surprised by his thoughtful gesture. Maybe he's trying to buy my silence after the recent coke bust. I'm suspicious of everyone right now.

"Thanks, Nathan, that's very sweet of you."

"God, it's disgusting out there, I can hardly breathe. It must be a hundred and forty degrees."

"I know. That's why I'm in here and not out there."

"So, what's new? Have you attended any fabulous parties that would make me jealous?"

"No more parties. I've been working every weekend."

"I guess the big IPO is coming up."

"Hmm." That's the last thing I want to think about.

"Sorry, did I say something wrong?"

"No, I'm just really tired of talking about it, that's all. How about you? Anything new in your life?"

"Actually, I have some pretty amazing news. My wife is expecting our first child."

I stare at Nathan, baffled. His first child? Billing three thousand hours a year doesn't give you much time to conceive a baby . . . If there are about eight thousand, eight hundred hours in a year and they say almost a third of that time is spent sleeping, Nathan had to be spending every waking hour at the office to make his billable hours add up. But because time spent reading emails, filling out time sheets, attending practice group meetings, surfing on the web, and snorting white powder isn't billable, he would have to be in his office on the clock from dawn until very late at night six days per week, with almost no time for meals, bathroom breaks, or sex.

"Congratulations, Nathan. That's wonderful news."

"I know. It really is."

"I'm sure you'll make a wonderful father," I say reluctantly.

"Catherine, I've been meaning to explain . . ."

"I really don't want an explanation, Nathan. You're free to do whatever you want."

"Just so you know, I'm not an addict. A friend of mine introduced me to it recently after a dinner party and I've only done it a few times since. It really gives you a boost."

"You talk about it like it's a new espresso blend. You could get caught or, worse, addicted. And you could lose your job over this."

"I know. I've quit. I hope you believe me." He looks totally shamed.

I have the sudden realization that maybe I shouldn't be

so self-righteous. After all, we're both dabbling with illegality; it's just that Nathan's comes in a tiny Ziploc bag and mine comes in the shape of a manipulative boyfriend.

"Have you ever tried it?"

I try to relax my tone. "No, not interested. I certainly don't need the adrenalin boost; I already have Bonnie breathing down my neck. She should be labelled an illicit drug."

He chuckles as he takes a bite of his sandwich. It's the first time we share a laugh.

"Hey, did you hear the good news about Antoine?"

"No."

"He just brought in a major deal for the firm—the privatization of a large French company. Lucky bastard has good timing. He's up for partnership this fall."

"Really? That's great." Despite his bizarre behaviour before he left for Paris, I'm happy for him. He deserves every ounce of his success.

"It looks like he really scored big. This deal is so huge that the entire Paris office will be mobilized for it," he says with a look of envy.

"How do you know all this?"

"He told me over the phone yesterday."

It hadn't occurred to me before now, but Antoine never called me for updates about the New York office. After our big run-in the night of the concert, he probably decided it was best to keep in touch by calling Nathan instead. It's odd that it would bother me but it makes me feel sad.

"Are you okay? You seem a bit off. Hope you're not concerned about all the rumours going around. I don't think we have anything to worry about, we're way too low on the totem pole to matter."

"No, it's not that. I'm just tired. This IPO is killing me."

"Hey, look on the bright side. At least you don't have to worry about your billable hours," he adds eagerly. "I'll catch you later."

The bright side? The bright side of what? I decide to take a lap in the hallways to stay out my office for as long as possible. Jeffrey's request has shaken my self-confidence to the core. I'm probably totally unfit to practise law. And what's the point in working like *un chien* anyway? Maybe Madame Simona was right; I should find another career. I walk aimlessly for a while trying to make sense of my life before my thoughts are interrupted by Bonnie's screeching. She's in Scott's office.

"I can't believe this. Catherine's working for me, not you!"

"No she's not. Catherine's doing work for me on the Browser deal, so she can't work on your new acquisition, sorry."

Bonnie storms out of Scott's office and down the hallway, the buckles on her black Gucci dominatrix skirt swinging from side to side.

Great, on top of everything, now I'm witnessing the battle of the warlords first-hand. For once, I want to throw myself at her stilettos and plead with Bonnie to give me work so I can avoid having to deal with Jeffrey. You know it's bad when . . .

I stop back at the library to pick up my things and the phone rings; Harry Traum's name appears on the screen. Given that I'm the only person in the room, I debate whether to pick up the line before it stops ringing. I take a few more steps toward the exit when the phone rings again. Paranoid there may be security cameras and he can somehow see me, I pick up the line.

"Hello."

"This is Harry Traum. I need research done right away. I'm going to court in a few hours. This is urgent."

"Well, um, not sure I can help out, Mr. Traum. I'm tied up at the moment with a large transaction."

"It'll have to wait. This is more important."

"I'm afraid I really don't have the time. Perhaps I could find someone else to help you?" I answer hesitatingly, knowing that this is risky. Given that I haven't had a decent night's sleep in about a month and my nerves are as frazzled as my hair, I decide to stand my ground.

"Do you know who I am?" he shouts into the phone. "Do you?"

"Yes, of course . . . Do you know who *I* am?" I reply, shaking.

"No."

My mind races for a split second. There are no hidden cameras. He doesn't know who I am.

"Sorry." I hang up the phone and run out of the library, shocked by my brazen stunt.

The next morning, Rikash shows up at the office unshaven and reeking of cigarettes and liquor. He has dark circles under his eyes and looks more dishevelled than I do.

"Rikash, what happened to you? You look horrible."

He walks into my office, shuts the door, rolls up in the fetal position on the floor, and begins to weep.

"What's wrong?"

"This is horrible, Catherine, horrible." I crouch down beside him, teetering in my heels as I rub his shoulder comfortingly.

"What? Please, tell me what happened!"

After rocking back and forth on the carpet for a few moments, he finally speaks.

"Can we go outside for a bit? I need a smoke."

We leave the office without letting anyone know where we're going. With the way I feel and he looks, they can just deal with it. He lights up, offers me a cigarette, and I accept. He puts his jacket on his shoulder and an arm around my waist.

"Dimitri stole my documentary."

"Oh my god, why? What happened?"

"We were out on Saturday night at some club and I guess Dimitri got jealous that I was talking to someone else. You know me, I'm an extrovert; I enjoy being the life and soul of every party. I don't think he could handle being with someone so outgoing. Anyway, we went back to my place, had a big fight, and he stole my laptop and my camera while

I was sleeping. My laptop had all the rough cuts from my film on it."

"Rikash, I'm sorry." My heart sinks at the news.

"And like a total idiot, I was keeping the backup copies in my camera bag. I wasted the last year and a half of my life making this film. I'm such a bloody fool."

"I can't believe it. Did you call the police?"

"No, not yet."

"Why not?"

He lifts his shoulders. "I guess I'm still hoping he might come back."

"Rikash, he stole your laptop. You think that he's actually going to come back?"

"I don't know. I'm a bit messed up at the moment." His eyes well up again. "And my poor brother, he'll be crushed. I was hoping to sell the rights to my film to help him get through school. My parents can't help out, they don't have a dime."

"I can lend you some money."

"Dah-ling, that's very kind, but I could never."

"Come on, it would be a loan. You can pay me back later."

"Thank you, but I have some pride, you know. I have lots of friends in Mumbai, maybe I'll live with them for a bit while I figure things out. Perhaps moving back is the best option."

"Rikash, I don't want you to go. I'll be lost without you." I look at him and tears start rolling down my cheeks. "You're not the only one who was taken for a ride, *mon ami.*"

He eyes become as big as saucers. "What do you mean?"

"Jeffrey. He used me, Rikash. He's a scumbag and a thief."

"What?"

"He asked me to help him steal from his company."

"But why? Isn't he making enough money as it is?"

"He's greedy. For some people, it's never enough."

He stops in the middle of the sidewalk to put his arms around me and I start to cry.

"I'm so sorry, sweetie. You should turn him in. He deserves it, the bastard."

"I don't know what to do about it."

"Hitchcock once said that revenge is sweet and not fattening. I think that the master of suspense might be on to something, don't you think?"

A million images flash through my mind.

"You just gave me a great idea." I bow my head as if in worship. "You're *my* master now."

❖

"Hi, Jeffrey, I thought things through over the weekend and I've decided to play ball. But only if you do me a small favour."

Faking pleasantries with Jeffrey is impossible right now, but I need to make sure I've got everything documented. I put him on speakerphone and turn on the Dictaphone.

"Sure, baby, whatever it is, you got it."

"A good friend's brother is studying to become a software engineer in India and desperately needs a job to pay for his tuition. Can Browser hire him?"

"Absolutely. We're always on the lookout for fresh talent. Consider it done."

"Perfect. So, you'll send me the written confirmation that I have your permission to transfer shares to your secretary and I'll have Sandy at the Swiss Bank set things up. You've got everything arranged so that you can transfer the money back to your personal account?"

"Of course. My accountant is the best—he does this sort of thing all the time. I'll sell the shares right away, and before you know it, you and I will be lounging on the beach in St. Barts, baby. It'll all be worth it."

I turn off the Dictaphone. Gotcha. The only place you'll be lounging, *connard*, is on a bunk bed in jail.

Chapter 35

I show up at the office the next morning wearing my new Dior suit with a red silk scarf tied around my neck, smelling of J'adore, and feeling invincible. I stride confidently by Bonnie's office holding my Edwards & White coffee mug, then stop dead in my tracks in front of her doorway.

"Good morning, Bonnie, how are you today?"

Startled, she looks up and lifts her reading glasses. She stares approvingly at my outfit.

"Hello, Catherine. I'm fine. How are you?"

"Just fabulous."

I'm not going to let some swindling conman throw me off my game or destroy my self-confidence and career. I walk back to my office, settle into my chair, and call Rikash.

"Shut the door. How are you feeling?"

"Terrible. I haven't slept in almost a week."

"That makes two of us. I've got some good news for a change. Your brother has just been hired by Browser as a software developer."

"What? But he hasn't even started school yet."

"Doesn't matter. I want you to phone him immediately and tell him that someone from Swiss Bank here in New York is waiting for his call. He needs to open an account as soon as possible. Can you take care of that for me?"

"Open an account at Swiss Bank. But why?"

"Don't ask any questions, just do it."

"I hope you're not engaging in anything risky for my sake. I don't want to jeopardize my good karma; god knows it's been damaged over the years and I've been desperately trying to get it back on track."

"Don't worry, your karma is totally safe. Just call your brother and tell him to call Sandy Mercer at Swiss Bank. His number is in our client directory."

"Okay, okay. I'll do it. You're looking very confident

in a badass kind of way today." He arches his eyebrows quizzically.

"Yes, confident that things will be put right. The account needs to be opened by noon tomorrow, so tell your brother to phone right away. We'll also need to fax him some documentation, so tell him to find a fax machine."

I take a large swig of coffee before I pick up the phone to call the Swiss Bank account manager.

"Hey, Sandy, ready for the big day tomorrow?"

"Yeah, man, it'll be crazy. This IPO is real hot."

"Listen, I have a new name to add to the list of participants in the international directed share program. Jeff Richardson asked me to add a software developer from India."

"Another one of those Indian whiz kids, huh?"

"Exactly."

"Okay, what's his name?"

"Nitesh Chandra."

"Got it. Do you have an account number here at the bank for me?"

"No. Not yet. He'll be calling you later today to handle that; he's to receive four hundred shares."

"Those guys are really raking it in, aren't they?"

"They sure are. Oh, and Sandy, before I forget, did you get the request I forwarded from Jeffrey Richardson?"

"Yup, got it right here. Eight thousand shares to an account held by one of the secretarial staffers. She must be some secretary . . ."

"I'm afraid the account information is incorrect—the company has requested that those shares be equally allocated among all of the Browser support staff instead."

"Really?"

"Yes, they're being very generous. You're not questioning my authority now, are you?"

"No, ma'am, of course not. You're the boss."

"Sandy, you're my main man on this deal, so don't let me down."

"Have I ever let you down?"

"Never."

"Good. Please remind your client of that. I'm looking forward to getting a nice bonus this year."

"Don't worry; I'll definitely let him know."

❦

On the morning of the Browser IPO, I sit in our boardroom waiting for the financial news to appear on television. A female news anchor comes on shortly after the NASDAQ opening to report that the shares have skyrocketed to $105 from the opening price of $23 per share. Given the number of shares Jeffrey owns, he's now worth more than $100 million on paper.

I call Rikash in. "Tell your brother to sell his shares. He'll be making a nice little profit."

"Thank you so much for doing this. You have no idea how much this will help us out. Will this get you into any trouble?"

"No."

"What about Jeffrey. Will he find out?"

"Doesn't matter. Right now he's probably too busy drooling over the huge pile of cash he just made."

"You're my Lakshmi, goddess of good fortune."

As Rikash gives me a hug and rushes out, I see Maria standing outside the door, eavesdropping.

Great. Blabbermouth will definitely love this one. Knowing it would come in handy one day, I had made copies of Maria and Roxanne's incriminating boardroom conversation. I wait until she's gone for lunch and then leave the miniature cassette on her desk with a note:

> *Dear Maria,*
> *Let's not get nasty, shall we? We would both have a*
> *lot to lose.*
> *Catherine*

I walk past her desk later that morning and she nods humbly to acknowledge our implicit pact.

"Congratulations, Catherine. I heard the Browser IPO went very smoothly. Too bad you couldn't participate in the offering; I heard that the stock went above a hundred dollars this morning," Scott comments as we both make our way to the elevators to grab lunch.

"I'm just glad it's over so I can dig into new challenges."

He stares at me with a look of surprise. "Are you heading out to the Hamptons this weekend?"

"No. I'm heading to another beach for three days. I've decided to take Friday off. I hope you won't mind."

"Of course not. Going anywhere exciting?"

"Yes, Anguilla."

Chapter 36

"Guess who called while you were baking your tushy in the tropics?"

"Hmm, let me guess, Mr. Hyde?"

"How d'you know?"

"Lucky guess."

I knew Jeffrey would try to reach me in a fit of rage after he found out that the Browser shares were transferred to a group of secretaries. I had received several nasty emails during the weekend that I desperately tried to ignore. After I read the last one, I wrote a precise script for Rikash to follow when Jeffrey called for me at the office. I press for details.

"What did he say?"

"He screamed that it was an emergency and he needed to talk to you. When I told him you were unreachable, he threatened to call Scott and tell him you committed malpractice."

"How did you respond?"

"Exactly how you said I should. I told him that you had taped your last phone conversation about the share transfer and that you would notify the SEC immediately if he did anything to harm your career. He told me to fuck off and then hung up."

I'm convinced that if he found out, Scott would take my side and turn Jeffrey in to the regulatory authorities, but I'm relieved that I don't have to spill the private details of our relationship. It's bad enough that Jeffrey's illegal request has caused me to put into question my professional judgment. I don't need to go through the painful exercise of exposing the personal side of this dreadful incident.

"Thanks for taking that nasty call, Rikash. You're a star."

Although I'm playing it cool, my heart sinks. It's disheartening to think that my relationship with Jeffrey went from pure bliss to vile threats so rapidly. I want to fly back to Anguilla and bury my head in the sand.

"The pleasure was all mine, believe me. I can't stand his guts. So how was the jaunt to the Caribbean? Any fun?"

"Fun isn't exactly the right word, but it was relaxing. I slept for more than twenty-four hours straight and in between sobbing sessions I got a massage, a seaweed wrap, and a facial. Let's just say that now I feel closer to being alive than dead."

"It's the beginning of the healing process. It means you're on track. It's all good from now on."

"How about you? How's your healing coming along?"

"Very nicely." He bats his long eyelashes. "I'm doing it the sexual way."

"Ms. Lambert, we're waiting for you in conference room 22J," a squeaky voice resonates from my speakerphone. The firm's recruiting coordinator, Joan Biltmore, is a petite woman with a steely determination and the demeanour of an army general. She had asked that I help interview law students for the firm's summer associate program—and now I'm regretting that I agreed. I'm in no mood to convince anybody to join the rat race in this loony bin.

At a pre-interview meeting for senior associates and junior partners, Joan provided us with the firm's guidelines for the interview process. "We're looking for a diversity of personalities who will contribute to the firm's continued success. Individuals with different cultural backgrounds and strong convictions who share our core values."

It was kind of unbelievable. Individuals with different cultural backgrounds? There are no more than 10 African-American lawyers in the New York office out of 420; perhaps she was referring to employment opportunities in the mailroom or the kitchen?

I arrive in the conference room as Joan is discussing the merits of selling one's soul to the firm. "We take a unique approach to forming our associates. Everyone gets lots of hands-on experience, all our attorneys are level-headed individuals who lead well-rounded lives, and the firm doesn't put a strong focus on billable hours, but rather on the quality of the work environment."

Pfff! N'importe quoi!

"Hello, Catherine, I was just explaining to Jonathan what makes Edwards and White such a special place to work."

"Ah, perfect timing." I flash my most winsome smile to make Jonathan feel all warm and tingly.

"Catherine is a senior associate in the corporate group. She also speaks French and worked in our Paris office before joining us. I'll give the two of you a moment to chat in private."

"Corporate? That's what I'd like to specialize in one day," he gushes.

Given the state of my nerves, I'm dying to tell him to just forget about it and run for his life while there's still time, but I bite my tongue.

"Great! Please tell me about yourself," I ask, feigning undivided attention while ruminating about the three hundred unopened email and phone messages that piled up while I was away for the weekend.

He goes on about his academic achievements until my eyes glaze over. I want to scream, Gimme a break and get over yourself, honey, you haven't even graduated yet! Being an editor at the *Yale Law Review* only qualifies you to return Bonnie's dry cleaning. But now that I think of it, I'm sure he'll fit right into this narcissistic paradise.

"So, Jonathan, why a big law firm?"

"For the challenging work and excellent training opportunities."

"Do you have any extracurricular activities? Favourite sports?" I ask, trying to avoid plaguing him with substantive legal questions.

"I enjoy activities and sports that have a strong team-building component. I guess that's because I'm such a team player. I also enjoy activities that focus on endurance, strength of character, and loyalty."

"Is there anything else that interests you?"

"I *do* enjoy French wine and French women."

"Is that right? You have fine taste, Jonathan." His response reminds me of the crap Jeffrey fed me to pull the wool over my eyes, and I want to jump across the boardroom table and go straight for his jugular.

"But flattery can backfire sometimes, you better be careful. I'm afraid that it takes more than that to get a job here."

"I like to think of it as a career-advancing move."

"Well then, I wish you the best of luck in the advancement of your career because you're definitely going to need it."

I excuse myself—Jonathan is a total bullshit *artiste* and

I'm convinced that the firm will make him an offer despite what I have to say about the matter. I signal for Joan to go back in to finish this façade of an interview, make my way back to my office, shut the door, and, for the first time ever at work, start to fully weep.

I feel so empty. When will this feeling go away?

Chapter 37

"So Jeffrey finally stopped trying to reach me."

"It took him long enough, didn't it?" Lisa comments after taking a final bite from her spicy chicken at Tartine in the West Village. "How did you manage that?"

"I sent him an email that must've got to him; I told him that he was lucky that I hadn't turned him in after he asked me to be accomplice in his grand scheme and told him that I hadn't made a final decision as to whether I would notify the SEC."

"Will you? If you do notify the SEC, the information

416

will become public and everyone at the firm will know about it straight away."

"I know, but the last thing the corporate world needs is another thief running a public company. I've prepared a letter addressed to the SEC's director of regulatory investigations outlining the facts, sealed it, and put it 'in escrow' in my desk drawer until I feel ready to mail it."

It feels awful to say it out loud. I still have major trouble coming to terms with the fact that I fell into the arms of a fraudster.

"You're absolutely right, Catherine. I'm so proud of you."

The waitress arrives at our table with two slices of pie. "The two gentlemen sitting by the window are offering you dessert. How lucky are you ladies?"

Lisa waves at them in thanks.

"How sweet. Maybe we can ask them to join us?" she asks keenly.

"Sorry, Lisa, but I'm not really in the mood. In actual fact, there's almost nothing I'd like less."

"I understand. I'm glad you're going to that firm retreat in California. It will do you some good to get out of town. And who knows, there might be some cute boys at your hotel for you to hook up with?"

I laugh—Lisa knows I've never understood the expression *hooking up*. It sounds so unromantic to me, probably because the first time she said it, I thought it had something to do with plugging in my toaster or cable TV. It's been a running joke ever since. She smiles, glad to see she's made me lighten up.

She reads my mind and continues. "How does that French saying go again? *Un de perdu . . .*"

"*Dix de retrouvés . . .* One lost, ten found. Frankly, I'm not looking for anyone."

"What if you didn't need to look? There's Antoine, for example . . ." She throws me an inquisitive look.

"What about him?"

"Aren't you a tad excited to see him?"

"Hmm. I guess. He's doing really well for himself apparently."

"You brushed him off pretty quickly. I think he sounds like a great guy." She winks mischievously.

"I'm definitely not going there Lisa. It's bad enough I crossed the line with a firm client. Like I said, I'm not in the mood for men these days."

"Your call. Just try to enjoy yourself. I'm sure it will be a blast!"

"Yeah, like the kind of blast you get from a major propane explosion."

"Lighten up, *mademoiselle!* At least the weather will be great. You'll come back totally revitalized."

"I hope so. I need something good to happen in my life right now."

Two in the morning is probably not the greatest time to be packing for a corporate trip; your brain is a bit fuzzy and your fashion judgment tends to go out the window. A bit exhausted from a day of non-stop meetings, I throw two pairs of Havaianas flip-flops and two Eres bikinis in my suitcase (perfect for paintball *non*?). But what to bring for business meetings and dinners? I sit on my bed for a moment, posing like Rodin's *The Thinker*. I get an idea for a fabulous outfit: I dig deep into my closet to find the perfect skirt and shuffle about for at least half an hour before I remember that the lower part of my outfit is being dry cleaned. *Merde!* I try to find a different outfit, put some items together, but nothing is quite as wonderful as the outfit I had originally thought of. Maybe I could break and enter Madame Paulette's in the middle of the night to get my skirt back? I start pulling out and trying on everything in my closet until my apartment looks like it's been ransacked, but nothing really works. I am now seriously hyperventilating since Harry Traum is picking me up in less than two hours to take me to the airport. *Calm down, Catherine, take a deep breath. Ahhh!* Quite literally, everything is sending me over the edge these days. After I calm my jittery nerves, I pick out a light pink vintage leather jacket, a pair of Acne jeans, T-shirts, my new Dior suit (I never leave home without it), a black off-the-shoulder evening dress, Lanvin stilettos, workout clothes and two Diane von Furstenberg wrap dresses. I throw a few vintage necklaces and my J. Crew clutch on the pile and voila, I'm ready to go. *Ouf!*

At five sharp, Harry Traum's limo pulls up in front of my building. Most of my colleagues had flown out yesterday to get a game of golf in before the official firm meetings. My involvement with an overseas file had "forced" me to postpone my trip by one day and as an unexpected side effect had made Harry Traum my travel companion. His driver meets me in the lobby to help with my luggage. Inside the car, I fumble to make career-appropriate conversation despite my incapacity to speak English properly this early in the morning.

"The firm seems to be doing very well these days. We're quite busy in the corporate department. How are things in litigation?"

"I'm always busy. You wouldn't believe the number of corporate thieves there are out there."

Yes sir, I do believe it. I could've added another thief to the long list but decided to settle the score myself instead.

"I've heard some good things about your work, Catherine. Apparently, you're a smart cookie."

Well, this is nice to hear first thing in the morning. I try to restrain a beaming smile.

"Thank you, I've been working very hard. I hope it pays off."

"I may have a proposition for you," he says with an intense gaze.

Uh-oh. That's not so nice . . . A proposition? If he makes a come-on, I will die. Or Bonnie will kill me first.

"Um, what kind of proposition?"

"This is highly confidential, so keep it to yourself. A few senior partners and I are about to leave and start our own firm and I'd like you to join us . . . as a junior partner."

I stare back at him with my eyes popping out of their sockets. I can't believe I'm being offered a partnership position! All six and a half years of gruelling hard work flash before my eyes. Harry continues to talk about the kind of files I'd work on (interesting), the pay (very interesting), and my stake in the new firm (very, very interesting). But after my initial excitement wears off, I notice a gnawing feeling in my stomach. Something's wrong, but I'm not sure what. I gaze out onto the highway trying to focus my thoughts as he continues to speak. This could mean more money, prestige, and getting out from under Bonnie's iron grip. But in the weeks after the Browser debacle, I've been feeling differently about my career. Do I really want to continue working these crazy hours and cater to the endless and often impossible demands of clients and those more senior in the food chain?

"We're opening up a white-collar crime defence boutique and your experience would complement that of the litigators."

"I'm very flattered by your offer, Mr. Traum, but I'm not sure I'm ready to make a move yet. Can you give me some time to think about it?"

He stares at me with a look of bewilderment.

"You're not telling me you're loyal to that firm, are you? With a bunch of assholes running the place? Do you think for a second they would be loyal to you? You're just a cog in a well-oiled wheel, my dear. Just make sure you remember that."

His words actually send shivers down my spine. I'm not naïve enough to think that associates like me aren't dispensable. But given the amount of effort I've put in and my commitment to the firm, I guess I do expect a certain degree of recognition in return.

"I'll remember that, thanks."

"Take as much time as you need, Catherine," he says sombrely.

As he looks out the tinted window, a pained expression comes over his tired features.

"I've worked my ass off for the last thirty years and what do I get in return? Zilch. Year after year, I brought in major clients, won cases that everyone wrote off as lost in advance, rewrote the law in the Court of Appeal and in the Supreme Court, and what for? They treat me like I'm some beat-up old car ready to be parked in the used lot."

Unsure if I should say anything, I listen in shocked silence. Despite his rough exterior and tough-guy antics, Harry looks like a wounded puppy.

"They don't appreciate what I've done for them. I went

through two triple-bypass heart surgeries because of those jerks. I've been the biggest rainmaker in the history of the firm and now they're trying to push me out. Can you believe it?" He stares at me incredulously. "What a load of crap, those ungrateful sons of bitches. You know what, they can go fuck themselves. And you know what the saddest part of it is? I'll take most of my clients with me and make more money on my own. A bunch of backward-thinking, short-sighted, greedy monkeys. That's what they are, a bunch of fucking monkeys."

I feel awful for him. He looks like a fallen rock star whose song is no longer being played on the radio. Why doesn't this sixty-year-old man with millions in the bank and decades of hard work behind him look forward to relaxing on the back nine? Despite his immense success, his enviable reputation, and all his money, he looks miserable. It occurs to me that he may have lost his temper recently not because of his divorce but because of the pressure of being pushed out of the firm. It crystallizes a worry that's been brewing inside me—I don't know if I want this.

We arrive at the airport and check our luggage in the executive-class line up.

"I've upgraded you, Catherine. You'll be sitting with me in first class."

Wonderful, my chances of resting after a sleepless night are now nil.

"You don't have to do that, I can sit in economy. I'm sure you have lots of work to do and I wouldn't want to be a bother."

"No, no bother at all. I have thousands of these upgrades and I never use them. And besides, you can help me prepare my speech."

"Your speech?"

"I've been asked to give a speech at the opening dinner tomorrow night."

We take our seats at the front of the plane. Harry sets his litigator bag overflowing with briefs and case law at his knees, pulls out a manila folder, and begins to voraciously read between aggressive sips of coffee. Staring at him, I realize that he's a human working machine and that this is what's expected of firm partners: work and more work. I can almost hear my inner Rikash: *Are you sure you want to become a partner? It's like climbing to the top of Mount Everest in your monokini, honey: it gets real cold at the top. The problem with the rat race is that even if you win, you're still a rat. And if you do make it to the big time, please remember that pigs get fat, but hogs get slaughtered.*

The fact that Harry's about to be sent to the slaughter-house is bringing Rikash's comments home.

Given his relentless work ethic, I feel slightly embar-rassed to pull out the *Vogue* from my handbag, so I decide to flip through the airline magazine instead.

"I know it was you who hung up on me in the library, Catherine," he blurts out. "I recognized that French accent of yours."

Oh god. As the pilot makes his announcement about our impending departure, I suddenly feel queasy. I grab a tissue from my bag and hold it tightly over my mouth. Please god, no, not now. I start thinking of anything that might help keep my mind off this nauseating feeling in my stomach: that great Yves Saint Laurent jacket I spotted at Bergdorf's, the fresh Provence air I breathe when visiting my mother, and the taste of ginger ale on my lips.

"Don't worry, kiddo, I'm not upset about it," he says after taking another sip of his coffee. "I think what you did was pretty gutsy. I was actually very impressed. You've got to learn to protect yourself in law. That's partly why I'm offer-ing you a job."

The engine makes its final roar and the plane moves for-ward on the runway. I turn to look out the window, hoping that it will help my queasiness, and to my dismay, I barf all over myself and Harry. Even his manila folder isn't spared. The flight attendant rushes to my rescue with a warm cloth and crushed coffee beans to alleviate the smell.

"I'm so sorry, Mr. Traum. I don't know what came over me," I say, wiping his folder.

"Don't worry about it, dear, my four-year-old grand-daughter does this all the time."

Completely mortified, I stand up from my seat and hurry to the lavatory. Oh my god, I can't believe I just threw up on a senior partner who knows that I hung up on him. *Ah, merde!* After twenty minutes of splashing cold water on my face, I decide to go back to my seat. Harry seems unbothered by my upset stomach and is deeply engrossed in his speech.

I turn to catch a glimpse of the man sitting across the aisle. He has his *Maxim* magazine folded so that no one can see the big-breasted babe on the cover. He's hold-ing his reading glasses over the tip of his nose as if he's actually reading *The Economist* while staring at my legs. I immediately pull out a copy of the *New York Law Jour-nal* to make sure he has absolutely no interest in engaging in conversation and put in my iPod earphones. When we arrive in San Diego six hours later, I feel disgusting and wretched; my clothes are stained and reek of throw up, my hair is a mess, and my face is white as a sheet.

Outside the airport, dozens of buses with banners bearing the words *Edwards & White* written in big bold letters wait for us at the arrivals gate. Lawyers from all over the globe are being reunited for team-building exercises.

"Catherine, you may want to sit at the front in case you need to throw up again," Harry says as soon as we set foot on the bus, his loud voice booming over the crowd.

Great. More than a thousand lawyers will soon find out I threw up all over Harry Traum. I'll never live this one down. *Ever.*

The next morning, after all my colleagues have taken turns making fun of me, we make our way by bus to a large conference centre for our exercises. Looking around, I wonder whether Harry has made any offers to other lawyers in our group.

About halfway there, Nathan cracks open a can of beer.

"Isn't it a bit early to start drinking?"

"Nah. Are you kidding? This is just the right time of day."

It's the first time I've seen Nathan let his hair down and it's kind of endearing. He's obviously letting off steam from a high-pressure practice and the upcoming stress of becoming a father.

"We're competing with Clifford Chance and Baker Mackenzie for first place in the international rankings," Scott says to Nathan, sharing his bench seat.

"Is that right?" Nathan replies, visibly uninterested, while ogling a young female lawyer from the Prague office sitting across the aisle from him.

"This retreat will be great to get everybody psyched up so we can crush them next year."

"Yeah, hmm. Wonderful idea," Nathan concurs, still staring at the eastern European beauty.

A few minutes later, I notice two stunning, well-dressed associates with British accents sitting a few rows behind us. God, I need to change the topic, *fast*.

I stare at one of the two men; he is impeccably dressed, has tousled hair, and deep, penetrating green eyes. When he catches me staring, he walks over and takes a seat in front of us.

"Hello, I'm James. Which office are you from?"

"I started in Paris, but I work in New York now."

"Lucky you." He smiles and reveals dimples the size of the Grand Canyon.

"How about you? London, I assume?"

"Yes. You're very perceptive," he adds jokingly. "I like that in a woman."

My face begins to redden.

"Welcome to the United States."

"Thanks, I'm very happy to be here. So I hear there's a big gala this evening."

"Yes, I believe so," I add nonchalantly.

Who am I kidding? Of course there's a big to-do tonight. I puked all over the evening's opening remarks.

"Could I have the pleasure of your company for dinner?" the Brit asks, now in major flirting mode.

Listening to our conversation, Scott chimes in.

"We'd love to have you at our table tonight."

You can say that again. We'd love to have you *period*. Maybe Lisa was right about finding someone here to take my mind off Jeffrey.

We arrive at the conference centre, where Antoine is waiting in line to take his seat. He is dressed in a sharp khaki linen suit with a blue checked shirt and is tie-less. He even has a bit of a tan that makes him look a lot healthier than when I last saw him. He walks over as soon as he sees me and I feel a slight pinch in my stomach, given that our last conversation was more than heated.

"Hello, Catherine, how are you?" His friendly tone makes me relax.

"Antoine! I didn't think you would make it. I heard that you're spearheading a major privatization for the French government."

"Things have slowed down a bit, thank god . . ."

He smiles warmly and my eyes are drawn to his light blue Hermès pocket scarf, his graceful gestures, and his broad smile. It's clear that the move to Paris has been good to him.

"It's taking a bit longer than expected to get the trans-action started."

"Enjoying Paris, I hope?"

"Absolutely. Everyone in the office really misses you."

"Really?"

I'm thrilled. Ever since I moved to New York, it's been difficult staying in touch with my former colleagues and I thought that they might have forgotten about me.

"Are you attending the dinner tonight?"

"Mais oui."

"I'll see you there. I'm sitting at your table. Scott saved me a seat." He winks.

I've changed my mind; this corporate retreat is going to be highly enjoyable after all.

"I can't believe you asked him to sit at our table," Bonnie whispers loudly to Scott with pursed red lips. "He doesn't work with us anymore. He should be sitting at the Paris table." She's clutching her evening bag so tightly it looks like a leather ball.

"What's the big deal? He did a tremendous amount of work for me and I happen to like the guy," he shoots back.

She turns away and doesn't respond. It's obvious that Scott failed to consult with her before inviting Antoine to join us. I just hope this doesn't turn into World War III at our table.

"Hello, Catherine." James stands next to our table looking dashing in a tailored suit and light pink tie.

"Ah yes, hello, James."

"Is this seat taken?" he asks, pointing at the empty seat next to me.

"No, please go ahead."

"I wouldn't want to risk taking a seat from a New Yorker. Could get my head chewed off," he says, positioning his serviette on his lap.

"I'm not a native New Yorker. I'm French, remember?"

"Ah, yes. Sorry. A French woman, just my luck."

We engage in a long conversation under the watchful gaze of my office colleagues. Antoine is now sitting across the table next to Bonnie, who has exaggeratedly moved her chair away from his and completely turned her back to him while talking to Scott. As soon as Nathan finishes his glass, he gives me the thumbs-up while signalling for the waitress to bring more wine. As she comes closer to the table, he whispers something in her ear and she stares back at him, flushed. He puts his arm on the small of her her back as she refills his glass for the fourth time. This evening is about to get *very* interesting.

After I've been speaking with James for about twenty minutes, Antoine interrupts our conversation.

"Catherine, can you please introduce your guest? I don't believe we've met."

"Of course, sorry about that. Everyone, this is James from the London office. He specializes in structured finance."

"*Shtructured finanche?*" Nathan remarks. "I was in the *shtructured finanche* department at my last firm. That's really b-o-r-i-n-g stuff. I had to drink about twenty coffees a day just to stay awake. You couldn't pay me enough money to do that type of work again."

"I don't see anyone waiting in line to make you any offers, Nathan. James, how many lawyers are in your office these days?" Scott asks, attempting to steer the conversation in a different direction.

"Even if I did receive an offer, I wouldn't accept it. I hated it," Nathan says, his voice getting increasingly louder. "To top it all off, I worked for the biggest asshole on the island of Manhattan. *Josh Green,* a loser with a capital L."

"Nathan, he's hardly a loser," Antoine replies politely. "He's the top-ranked American lawyer in the field."

"Yeah? Well he's also the top jerk in America."

Scott stands from his chair and signals to Nathan to follow him. Poor Nathan is about to have a little chat.

"Please excuse my colleague. He's had a bit too much to drink today."

"Oh, no worries. I didn't take it personally. Besides, he's quite right. I'd much rather be a DJ in a nightclub, but my parents would probably disown me."

After Scott and Nathan leave the table, Bonnie chimes in. "Can you believe Nathan's behaviour?"

"It's no big deal. I mean, this is only an internal dinner," Antoine responds.

"No big deal? You've got to be kidding. Did you hear what he said? We're damn lucky it's only an internal dinner. He should be fired."

"You can't be serious. He's the top billing associate in the office and his wife is expecting. We can't do that," I chime in.

"What do you mean by *we*, Catherine? I'm afraid you're not involved in any decision-making for the department."

"Okay, then *you* shouldn't do it. He's had too much to drink. It's not the end of the world."

"Do you think I'm going to follow employment recommendations made by someone who flaunts herself half-naked at low-brow parties in the Hamptons?"

The tension at our table is so palpable that it could be cut with a knife. I think long and hard before responding to her nonsense but having Harry's offer in my back pocket gives me the courage to push back.

"Being half-naked at a Hamptons party is more appropriate than half-naked at client meetings, don't you think?"

Antoine and James turn my way, dumbstruck. I smile

back triumphantly at Bonnie, whose face is now the same colour as the soles on her Louboutin sandals. She tries to change the subject by bringing up an important acquistion she's working on.

After my blood pressure returns to normal, I feel a bit remorseful for snapping at Bonnie. Despite her ludicrous behaviour, I know she's fought against sexism and the old boys' club rules to get to where she is today. What woman can silently tolerate years of relentless backstabbing, aggression, and raw competitiveness without losing a bit of her soul in the process? And there's the old double standard: if a professional woman acts consistently with female stereotypes, she's considered a pushover. If she goes against it and is overly aggressive, she's considered a bitch. No matter how you cut it, it's a tough place to be.

After dessert, Scott has returned to the table but Nathan is nowhere to be seen. As we sip our coffee, Harry Traum addresses the heavily liquored crowd with his (puke-covered) opening remarks. Tipsy, I start to lean into James and I can feel him doing the same.

"Good evening, dear colleagues," Harry's voice silences the crowd. "We would like to begin this evening by saluting some great talent at our firm."

James stares into my eyes and I shake with that titillating feeling you get from flirting with an attractive stranger. The immediate physical attraction has every blood cell in my body racing furiously to my heart. My thoughts are interrupted by the applause of the crowd.

Harry calls a few senior partners to join him on stage to announce that they will hand out fifteen lifetime achievement awards. A projector provides pictures of each recipient as their names are called out. It takes me a few minutes to awaken from my lustful stupor to realize that, of the fifteen people recognized this evening, not one is a woman. I feel a profound sadness swell up inside at the thought of all those extremely dedicated and talented women who have contributed so much of their lives to the firm. These are women who made it to the top of a male-dominated firm, who've made innumerable personal sacrifices, who haven't had the benefit of having a "wife" taking care of them at home, and who are obviously invisible to those handing out the awards. What message is the firm sending to the women filling up half the room? Will this motivate them to put on a smile and a suit every morning and to fight one for the old boys? My body stiffens and my head spins. Will things be any different if I accept a job with Harry Traum? The reality is: probably not.

"Now, I'd like to take this opportunity to let all of you know that we've beat a new record on the number of deals we've taken on at the firm: a mind-blowing six billion dollars' worth of transactions. Congratulations to all of you for this incredible achievement."

A collective moan that borders on the orgasmic emanates from the crowd. Bonnie's face lights up as though this message was directed at her. She throws her head back, removes the shawl from her shoulders à la Dita Von Teese, and glances up at Harry with her naughtiest bedroom eyes.

"Before I begin with my speech, I just want to thank somebody in the room for altering the direction of my opening remarks." He presses his reading glasses on the tip of his nose. "I had the pleasure to share my flight to California with a woman from our office who was recently transferred from Paris."

Ah, non, c'est pas vrai! I feel more than two thousand eyeballs turn toward me and I want to die.

"Yes, many of you know Catherine Lambert from her outstanding work in corporate law, but what you don't know is that she hurled her breakfast all over my speech on our way down here and I was forced to rewrite what I was going to say."

Loud laughs come from the other side of the room. I recognize my former French boss's voice. *"Bravo, Catherine, bravo!"* Bonnie and Scott glare at me in disbelief. I want to crawl under the table.

"I have to say that she was a really good sport about the whole thing and, in my book, she gets extra points for that." A roar of applause fills the awkward silence and Antoine lifts his glass to me. James presses his hand on my shoulder and smiles broadly. "Well done, Catherine. Well done."

"Yes, before that little incident, I was going to talk about the firm's international rankings and so on," Harry continues sombrely. "But I decided to say a few words about the virtues of loyalty and unyielding dedication."

I take a large gulp of wine to numb my embarrassment. It then occurs to me that Harry's about to give his last Edwards speech and will probably take this opportunity to vent some of his frustrations publicly. This makes me smile.

After he discusses the values of loyalty and dedication in one's career, he starts to walk across the stage like an evangelistic preacher. "When I started out at the firm more than thirty years ago, it was a small litigation boutique with no more than a few dozen people. It was very collegial at the time." He pauses, smiling nostalgically. "Those were truly the golden days of the firm. We fought like hell in court and we were loyal to our clients and they really loved us for it. Then the firm grew and started opening offices left, right, and centre and we sort of lost that intimate feeling. To my chagrin, people started becoming selfish, worried about the size of their take-home profits . . ." His voice trails off and this generates an exchange of red-faced glances and a few dry coughs at the senior partners' table. "And then after a while this selfishness turned into flat-out greed." He looks like Michael Douglas in a scene from *Wall Street*. Just when I expect him to launch into Gordon Gekko's greed speech, he stops in his tracks in front of the managing partners' table and continues his spiel: "But the greed I'm referring to turned out to be a back-stabbing, screw-you-up-the-ass kinda greed." I turn to Bonnie and Scott, whose faces have now dropped into their chocolate cake; Bonnie has even covered up her cleavage with her shawl.

"This is why tonight I say to you, *Au revoir*, farewell, you buffoons! I'm leaving you to start my own firm and I'm taking about fifteen of your esteemed colleagues with me . . . So good luck with everything!" He exits the room dramatically and a sudden hush comes over the audience. Like in an episode of *Survivor*, everyone looks at their neighbour wondering who the fifteen "traitors" are. I pretend to play with my evening bag, trying to look innocent.

After ten minutes of dead silence, Bonnie rushes out of the room and Scott follows her. Antoine comes to sit on our side of the table.

"Wow, I guess that was unexpected!"

"Hmm, yeah," I respond. "But there's been talk about him leaving for a while, so I guess he just made it official."

"You can say that again!" James chimes in. We laugh a bit to break the tension.

"I can't believe he called the other managing partners a bunch of buffoons!" Antoine shakes his head.

"Oh, I've heard him call them worse things."

"Oh?" James retorts.

"Um, I was just kidding." Reluctant to violate Harry's trust after the whole divorce episode, I keep his monkey reference to myself.

"So, James, I see that you're in good company."

"I definitely am. There is a bright side to this evening after all."

"Catherine isn't only charming, she's a damn good lawyer too." Antoine smiles my way.

I look up at Antoine, shocked. I never thought he'd

compliment my legal skills. This whole evening feels surreal.

"Can I buy you guys a drink? I think we could use one, don't you think?" Antoine points toward the bar at the back of the room.

"I'd say so." James looks at me to confirm that I'm on board.

"Yes, it sounds like a great plan."

As soon as we get to the bar, Antoine starts talking business with James. "I recognize your name from the international file database. I think you're representing one of my clients."

They exchange client stories over dirty martinis while I mull over the job offer I received earlier from the anti–Gordon Gekko. Frankly, after what I've witnessed tonight, my inclination is to apply to become a J. Crew customer service representative. At least I'd get first dibs on their new collections and great discounts. I gently excuse myself to catch up with a few colleagues from Paris.

As I make my way back to my room around midnight, James is waiting for me in the lobby.

"How about a nightcap?" He raises an eyebrow.

I hesitate for a moment and look around the room before answering. Seriously, though, what do I have to lose?

"Okay."

He follows me to my room and we fumble through the mini-bar to find something to drink.

"White wine?"

"Perfect."

"Sorry about talking shop with Antoine tonight."

"Don't worry about it, that's his favourite topic of conversation."

"We didn't actually talk about work the whole time. He seemed more interested in discussing British bands. He's extremely knowledgeable about music."

"Really? I guess I tuned out at that point. I was thinking about Harry's dramatic exit."

"That was quite a scene, wasn't it?"

"Hmm." He pours wine into my glass and stares at me with puppy-dog eyes and approaches to kiss me tenderly. He looks as delicious as a box of Ladurée macaroons.

"You're very pretty, Catherine."

"Thank you, James."

He then kisses me on the back of my neck. I immediately

tense up because it reminds me of the mess I got myself into with Jeffrey.

"We probably shouldn't be doing this." I push him away.

"I want you so badly, Catherine. I won't tell anyone, I promise."

I quickly calculate the odds of either working with or seeing him in the near future. What to do?

The phone rings and I try to ignore it while James continues to kiss me. It rings again.

"Hello?"

"I hope it's not too late to call?"

"Nathan, is that you?"

James stares at me with a look of terror.

"Yes. I'm in deep shit, Catherine. Real deep."

"What happened? Where are you?"

"In the bar downstairs."

"I'll be there in five minutes."

"It's Nathan. He's at the hotel bar and sounds terrible. I'm sorry, James, how about getting together tomorrow?"

"Can't this wait until the morning?"

"No, I'm sorry. It can't."

A crestfallen James picks up his tie and heads for the door after kissing me on the cheek.

"Good night, Catherine."

"Good night."

I stumble into a pair of jeans and a T-shirt and make my way downstairs to meet Nathan at the hotel bar. He's sitting on a stool looking dishevelled and appears to be in the final stage of sobering up.

"Hey."

"Are you okay?"

"Not really."

"What happened?"

"I drank too much and embarrassed myself in front of Bonnie. She and Scott both gave me an earful. I'm sure I'll lose my job over this."

"I was there, it wasn't that bad. Besides I'm sure they have other things to worry about. Harry Traum gave an exit speech that left them with major battle scars."

"So I heard. I'm sorry I missed it."

"It was like being in a movie. I'm not sure what this will mean for the firm going forward."

"It means we all need to run for cover. But right now I might not have anywhere to run to. I just want to keep my job."

"Nathan, I think you need to get some help."

"I know I shouldn't be drinking like that, but I got carried away. It's just that I have so much pressure to deal with. I'm totally exhausted. And you don't know my wife. No matter what I do, it's never enough."

"What do you mean?"

"If it's not a co-op apartment, it's a house on the beach, and this and that and the other thing. She wants me to provide her with this lifestyle I can't afford. I'm just doing what I can to make sure I'm on partnership track."

"Why don't you tell her that she's putting too much pressure on you?"

"Every time I try to talk to her, she rips my head off. And if she's like that now, I can only imagine what it'll be like after the baby is born." He drops his head into his hands.

"You need to join a support group when you get back, otherwise you're just going to dig yourself further into a hole."

"If I'm still employed after tonight," he replies, his forehead still leaning against the bar.

"I'm sure this will be forgotten in the morning. You have the top billables in the office. Scott won't want to let you go."

"Let's hope so. Thanks, Catherine, you're making me feel a lot better. I should let you go to bed, you have team-building exercises to attend in the morning."

"So do you. See you first thing tomorrow."

"Yes, commander." He jumps off the bar stool and stands with his legs apart, military-style, in attention pose.

"Good night, soldier. At ease."

Chapter 38

Y*our passion is waiting for your courage to catch up.* I replay Madame Simona's words of wisdom in my mind on my way to the hotel gym. I figure that running on the treadmill will give me an opportunity to unwind and, more importantly, figure out what that passion is.

The elevator doors open on the gym floor and my heart stops: a large opalescent grey banner boasts, *Welcome Dior Executives.* A long, narrow table is setup with tiny silver Dior gift bags meticulously arranged along the wall. I cross the hallway to get to the gym in a Petit Bateau T-shirt and shorts and pass by numerous chic women milling about sipping tea. I wonder if Antoine knows anything about this executive gathering.

After about ten minutes of painfully trying to run on the treadmill and staring at George Michael's "Freedom '90" video on MTV, random thoughts flash through my mind: memories of my childhood, *Didn't know what I wanted to be . . .* ; my meeting with Simona, *there's something deep inside of me . . .* ; my cousin Françoise's enviable job at Chanel, *there's someone else I've got to be . . .* ; my doubts about whether I want to stay at Edwards, *take back your singing in the rain . . .* ; my reluctance to join Harry's new firm, *sometimes the clothes do not make the man . . .* ; and the way my face lit up when Antoine handed me the Dior file, *Now I'm gonna get myself happy . . .*

I'm suddenly hit with a lightning bolt: What if Pierre Le Furet, Dior's intellectual property director, is here? I could find out if he has a position available in his department! Without thinking it through any further, I jump off the treadmill, throw a towel over my shoulders, and sprint back to the elevators.

Back in my room, I take the quickest shower ever, throw on my Dior suit, a long rope of pearls, and some heels, quickly apply some makeup and a dash of J'adore for good luck, and head back out the door. I fetch my laptop and print my resumé in the hotel business centre, then slide it into an envelope. I head back to the floor where the Dior meeting is being held and catch a group of women trickling out of the conference room.

"Excuse me, is Pierre Le Furet here by any chance?" I ask the first woman who crosses my path.

"No, Pierre isn't here, I'm afraid. Why do you ask?"

"I have an important document for him," I respond, visibly crushed.

"His boss is here. Sandrine Cordier runs the legal department. You could hand it to her instead."

Oh, fantastique! That means I could go straight to the top without worrying about dealing with Antoine's client, who could blow my cover.

"Your best bet is to find out her room number. But you better hurry, our meetings are over."

I rush to the hotel lobby, bumping into a few lawyers from the firm in the elevators on my way down.

"Looking very chic there, Catherine. Going anywhere special?"

"I sure am," I reply, running out of the elevator.

I approach the concierge desk and wait impatiently for the man to notice me.

"Can I please have the room number for Sandrine Cordier?"

"I'm sorry, miss. We cannot give out this information, but you can call the hotel operator, who will connect you to her room."

I pick up the hotel house phone in the lobby under the quizzical gaze of my colleagues.

"Madame Cordier?"

"Yes."

"*Bonjour*, Madame Cordier, my name is Catherine Lambert. I'm a lawyer staying at this hotel and I noticed that Dior is holding executive meetings here. I was wondering if I could hand you a copy of my resumé? I have relevant experience that could interest you."

Woody Allen says that eighty percent of success is just showing up; I say that ninety percent of success is simply being bold and asking for what you want.

"I'm very tired right now, Catherine," she replies after a long, awkward silence. "Why don't you meet me in my room around nine tomorrow morning so that we can talk? I'm in room two zero nine."

"That would be perfect."

I get back to my room and dive on the bed, thrilled with my feat of tracking down Dior's general counsel. I have visions of working with the world's greatest couturiers. After a few moments of daydreaming, my mood swiftly changes and I start having doubts. Am I ready to throw in the towel on private practice at this point in my career? I've invested so much energy getting ahead at the firm. And I need to tread carefully: Dior is an important client and if my plan backfires, I could find myself answering the phones, "This is Catherine, thank you for calling J. Crew." Despite my earlier inclination, I don't really relish the thought.

I try Lisa to get her opinion, but I get her voicemail so I pick up my messages instead. Hearing my colleagues' voices brings me back to reality.

"Hi, it's Nathan. Thanks again for your support yesterday. Just spoke to Scott and I still have a job. See ya later."

"Hello, Catherine, it's Antoine. Are you free for dinner tomorrow night? There's nothing on the retreat schedule and I have something important to discuss with you."

Curious about his message, I return Antoine's call and accept his dinner invitation. After all, I better remain on his good side in case I need a reference for Dior.

The next morning, I arrive at Sandrine's room at 8:56 with my resumé in hand. A pile of Louis Vuitton luggage is stacked by her door. I take a peek inside. The room is deserted.

"She left," the porter says while unsuccessfully attempting to fit all the suitcases on a trolley.

"Where did she go?"

"The airport."

"Did she leave any messages?"

"Not with me, she didn't. Maybe you can catch her downstairs. She only left a few minutes ago."

I rush down to the lobby in my stilettos and catch a glimpse of a woman in a beige trench coat carrying this season's black patent Dior bag getting into a Town Car. She signals the driver to move forward while talking on her cell phone.

I stand on the sidewalk out of breath and crushed. How could she forget our meeting? I sulk back to my room and try not to feel disappointed. Sandrine Cordier is dealing with one persistent lady.

❧

Later that night, I meet Antoine in the hotel lobby. He's wearing a crisp white linen shirt with designer jeans and his signature Vetiver cologne. His scent transports me back to our first meeting in New York.

"Where are we having dinner?"

"I made reservations at a new Italian restaurant downtown. You like pasta, I hope?"

"Love it!"

We sit at opposite ends of the cab's back seat and he keeps shooting me strange looks. Does he know what I've been up to?

The restaurant is a quaint trattoria on a quiet, leafy street. We're directed to a table in a corner with a traditional red-and-white-checkered tablecloth.

"This is a great spot. How did you find it?"

"I asked the concierge at the hotel. He told me that it's one of the best places in town."

Best places in town? I wonder why Antoine would take me to such an upscale restaurant. Is he wining and dining me so that I'll volunteer to work on his privatization?

Before we're handed the menus, Antoine signals the waiter to come to our table.

"Please bring your best bottle of champagne."

I guessed wrong; he wouldn't order champagne to get me to work for him. He usually makes those demands by email late on Friday night when I'm trying to unwind.

"Best bottle? Are we celebrating something?"

"As a matter of fact, we are." He smiles warmly. I'm surprised by the relaxed tone of his voice; he seems uncharacteristically laid-back; it must be the fresh California air.

"Really?"

"I just found out that I've been made a partner."

This comes as no surprise, I knew he would make it. Unlike me, Antoine seemed to have partnership tattooed on his heart.

"Congratulations! That's great news. I'm so happy for you!" I lift my flute.

"Thanks. It hasn't come easily." He meets me halfway and we clink our glasses.

"I know. Everyone knew you would get it."

"You never really know for sure until it's set in stone."

Antoine's relaxed demeanour allows me to open up. "True enough. I don't think I have it in me, to be quite honest."

"Sure you do."

"Not the willingness to make the sacrifices that you've made. You practically live at the office and I don't think I can go on much longer working those gruelling hours."

"It takes its toll, doesn't it?"

"It does. And I don't want to wake up ten years from now with work being the only important thing in my life."

Antoine stares down at his serviette while playing with his fork. I'm such an idiot.

"Oh god, I put my foot in it. I didn't mean you. I'm just talking about me and my life."

"No. No. You're right, Catherine. You're totally right."

And it dawns on me. I *am* right; I can't imagine spending every waking moment of the next fifteen years of my life chasing billable hours and new clients for Edwards & White. Maybe a job at Dior would be just right for me. I want to tell him that I'm seriously considering leaving the firm and I'm dying to work for one of his clients, but I keep my mouth shut and change the subject.

"So are you enjoying the Paris office?"

"It's great, but it isn't New York." He looks away for a moment before he continues. "Just so you know, the decision to move there wasn't mine."

"Whose was it?"

"Harry's."

I had a feeling Antoine had been pushed out of New

York, but why would Harry ask one of the top lawyers in the office to leave when he himself was leaving anyway?

"Bonnie made him do it. I guess she felt threatened by my close relationship with Scott and my ability to drum up business."

"I had a feeling it wasn't your decision. You didn't seem too excited about going to Paris."

"No, I wasn't. Unfortunately, Scott wasn't able to make Harry change his mind. I told you the place is a war zone."

"I just never thought the politics were *that* bad."

"They were and they still are. That's why I suggested Bonnie be your warlord. It's always better to have her on your side," he says sarcastically.

"I'd prefer not having her around, period."

He smiles. "She's a very good lawyer."

"I know, but I find her very intimidating. I cringe every time she asks me to do anything."

"Why?"

"It's never good enough. I don't think my ego can take any more of her criticism. Do you know that I walk through reception fifty times a day to avoid walking by her office?"

"Really?"

"She scares the hell out of me."

"Is that what people say about me?" he asks, staring at me fixedly.

"Well, um, no. Not really."

"Come on, Catherine, I'm not stupid. Tell me what people say behind my back."

I hesitate for a moment before answering, but given his upbeat mood I take a deep breath and go for it.

"I've heard it said that you have a highlighter up your butt."

He laughs out loud.

"Really? That's hilarious! I love it! What else?"

"Rikash told me you helped him out with a script. He thinks very highly of you."

"I was looking for the dirt, not the compliments. I know people say that I'm an uptight workaholic."

"You *do* spend a huge amount of time at work."

He picks up the votive candle from the table and rolls it awkwardly between his palms.

"Not like you. You were always out at glamorous parties."

"Because Scott asked me to go. And most of them turned out to be pretty unglamorous, believe me."

"I'm sorry I was so hard on you, Catherine. I know Mel was quite an ass."

I stay silent. Mel wasn't who I had in mind. I think about the concert with Jeffrey at Carnegie Hall and how he had made such an impression on me that night. I look across the room and feel a knot in my stomach.

"Catherine, are you okay?" he asks, concerned.

"Sorry. I was daydreaming for a second."

He takes another sip of champagne before blurting out: "I have to tell you that, well, I know all about Jeffrey."

Not expecting him to be so in tune with my thoughts, I nearly jump from my seat. I look away for a moment before he catches my gaze.

"Who told you?"

"A little bird."

"Rikash."

I'll kill him.

"Out of concern."

"Concern?"

"Rikash was worried Jeffrey might be a womanizer so he called to ask me if I knew him. I googled him late one night at the office and we both saw that he was probably going to be bad news."

"What? Why?"

"His last job was CFO of a media company that spun

off its Internet division."

"What's so bad about that?"

"There were allegations of insider trading against him."

I sit back in my chair, mortified. My mind spins; Rikash had suggested I do a background check on him before I went away with him to the Hamptons. How could I have been so naïve?

"How did he become the CFO of a public company?"

"He must have cleared his name. Otherwise they wouldn't have allowed him to take that position."

"Why didn't either of you tell me?"

"I tried. I sent you that email about trusting but verifying, remember?"

"And you expected me to understand what it meant?"

"I was trying to be subtle."

I go back in my mind to that precise moment when I received Antoine's email and I had brushed him off as being annoying. How wrong was I to think that Jeffrey had it together and not him? I try to clear my name with dignity.

"Just so you know, I've written a letter to the SEC that recaps all the facts. This isn't being buried under the carpet."

"I didn't expect it would be. You're doing the right thing, Catherine."

"I know. Does Scott know?"

With all the backstabbing going on at the firm these days, it's hard to know whom I can trust. I squirm in my seat thinking that Scott might know about my personal *catastrophe*.

"No. You can trust me, Catherine. *Really.*"

The tension in my lower back dissipates. Antoine is on my side.

"You guys were right to be suspicious about Jeffrey. What an asshole."

"I'm sorry."

"It was like being dragged through gravel. It really hurt." I pause and try to collect myself but the pain is still raw. I quickly change the subject. "Anyway, it's over and I really don't want to dwell on the past. I'm about to make a fresh start."

Conscious that the alcohol is going to my head and I'm about to say things I shouldn't, I change tactics. The champagne makes me brave enough to pry into his personal life.

"So are you seeing anyone?"

"No."

I'm surprised by his response; he's got the looks, the brains, and now the power, so I assumed women would be throwing themselves at his feet.

"Really? A great catch like you? That's unbelievable! I guess you've been too busy working on that big privatization . . ."

He stares at me from across the table and puts an arm around the back of his chair. He pauses for a long moment before taking a large gulp of champagne.

"Catherine, I really don't give a shit about that client or any other file for that matter."

I stare at him, speechless.

"I have way more important things on my mind." His dark eyes seem to look right through me.

"Oh."

"And that whole googling Jeffrey business."

"Yeah?"

"I did it because I was jealous. I didn't want your relationship to work out."

I lock eyes with him, my heart beating fast. I've always been attracted to Antoine, but I never expected it to be mutual. And besides, he was always more of a thorn in my side than a love prospect. But something's different about him now—he's so much less tense.

"Really?" I skip back to our exchanges, zeroing in on some of our emails and conversations.

"And is that why you ignored me in the photocopy room after I had sent you that flirty email?"

"I thought you were just playing with me."

"And is that why you took the Dior file away?"

"Mmm-hmm. I guess so." He stares down at his plate. "I was upset that you were spending a weekend in the Hamptons with Jeffrey."

"Really?"

"It was incredibly inappropriate, and I apologize. But to tell you the truth, I was afraid to tell you how I felt because I was leaving the country and I didn't want to get hurt."

His vulnerability makes my heart stop and my eyes open—he's an incredible man.

"What's so different now? You're still on another continent."

"I don't want to lose my chance to be with someone so amazing."

He stands up from his chair and leans into me. I feel weak in the knees.

"Can I kiss you?"

Without thinking about it, I nod. He grabs my arm and pulls me in closer. Being a bit tipsy helps keep my inhibitions in check and I let myself lean forward—my right hand reaching for his black curls—and passionately kiss him back; having his lips touch mine seems so perfect.

The waiter pretends to ignore us until Antoine signals for him to bring another bottle of champagne.

"We have something else to celebrate," Antoine says to the waiter.

"I don't think I can drink another glass," I say.

"Okay, we're taking it to go."

He reaches for my hand and tenderly kisses the tips of my fingers. I'm overcome with elation.

"You have no idea how often I've dreamt of this moment."

We wake up the next morning to the sound of the alarm clock.

"How about breakfast in bed?" Antoine asks.

"Shouldn't we at least make an appearance at the firm's team-building exercises?"

"The firm? What firm?"

"The one that just made you a partner!"

"Ah, yes, that one!"

He wraps his arms around my shoulders and the warmth of his touch makes me feel giddy.

"What are we going to do about this, Mademoiselle Lambert?" he whispers in my ear while caressing my hair.

I remain silent for a long moment. I don't tell him that I've been awake half the night asking myself that same question; that I can't take any more heartbreak than I already have, that I want to be with him, but I'm unsure whether I could bring myself to move back to France for the sole reason of being with a man and that, on top of all this, I'm desperately thinking of leaving the firm and even spoke to Dior's general counsel about applying for a job.

"I think I might have a plan," I whisper back.

"Really? Are you going to share the details?"

"If I did, I might have to kill you."

"You already have with that smile of yours." He tickles me. "I only have six months to live unless I see you again very soon." He turns my body so that I face him and becomes serious.

"I really mean it, Catherine. I want to be with you and a long-distance relationship might be difficult. Move back to Paris. I'll make it worth your while, I promise."

I fall back on my pillow as he kisses me tenderly all over.

A moment of deep happiness comes over me. Whatever this is, it's not hooking up.

Chapter 39

"So how was California, dah-ling? Meet any cute boys?"

I stare at the floor and try not to blush.

"Okay, what's his name?"

"Rikash, shut the door."

"Oooh, this sounds juicy."

"You can't tell anyone about this, okay? No hints, implications, nothing."

"Okay, okay. Are you having an affair with Harry?"

"Ew, of course not. We did get quite cozy though. I threw up all over him on the flight to California."

"I heard. The entire firm heard. Go on."

"I was about to tell you that something, um, happened with Antoine."

"Oh, dah-ling." He waves his hands in the air. "You've finally come around."

"What do you mean?"

"We all knew that he liked you. I caught him staring at your picture on the firm's website more than a few times."

"Funny, I always thought he disliked me."

"It's quite the opposite, pumpkin."

"He told me about you two googling Jeffrey."

He crinkles up his nose. "I'm so sorry, I didn't mean to spill any information, I was doing it out of concern."

"I know. You're a good friend."

"But he's in Paris. Long-distance relationships are very complicated."

"I think we can manage."

"Couldn't you simply transfer back to your old job in the Paris office?"

I lower my voice. "Something pretty amazing happened in California that got me thinking."

"Oh really?" he whispers back and raises his eyebrows dramatically. "What?"

"Dior was holding executive meetings at our hotel and I spoke to their general counsel about applying for a job."

"Dior? *Oh my god!*" He does a pirouette over a stack of files.

"Shuuush, not so loud! Isn't that incredible? It would be the best job ever!"

"So when's the big interview?" He places my face in his hands.

"Um, that's the problem."

"Oh?"

"She left the hotel before I could hand her my resumé."

"Oh, sweetie, that sucks. But Antoine docs legal work for Dior. Why doesn't he put in a good word for you?"

"We talked about this before we left California and we decided that given his recent promotion as a partner, it would be best if I pursued the Dior job on my own. Otherwise, it might put him in tough spot with the managing partners."

"But I don't understand . . . So many lawyers leave the firm to go work for their clients. It's usually seen as a good thing, isn't it? A way to ensure the legal work filters back home. But I can help get you that legal job at Dior. Let me try to work my magic."

"No, no, Rikash, no crazy pranks, please. This is my big chance."

"Trust me, dah-ling. Have I ever let you down?"

The next morning Nathan walks into my office looking dejected.

"Hey, what's up?"

He shuts the door and throws himself into one of the chairs in front of my desk.

"I feel like crap."

"Why?"

"I didn't make it, Catherine. I didn't make partner. Scott just told me a few minutes ago."

"I'm so sorry, Nathan. I'm sure you'll make it next year."

"That's not the point. Do you know how fucking hard I've worked for the last seven years? How many goddamn hours I've billed?"

"Did he say why?"

"He said I didn't do enough work for this and that partner who's a heavy hitter and this and that partner who pulls more weight on the partnership committee, that I needed to prove that I can market my practice, blah, blah, blah, whatever. It's a political game, Catherine. It's all bullshit."

"But you billed more hours than anyone else in the department."

"I know. That's what's so sickening. I don't want to do this anymore, Catherine. I just want to go jump off a bridge."

"I can sympathize." I pause, considering my next sentence. "I'm really tired of this too. I'm sort of thinking of leaving the firm."

I can't believe I've said this out loud to Nathan and without even having another job lined up, but it cements my feeling that Edwards & White is not for me. And Harry's firm wouldn't be any different.

"I'm not surprised. This is no place for someone like you."

"Please don't be discouraged over this, Nathan. It's not worth it."

"Easier said than done."

"If it makes you feel any better, I read an article in the *New York Law Journal* that said lawyers are among the most depressed people in America."

"Really?"

"Uh-huh. Depression, alcoholism, drug abuse, divorce, and suicide. We're an unhappy bunch."

"At least we beat the dentists."

I'm relieved to see him crack a joke.

"So what are you going to do now?"

"I have no clue. If I had one ounce of pride, I'd leave, but I've invested so much time in this place, I can't just throw it all away. I can't believe it." He drops his head into his hands and begins to sob. "What will I tell my wife? She'll be furious."

"Are you doing this for you or for your wife, Nathan? She's supposed to be supportive. That's why she's your wife, remember?"

"I know. But this is so embarrassing."

"No, it's not. You could find another job in a minute if you wanted to. You're a great lawyer."

I try my best to encourage him, even though I know that lawyers who don't make partnership after a certain number of years are being sent a not-so-subtle message about their prospects at the firm.

"Why don't you go work for Harry?"

"He didn't offer me a position," he answers, looking even more dejected.

"So what? Maybe he thinks you wouldn't leave the firm. Call him!"

"Hmm. Not sure. I need to think about it. But thanks, Catherine. You're the best."

After Nathan leaves my office, I wonder why it is that I can get everyone else's career on track but mine. I take a walk along the firm's spartan hallways and look at the portraits of the founding partners, Messrs. Edwards and White, with bemusement. Why did I become a lawyer any-way? I get a flashback of gruelling law school exams, endless hours slaving over legal documents, the painful prepara-tion courses endured to be admitted as a lawyer in Paris and New York. If Nathan didn't make partner, do I really stand a chance? Is leaving the private practice of law the right decision? A junior associate from the litigation group walks by and confirms my decision.

"Love what you're wearing. Great outfit."

Chapter 40

Absence might make the heart grow fonder, but it's turning mine into cheese fondue, thick and heavy. Although it's been less than a week since we left California, I miss Antoine dearly and the only thing on my mind is getting across the Atlantic as soon as possible.

"You'll never guess what happened today."

"No, but I have a feeling you're about to tell me," Antoine responds jokingly while pointing his finger at the tiny camera. I can see his warm smile thanks to one of the miracles of modern technology: a webcam.

"Both Bonnie and Nathan announced they're leaving Edwards & White to join Harry's firm."

"You sound surprised."

"Um, hell no!"

"You're starting to talk like a local. It's definitely time to get you back to France."

"Believe me, I'm working on it!"

"Aren't you glad you declined Harry's offer? You'd be working for Bonnie again!"

"Ha! It's the best move I decided *not* to make."

"Any news from Sandrine?"

"No. I sent her an email with my resumé, but she didn't respond. Rikash is now working on some diabolical plan to get me an interview. I'm a bit worried."

"I wouldn't be! He's probably out filming a short documentary on your life to send to the legal department."

"That would be the most depressing film ever."

"Gee, thanks a lot!"

"Um, I mean it would be all about work, until the fairy-tale ending."

"Now that sounds a *lot* better."

"I'm having lunch with Lisa and her boyfriend, Charles, tomorrow."

"I wish I could join you."

"So do I. She can't wait to meet you."

"Where are you guys going?"

"Artisanal Bistro."

"That's one of my favourites! This is really painful. I miss you, Catherine."

I say nothing in response.

"Catherine? You're going silent on me."

"I'm sorry. I'm finding this really tough too."

As soon as we sign off, I receive a text message.

Close together or far apart, you're always in my heart.

A.

XXXX

I meet Lisa and Charles at Artisanal and the strong smell of cheese takes me back to my childhood. I inhale deeply while we wait to be seated. Charles greets me with two kisses on the cheek; he's tall with dirty blond hair, a freckled nose, and straight white teeth. He's wearing khaki combat pants and a leather bomber jacket and could be a model for the J. Crew catalogue. He graciously pulls out my chair as I take a seat at our table.

"Finally I get to meet you, Catherine. I've heard so much about you."

"Yes, and I've heard so much about you."

"I'm sure you have. Lisa has probably complained about how bad a boyfriend I've been," he responds jokingly, and reaches to hold Lisa's hand. I notice the diamond glittering on her left ring finger.

"*Mon dieu!* Lisa! You didn't tell me!"

"Yes." She gazes at Charles lovingly. "We're engaged!"

He kisses her tenderly on the lips.

"Congratulations! I'm so happy for you!"

She glances at Charles before continuing with the details.

"We'd like to get married in France."

"Really?"

"We were wondering if we could hold our wedding at your mother's house since we want to do it by the water."

I flash back to Madame Simona's mention of a wedding by the water: it was Lisa's wedding she was referring to. And, actually, I feel a rush of happiness for her—she deserves this.

"My mother would be thrilled."

"You're sure she wouldn't mind?" Charles asks.

"Positive."

"Thank you so much, Cat!"

"Yes, thanks, Catherine," Charles chimes in.

"I want you to be my maid of honour."

"I'd be very happy to."

"We have to go shopping for my dress! Maybe in Paris?"

"Absolutely! And I'll take you to Fifi Chachnil's shop for some beautiful French lingerie."

Charles looks pleased with my suggestion.

"Yeah, that sounds great!"

After he says this, I stare into my steak frites. I try not to spoil their big moment but can't help feeling sad that Antoine isn't here to celebrate the good news. Lisa guesses what I'm thinking.

"You miss Antoine?"

"Yes, very much so."

After our lunch, I walk back to the office hoping Rikash made some headway in his grand master plan. The firm has been eerily quiet since Harry announced his departure and I just want to get to Paris as fast as I can.

❖

I sit in my chair daydreaming about Paris when Rikash catches my attention.

"Look what just came for you. They're gorgeous," he says, placing a large bouquet of white calla lilies on my desk.

"Thanks, Rikash."

I tear open the envelope and find a handwritten note:

With all my love.
Antoine

I never expected Antoine to express his feelings so quickly, and I'm deeply touched. I've spent the six longest and most painful years of my life working ridiculously long hours, grappling each echelon of the career ladder as if my life depended on it. But I've been missing out on one of life's true pleasures: a rewarding relationship.

Rikash stares at me expectantly.

"So?"

"He's written something very romantic."

"Why the long face then?"

"I need to find a way to get out of this place."

"Come on, sweetie. I already told you not to worry."

"I'm getting more desperate by the second and I'm having trouble concentrating on my files. I have no drive left."

"You can't look desperate. You'll never get anything that way. You need to act as if you already have the job. Repeat this after me: *I am a fabulous diva and they will kiss my feet.*"

"What kind of mantra is that?"

"A sacred one from India. I repeat it in front of the mirror every morning before leaving my apartment. And you know what? It really works."

"Right. Sorry, Rikash, but I don't think my dream job at Dior will magically appear by repeating your silly mantra."

"Silly?" Rikash stares at me defiantly. "Are you calling my cultural heritage silly?"

"Of course not. I'm just not feeling it, that's all." I pull out a plastic glass and an emergency bottle of red wine from my desk drawer. "I need a drink."

"Don't tell me you're actually going to drink some of that cheapo stuff?"

"Yes, sir, I am. Desperate times call for desperate measures."

"You can say that again." He rushes out of my office without saying another word.

❖

The next day, I'm nursing a cheap wine hangover when the word *DIOR* appears on my office phone screen.

"Catherine? *Bonjour,* Sandrine Cordier."

I freeze as I hear her voice.

"Hello, Sandrine, so happy to hear from you. You remember me from our brief conversation in San Diego?"

"Yes, of course."

"I guess you couldn't make our appointment. You must be extremely busy."

"Yes, very busy."

"Are you calling to reschedule?"

"Not exactly."

I feel a pang in the pit of my stomach and expect the worst. I hold back tears.

"I'm calling because I just received a FedExed copy of your resumé printed on pink and orange silk taffeta with your initials engraved in gold letters. It makes quite a statement."

Putain! I can't believe Rikash went that far. My one chance at getting the job of my dreams and being with the man I love has just been flushed down the drain. I suddenly have visions of finishing the rest of my days locked in my New York office tied to a swivel chair, billing hours until my face turns blue while junior associates plot to have my desk blown up and my coffee poisoned.

"Oh."

"You are one *very* determined woman."

"Um, I can explain."

"There's no need. I just showed it to a few of the designers downstairs and they loved your idea. They were amazed that you knew about the colours from their upcoming collection."

"I'm so pleased they liked it." I go along with it despite having no clue about what she actually received.

"Can you be in Paris next Thursday for an interview with our CEO?"

There's a long pause. My heart beats at record speed.

"I have a position that might interest you: Monsieur Le Furet is retiring as our intellectual property director. I need someone to replace him and I see from your resumé that you've done some work in this area. It sounds like you would be perfect for the job."

A profound feeling of euphoria fills every inch of my body. I want to tell her that I'll even work for free, but I take a deep breath and remember Rikash's mantra; I can't appear too desperate. I'll never get anything that way.

"Yes, I do have relevant experience that could be interesting for this position. I'd be delighted to meet with your CEO."

After I hang up, I throw a miniature pink bottle of POP Champagne toward Rikash's cubicle. "You are amazing! Catch!"

"You have a well-stocked mini-bar in that office of yours. Do we have something to celebrate?"

"Oui, monsieur!"

He runs into my office, mini-bottle in hand. "So did it work?"

"It certainly did. I can't thank you enough, you're the best."

He lifts his hands in the air Olympic-champion style and then shakes the mini-bottle of champagne. As he opens it, the contents explode all over my office. I don't care.

"If I get the job, would you be interested in becoming my assistant? We could wage the war on international counterfeiters together."

"Not *if* but *when.* Remember the mantra, dah-ling. God, I think you'll need me in Paris to keep you in line!" He hugs me, then lifts me off my feet.

"This calls for a celebratory *soirée*. How about sushi at the Gansevoort Hotel? Dinner's on me."

He grabs his suit jacket and starts skipping down the hallway. "Ready when you are!"

I reach into my drawer.

"I'll meet you in the lobby in five minutes; I have an important letter to drop off in the mailroom first."

Acknowledgements

I would like to thank my family and friends for their love and support—especially my parents, Colette and Réal, who've always been my biggest fans. *J'adore New York* would never have seen the light of day without the encouragement and generosity of Isabelle Rayle-Doiron, Marie-Claude Germain, and Daniel Bourque.

Un gros merci to my editor, Kate Cassaday, for her unshakable enthusiasm, dedication, and impressive *savoir-faire*.

To the rest of the team at HarperCollins, Catherine Mac-Gregor, Jennifer Lambert, and Iris Tupholme, who helped make a dream come true.

A warm thank you to Professor Charles Ellison, whose generous spirit showed me the way to creating a life filled with improvisation.

A special thanks to a psychic named Christine, who stopped me on the streets of Manhattan one dreary November afternoon to tell me I was missing my calling.

To all who provided encouragement, feedback, and inspiration along the way: Simon Laflèche, Atul Tiwari, Denis Boulianne, Gérard Vannoote, Caroline Lemoine, Line Rivard, Dominique Fontaine, Marie-Josée Fournier, Geneviève Guertin, Julie Drapeau-Crevier, Pascale Bourbeau, Michel De La Chenelière, Caroline Fortin, Yanic Truesdale, Marcy Jezak, Robin Sowers, Joelle Reboh, Olivia Commune, David Jurado, Claude Commune, Isabelle Lamarre, Carolyne Van Der Meer, Rossana Sommaruga, Myriam Caron-Belzile, Julie Rivest, and Daniel Laporte.

And particularly to Patrice Commune for his *joie de vivre*, patience, and immense support throughout this exciting journey.